# SARLAN

## VOLUME ONE

### INDIE D

**Grosvenor House**
**Publishing Limited**

This book is published by
Grosvenor House Publishing Ltd
Link House
140 The Broadway, Tolworth, Surrey, KT6 7HT.
www.grosvenorhousepublishing.co.uk

This book is a work of fiction. Any resemblance to
people or events, past or present, is purely coincidental.

A CIP record for this book
is available from the British Library

ISBN 978-1-80381-888-7
eBook ISBN 978-1-80381-889-4

*This book is dedicated to my partner*
*Nathan, whom I love,*
*incredibly a lot...*

'It's just going to take time.
If it's out there,
I'll find it...'

**The Puppet Show
M.W. Craven**

'Energy can neither be created nor
destroyed, only converted
from one form to another.'

**The first law of
thermodynamics**

# PROLOGUE

*The last of their kind*

It hadn't occurred to Gee to place any importance on the fact that she was the only one of her kind in the world. Why would it? The leaves on the ground were especially crisp that morning – that was all that mattered to her. To the untrained eye, Gee was merely a mossy-grey dog with small antlers, just a little larger and more wolf-like than a standard dog.

Gee's lip curled, revealing some large teeth, as she stood shaking her spindly legs, huffing and snorting. Delicate swirls of steam spiraled from her long snout as she patted at the ground, little pockets of dirt bobbing up around her. She turned and limped over to two figures shuffling down the forest path, a green leaf lodged in her cloven hoof.

'Again? Really?' A soft, wearied voice found its way into Gee's large pointy ear, as a silver curl flopped in front of her face.

A hand moved to Gee's hoof, freeing her from the annoyance.

Relief. Gee wagged her tail.

'Maybe just stick to the brown ones now, okay?' Gee licked the face of her liberator.

'Okay...yup. Okay, thank you, Gee.' The woman smiled and craned away from Gee's sloppy thanks.

Gee trotted off.

Dhalia Fourlise peered down at her thirteen-year-old daughter Feina and attempted to tuck her frizzy brown curls back under her little straw boater. Feina flapped away her mother's hands as they both turned to see Gee shaking a limp green leaf in her jaws. She was not about to allow her hoof to be conquered again. She leapt around, squeaking and kicking up a small tornado of detritus. They laughed.

A chilly gust of wind swept down the path and the pair felt their precariously positioned straw hats begin to lift from their heads. They grabbed at them, squinting over to see Gee, wild with excitement as the leaves began to swirl.

'Get 'em, Gee. Go on, get 'em!' they gushed. Gee snapped at her crispy opponents.

Dhalia buried her icy hands in the pockets of her soft pea-green coat, brushing her numb fingers against an ornate silver dagger sheath attached to her belt. The light faded as an airship floated in front of a small patch of sun which hung over the distant city. The pair shivered.

The biting wind gusted past them once again and Dhalia watched Gee stop up ahead to sniff the air, her face scrunched in discomfort. The wind had picked up a distinctive smell, making the hairs on their arms prickle. Dhalia looked over to see Gee sniffing the ground, the ridge of fur along her back spiking.

'Gee?' said Feina, her brow furrowing as she watched Gee stiffen and her throat begin to glow.

Dhalia gasped. She grabbed at Feina's coat and quickly pulled her daughter behind her.

Their breath left them, as a silent, white stream of light rocketed through the trees and hit the side of Gee's head, piercing her right eye.

They stood there for a moment, numb, at the sight of Gee's lifeless form on the cold ground.

'GEE!' Dhalia launched forward screaming, then skidded to a stop as she saw a fog-like substance slither out of the forest, and travel along the ground, surrounding Gee's frozen body. She spun back, clasping Feina's trembling face.

'You have to listen to me, Fei!'

'I ca... I can't... I...' Feina spluttered through her tears.

'Fei, listen to me! Whatever happens, you must stay as calm as you can. Do you hear me? Your life depends on it! Tell me you hear me!' Dhalia insisted, trembling.

Fei nodded. 'What are you going to do?'

Dhalia wiped away Fei's tears. 'What I must. I love you. Look after them for me.'

'Mum, no, what are you doing? No!' Fei reached forward, grabbing at her mother's coat as Dhalia whispered, 'Cidisadain.'

'MUM, No...' Fei's words vanished. Silenced. As her mother's voice and body fell behind a veil, cloaking her.

Speechless, the girl charged forward as her mother splayed out her hand behind her.

'Cuilbach,' Dhalia muttered under her breath, a tear falling down her cheek. Finding herself forced back, Fei watched gasping from the ground, as her mother stood firm above her, staring into the forest.

'Took you long enough,' Dhalia hissed, her hand clenched round the hilt of her dagger.

'Well, unlike you, Fourlise...' The glistening face of a young woman emerged from the forest, the fog slithering round her body. '...I am in no rush at all.'

'Mum, no!' Fei screamed into nothingness.

The strange woman's face was emotionless as she raised her hands, which began to glow. Dust and dry leaves swirled around her, as piercing beams of white light shot from her outstretched hands.

Dhalia thrust her dagger into the line of fire as the light pelted into it, sending her skidding back.

Fei panted as her mother's boots ground to a halt within arm's reach. She thrust her hand out, only to be obstructed by the veil. She cried out.

The glistening woman cackled as a violent battle began, white streams of light hurtling between the combatants. Dhalia swung the dagger round, absorbing the light into her blade.

'MAICHORRA!' she roared.

A colossal shockwave careered into the other woman, sending her spinning backwards into the forest. Dhalia fell forward onto her knees, her hands shaking.

'Mum...' Fei whimpered on the ground.

Silence fell as the pair watched the fog part, revealing the woman kneeling low to the ground, her hands buried in the dirt, arms bent and teeth bared.

Dhalia gasped.

'ORCHASAYIS!' the woman bellowed.

Fei screamed as she watched the shockwave from the woman slam into her mother's chest, firing her backwards. Dhalia blasted into a tree, her back cracking on impact as her iron grip loosened, and the dagger fell away. She plummeted to the ground, winded, gasping, paralysed.

Tears streamed down Fei's face as she watched the woman kick her mother onto her back.

'Mogalort,' Dhalia whispered.

Fei shook, her jaw clenching and her face wet with despair as she whispered. 'I love you too.' And closed her eyes.

Dhalia felt a sharp force punch into her chest. As her sight began to leave her, she rested her gaze on a small patch of snowdrops where Gee had fallen, her body gone.

She smiled and let her eyes close.

Fei's silent tears trickled down her face as the woman pulled Dhalia's dagger from her chest. The woman's mouth quivered, blood dripping down the blade as she turned to look in Fei's direction.

'I may not be able to see you now child, but I know you are there. And if anything is ever to rise in you, believe me, I will find you.'

Fei's nails clawed at the dirt as she watched the woman take a last look at her mother's lifeless body, then leave her lying on a bed of crisp brown leaves.

Dragging herself over to her mother, and touching her pale face for the last time, Fei sobbed, her tears pooling in the folds of Dhalia's soft pea-green coat.

A dim yellow glow rose on the horizon, as the strange woman floated through the forest. She stopped at the cusp, looking out past Suga Valley. Grass waterfalled into the lush fields that stretched out towards the rising sun. With the dagger in her palm, she moved forward to the edge.

The woman thrust the dagger above her head, catching the sun's rays on the blade. A thin yellow beam of light gleamed in the distance to her left, fixing on a spot. She stared in its direction and began twisting the blade around.

The beam did not waver.

The woman smiled.

# CHAPTER ONE

*13 years later*

The ground rumbled. Tiny cracks made their way across the field as small rocks and lumps of dried dirt skipped around the parched yellow patches of grass. A huge, dark grey cloud crept along the ground, cascading down the side of Suga ridge, dodging rotten old tree stumps and broken park benches consumed by weeds. A whirring noise hummed within the cloud, growing louder.

The cloud climbed up and over the remnants of an old children's playground, toppling over the side of the battered wooden fence and creeping across the rusty see-saw. The whirring noise grew louder, sounding like a very old, very used fan.

A small wooden archery target shot out, sending heavy grey contrails swirling away from its battered metal propellers as it zig-zagged. A small, thin arrow shaft wedged in its centre.

Two more flying targets, one just ahead of the other, soared out of the cloud – thick with grey on their exit, the slightly slower one with a large chunk missing from its body. The other had a long gash through the wood.

Then another appeared. This one was dragging itself across the ground, bumping over small, hard mounds of earth, a long, thin dagger sticking out of its bullseye. Finally, the most battered and crumpled of the five targets appeared, jerking through the air as it flew.

The ground rumbled harder, and vibrations soared across the valley, as a very small girl, astride a very chunky horse, hurtled out of the cloud. A leather gas mask covered her face and another long, thin dagger (similar to the one buried in the target) was strapped to her belt. She caught sight of the daggered target, which had landed rather dramatically to one side, over a rock.

'YES,' she breathed.

The horse pricked its ears as the girl punched a celebratory fist in the air. Clyde's huge hairy black hooves sent shockwaves through the ground as he charged along. His ears were pointed firmly forward, as he snorted swirls of steam through his little nose covering. He was not the nimblest of steeds, but there was no denying he could run at a fair pace for a fair while, considering his robust stature. The girl riding him had long, curly dark brown hair that flapped haphazardly in the wind, occasionally whipping her in the face. Which was annoying, and stung.

Subtle strands of silver spiralled through her frizzy curls, which had been stuffed under a small boater.

She had endeavoured to pin the hat to her head and was now clinging on to it for dear life. She wore dark brown corduroy trousers, fitted at the bottom but puffed out a little at the thigh; black knee-high boots, with a small heel and the fewest laces she could find, and rather worn, black braces over a large white shirt. She had rolled her sleeves up to her elbows, revealing small but muscular forearms. Although slight, she was strong. She had to be, to manoeuvre Clyde.

Twenty-seven-year-old Feina Fourlise, known as Fei, removed her gas mask, to reveal a young, blue-eyed, pale, freckly face. She had never considered herself pretty; 'striking' she thought, was much more fitting. She did smile a lot though, which gave her a pleasant glow. Grinning, and grabbing the reins in one hand, she strapped her mask to the saddle and twisted round to watch the grey cloud behind her.

Two small beams of light appeared, growing brighter as the greyness dispersed. Another girl, a little taller and skinnier than the first, rocketed out on a small, rusty motorbike. A crossbow strapped to her back. The blurry wheels dug into the ground as steam and sparks showered from the back. She too wore a leather gas mask, secured around her auburn hair which was arranged in two buns. She manoeuvred skilfully, and apparently nonchalantly, over large rocks and humps on the ground as she careered along.

Fei waved. The second girl, noticing Fei's flailing arm did not react, other than to pull up her gas mask, revealing a much younger, tanned, but still a little freckly, cool face.

She gave Fei a thumbs-up, then promptly popped her hands back in her pockets.

Considering her tall, gangly-ness, sixteen-year-old Cora Fourlise was perfectly balanced on her bike. She peered down at her watch, beneath the sleeve of her long pea-green coat, the only one that fitted over her long, cream, biking skirt.

Fei pointed at the targets, then signalled a 'two' with her fingers. Cora raised an eyebrow and veered beside Clyde, still moving at speed as she lazily rearranged her cream tights, which, shockingly, had no holes in them.

'Doesn't count. He can see in there, I can't!' Cora shouted.

'Uh, yes, it does! And neither can I!' Fei bellowed in return.

'Didn't see it, Fei. Didn't happen.' Cora grinned and gave her sister another thumbs-up.

Fei frowned.

Thundering away from the city, the girls raced parallel to Suga forest, which sat at the top of the ridge, stretching down as far as they could see. A tall wooden fence now surrounded the forest, with signs reading 'NO ENTRY – TOK ZONE' plastered every ten metres. Fei gazed over the fence to see a little dirt path, with weathered, dying trees on either side.

*CLAP!*

Both Fei and Clyde jumped, as a small, thin arrow smashed into the middle of one of the flying wooden targets in front of them.

'HEY!' Fei yelled and Cora signalled a 'two'.

Cora's smugness dissipated as she watched her sister turn to look over the fence. She steamed forward, swung out and in front of Clyde, grabbed hold of his bridle and pulled back. Clyde snorted in frustration. Fei turned to see Cora in front of them, her head cocked and her arms crossed. Clyde gave Cora's rigid stance a gentle nudge.

'How have we found ourselves here...again?' said Cora. Fei shrugged and picked at a fraying thread on Clyde's saddle.

'I dunno. I don't even *want* to come here... It just happens.'

'Well, it can't keep happening. It's no good for either of us.'

'It's just... it's hard to believe it's been so long... It all smells the same, just looks totally different.'

Cora sighed, gazing at the large 'Danger' sign on the fence, which seemed a particularly annoying shade of red today. The small patch of scrubby grass beneath Clyde and Fei began to bloom. Little shoots of new grass pushed themselves through the mounds of yellow fuzz.

'I just wish we knew more.' Fei felt her eyes watering and Cora examined the fence, noticing a small crevasse in the bottom.

She scanned either side of the ridge.

*There's no one around.*

Fei watched as a large grey cloud rolled closer and closer to the city in the distance. 'I have this perpetual blank space in my mind, filled with all the questions I know will never get answered. I know Dad hasn't told us the whole story, I can just tell.'

'Dad's always avoided answering questions – there's no reason he would give us more details now, and were wasting time wondering. We'll just have to find out for ourselves,' said Cora, marching towards the fence.

'I guess.' Fei strained to hear, as Cora's voice faded a little. She swung round, to see Cora marching towards the forest.

'Cora!' In a panic, Fei slid off Clyde's back and hurried after her.

She stumbled over her feet, her hand on her dagger, scanning the area.

They were alone.

'There's no more risk in here than in the city,' said Cora, shrugging. She reached up to hold on to the fence while she jimmied her foot into the crevasse she had spotted, when she felt a hand grab her arm, pulling her back.

'Cora! No!'

'Why not? No one's been behind here in years. There might be nothing in here, for all we know.'

'Yeah, for good reason!' Fei nodded at the large red warning sign.

'You're really bothered about them?'

'Uh, very much so, and you should be too! There's too much grey in there and I'm not gonna risk it with you here.' Fei turned back towards Clyde. 'Besides, it's basically constant night-time in there, we'd literally be asking for it.'

'But you've killed loads before,' said Cora, getting a little bored of the same conversation. Fei leant back against Clyde's tree-trunk of a leg, her face sour.

'Three. I've killed three, and it was a bloody task.' They both looked down into the valley and saw the grey migrating towards them. 'It's not worth it, not right now at least, with you here, and not...today.'

Cora sighed, as tiny purple flowers flickered through the grass beneath Fei's feet.

'We'll figure it out one day, I promise. Toks don't scare me half as much as people do, anyway.'

Cora raised an eyebrow. 'When is one day gonna be *the* day? You've been saying that forever.'

'One day will be the day when the Earth's about to explode and humanity as we know it will cease to exist,' Fei chuckled.

'Righto!' Cora rolled her eyes.

'Umm, shun the non-believer... It could happen you know.'

Cora started turning back towards the valley when she felt Fei's hand on her arm again.

'Look, I really will one day, I promise. It's just, every time I think about going for it, I find myself reliving the trauma of that night... You're a lot stronger than me, and I'm *glad* you are, but it's just a lot to deal with, and I need time. One day, I promise, I'll be ready. Just promise me you won't run off in the meantime?' She clutched Cora's sinewy arm and gave her a tired smile.

'You can't stalk me forever,' Cora said, ambling away.

Fei smiled and leapt on to Clyde. 'Yes, I *can*. Also, you're my only friend, so you have to like me.' She grinned at her sister, who shook her head and rode off.

'Not your only friend...' Said Cora, whittling away.

Fei peered for a last time over the fence, allowing the smell to fill her nostrils. Her smiled faded and she pulled away on Clyde's reigns after Cora.

*** 

Valkyrios city wall, which looked large no matter how far away from it you stood, loomed as they approached. It was around a hundred metres high and could be seen for miles. Valkyrios's number-one Tok prevention system!

And to be fair, although it hadn't quite succeeded in keeping all the grey out (as around two-thirds of the city's residents suffered from a mild cough), it certainly prevented the Toks from getting in. A considerable issue that Valkyrios had experienced in the past as the city sat within Suga valley. It's soil rich with nutrients and its situation a short, rather pleasant journey from most neighbouring cities.

Ironically, the wall had now become Valkyrios's primary tourist attraction, with just about everything being sold within the city having some sister version of the wall, or in the shape of the wall: wall-shaped pastries, wall-shaped hats, wall-shaped sweets, and wall-themed shows to name a few. However, wall-shaped wheels and brassieres had been quite abandoned.

As the girls ambled along the vast, smog-filled West road, they watched a myriad of carriages, stuffed to the brim with produce and cars pulling carts of livestock and engine parts, make their way past them towards the enormous West entrance doors, which had been adorned with flowers, looping fabric, and an ornate banner with the inscription:

'WELCOME! HAPPY WALL FRANCES DAY!'

Even the usually bleak, sad looking trees that sat along the road had been covered in small lights and colourful little paper lanterns.

The girls stopped to examine this odd scene.

'Effort, much?' said Fei, grimacing at the coiled, dry branches of trees intertwined with red streamers.

'Not sure it was worth it,' agreed Cora.

Glamorous women, and men in shiny top hats, were greeted eagerly by the West Gate guards. One particularly large, expensive- looking black car pulled up. An elderly man in a suit got out, shook hands with the guards, and offered them all small glasses of port from a blindingly silver tray.

Fei's lip curled as she felt a tap on her boot. She looked down to see a dirty, crumpled piece of paper, with the cracked wax seal of the Prime Minister at the top. Picking it up, she shook her head as Cora peered over her shoulder.

7 PELHAM AVENUE
VALKYRIOS EAST

THE PRIME MINISTER

*To all Citizens:*
*I am writing to you to update you on the steps we are taking*
*to combat the Mage.*

*In the last thirteen years, everyday life in this city has changed dramatically. We have all felt the profound impact of the 17th day of December 1879 on our community.*

*This is why I am giving you one simple instruction: if you, or anyone you know, are aware of the presence of a Mage, you must inform the local authorities.*

*This rule must be observed, not only for your own safety, but also the safety of your loved ones and your community. If you are found to have broken this rule, the guards will be authorised to arrest you.*

*I understand the deep concerns you may have, especially in view of the substantial and dangerous power a Mage can wield against you. But rest assured, your government will do whatever it takes to protect you.*

*We have at all times sought to take appropriate measures to protect our thriving city. And we have seen considerable results since building our glorious wall, Frances.*

*Below you will find a list of features of the three main Mage groups: Cunning men, Witches, and Nathair.*

## CUNNING MEN

- *Typically, a shaved head*
- *Erratic or irrational behaviour; have been known to have drinking problems*
- *You may see them bury their hands in the ground*
- *Have been known to use their powers for the purpose of demonic possession.*

*WITCHES*
- *Socially distancing or antisocial behaviour*
- *They spend an excessive amount of time outside at night*
- *Abnormally coloured eyes – look for an amber or yellow tinge to the iris*
- *Have been known to steal – and eat – new-born babies.*

*NATHAIR (Possibly the most dangerous)*
- *Look for sudden growth of foliage beneath feet*
- *Some have been known to run flourishing horticultural businesses*
- *Sightings have been reported of Nathair flying or hovering*
- *Have been known to lose the use of their sight or hearing during the use of powers*
- *Known to influence mass suicide in towns and cities – look for those attempting to recruit members to various 'groups' or 'practices'.*

*Please, if you become aware of a Mage, DO NOT attempt to restrain them yourselves. We have very limited knowledge of their abilities, but we do know that they are extremely dangerous.*

*Once again, I urge you, please, to contact the authorities if you believe a Mage may be present; protect our city, save lives.*

'*Save lives,*' mocked Fei. 'I remember the day this came through the door. I've never seen Dad in such a rage!'

'You'd think they'd have more important things to worry about. Why did they never do one of these for

Toks?' asked Cora, as Clyde rested his heavy head on her tiny shoulder.

'Because after the wall was built, and everyone realised you could stay safe by just avoiding night-time and the grey, people stopped worrying about them,' said Fei. 'Besides, look at me, I'm clearly way more dangerous.'

'Yeah, you won't even turn the lights off at night. It's actually really annoying.'

They laughed, making Clyde's head bob up and down on Cora's shoulder. He decided this was not a sufficient place to nap, and promptly moved his head. As he did, Cora's smile faded, and she looked up at her sister.

'Do you think you'll ever be able to be, like, out in the open?'

'I dunno. It would be nice not to have to hide anymore, if only to disprove all this crap.' They both snorted as Fei crumpled the sheet of paper and threw it over her head, shocking Clyde out of his snooze as it skipped off his bottom. The began shuffling towards the gates.

Fei stopped. 'Actually you know what, you go on ahead, I'll just fly home!'

They both rolled their eyes.

The city was buzzing. Large groups of people bustled through the long, wide and usually a bit dirty streets. Stalls lined the main road through the city. Stalls from all different places, selling goods of all kinds. You name it - and it was also probably shaped like the wall. People had come from all around, it was a sight to be seen. The residents of Valkyrios had gotten used to the perpetual smell of damp and soot. It was such a treat for it to have been replaced with the smell of roasting meat and candyfloss. An odd combination granted, but certainly a much more welcome one. Small children gripped their parents' hands and buried their faces in large paper bags of sweeties as the sun bounced off the glorious gold carriages of the Ferris wheel that spun in the town square. Parents waved up at their children, who waved back as the odd pink cloud of cotton candy floated to the ground. Followed by wailing.

It was all somewhat overwhelming.

'Home?' Said Fei.

'Home,' agreed Cora.

Cora flung her leg over her bike, knocking a bag of sweets out of a small boy's arms. Wailing followed as Fei made after her, heaving Clyde's immense body along. They made their way down a side road, dodging merry groups of drunken celebrators.

'Didn't you say you had some stuff to pick up from school? I need to help Dad bring all the kit into town.' Fei nodded in the direction of the town centre as more folk began to bustle towards the merriment.

'Yeah, shouldn't take me long, but you know it'd be quicker if I went round the outside. Especially today. Just saying!' said Cora, as she began riding away.

'No! Especially not today. Too many distractions – the grey will be thicker today, with all the cars about,' said Fei as Cora rolled her eyes and spun round. 'Centre! People! Safer!' she shouted after her.

Cora gave her a thumbs-up and sped off. Fei watched Cora's little green jacket disappear down the road, disorientating drunk visitors as she swooped around them.

The glorious smells of the fair wafted up Fei's nose, as a sharp pop erupted from the town square, followed by another, then a chorus of 'oohs' and 'aahs' and the inevitable wailing. A splattering of pink and yellow sparkles filled the sky, the colours reflecting off the clouds of grey hanging above the city.

Clyde snorted, and Fei scoffed at the idea that the grey could be prettified. They made their way home slowly, Clyde dragging his heavy hooves.

# CHAPTER TWO

Fei led Clyde into his stable and heaved a mountain of hay over the door. laying a hand on his warm neck, she drew her clammy palm across her forehead.

So tired. Always so tired.

For someone aged twenty-seven, and of 'unique abilities', she knew surprisingly little about herself. Doctors had been out of the question since she'd sent one of their old neighbour Mrs G's seedlings shooting through her thatched roof when she was nine during a tantrum. Luckily Mrs G had found it wildly funny; Hercules, her ginger tabby cat, had not; but fortunately, due to Mrs G's unexplainable issues with memory loss, the following day she had forgotten the event. As much as Fei loved their home in the city, she wished they had stayed in the countryside; but, of course, being alive costs money, and gradually, after that fateful night, people stopped travelling beyond the city gates.

The familiar tinkle of the front doorbell reverberated round her father's dimly lit, dusty shop. The little plaque reading:

FOURLISE MOTORCYCLES
EST. 1879

had been knocked at some point, and now hung off the side of the cash desk. Fei moved it back into position, blowing away some of the dust. She looked around the shop floor, coughing. It was in even more disarray than usual.

'Dad?'

No answer.

The shop was attached to their house, separated by a glass-panelled door that had little grey dogs in its design. Fei pushed it open and stuck her head through.

'DAD?'

'Downstairs!' Henry's muffled voice floated through the door opposite, which led to his workshop. She crossed the room – dodging several still-to-be-packed engine parts – and made her way down the narrow, brick staircase. Peering down, her father was still nowhere to be seen, only the small, sooty, but warm and cosy workshop.

'Dad?'

She saw Hercules sitting on some blankets by the fire in the corner, his ginger stripes practically glowing.

'Hello, darling,' Henry's head popped up from behind a useless-looking motorbike, his head covered with a large iron mask. Henry winced as he scanned Fei's clothes.

'Oh dear, who's been in a tear-up?'

'Hilarious. What are you doing? The fete's started already, you were supposed to have everything ready.' She sat on an old wooden chair and steadied herself as it rocked under her. Henry waved a gloved hand, and, struggling to his feet after what Fei imagined had been a fair few hours of kneeling, began to clean his hands with an old cloth.

'I know, I was just finishing work on this beauty.'

His dirty white shirt sleeves were rolled up over his muscular, tanned old arms. He pulled off his mask, revealing a wide grin, and stared lovingly at the motorbike, his weathered face lighting up.

'Gorgeous, isn't it. Harry Dempsey from down the road was chucking it out, just like that!' He flung his arms, looking at her for agreement.

She laughed.

'An original 60s Stoker steam bike. Incredible!' He crouched again and began tenderly stroking the worn steam tank between the wheels. Shaking his head in amazement, he ran a dusty hand through his thick grey hair.

'She is a beauty.' Fei walked over and crouched down beside him, admiring the metalwork. 'But you're gonna miss the fete.'

'I'm not too bothered. Never really sell anything at it anyway.' He shrugged, pulling his mask back on, and returning to his welding. Small sparks leapt off the bike, making little singe marks on his shirt and trousers.

'Well, actually going to it would be a good start, and we *do* make a bit – it's better than nothing. Besides, it looks really busy this year.'

He shrugged again.

'We have to get out there more to have any hopes of making this somewhat successful.' She dropped her head and began playing with a stray exhaust pipe. 'Vendors from Leos might be there, with the new Merenial airship.' She peered at him.

'Really?' he said, whipping off his mask. 'Gimme five minutes!' He struggled up again, rubbing his stiff knees as he walked over to the sink and began splashing his face.

Small droplets jumped onto Hercules' back. His ginger stripes rippled as he peered round in discomfort. Another droplet landed on his nose. Snorting, he jumped down off the blankets, and strutted towards Fei with his tail up. She smiled and reached down to scratch between his ears as he proceeded to rub himself against her legs. She clutched round his soft tummy, lifting him up onto her lap, snuggling and scratching his head in her arms.

'God, Herc, you're boiling! How long have you been lying by that fire?' She buried her face in his fluffy neck.

'Dad.'

'Yeah?'

'Why is Hercules here?'

Henry stopped for a second, sighed, and sat down on the blankets by the fire drying his hands.

'What is it?'

'Um ... Hercules is here because Mrs G is here.'

'Riiight ... not that that's in any way an issue, but your face is suggesting otherwise.'

'Mrs G is here because two days ago she was banished from the city, on suspicion of being a witch.' Henry tapped his tired hands on his knees.

Fei drew back. 'What?! What evidence did they have?'

Henry stood up, throwing the cloth down behind him. 'Well, that's just it. This lousy neighbourhood reckoned they didn't see her enough, spent too much time inside alone they thought - 'antisocial' you might say.' Henry rolled his eyes.

Fei sat dumbfounded. 'You could say that about most old people. What makes her any different?'

Henry rubbed his forehead. 'You know how they all gossip till eventually everyone is convinced... Then everything they had seen her doing seemed suspicious – and she was reported and brought in.'

'Did no one mention her problems? Her memory?!'

'What do you think? Everyone in this city is so scared of Mage, they're even willing to persecute a sick old lady. The Prime Minister has a lot to answer to for, spreading that damn propaganda.' He threw a piece of rotten wood into the fire, then slumped back in his chair, burying his face in his hands. 'It's definitely got worse recently – it scares me to death whenever you leave the house.'

Fei sighed. 'So you went and found her?' She stood up, placing Hercules on the chair, which was too wobbly for him, so he jumped off and made his way back to the blankets by the fire.

'I followed the whole process. They couldn't find enough evidence to imprison her so they decided to do their best at just pushing her away – concluded she was too delicate and assumed she would not be able to "wield as much power at her age",' he mocked. 'She was banished last night. I followed the guards and watched them shove her through the North gate and lock it behind them.

I went out later, found her and smuggled her back here. And this is where she'll stay, in the safety of the workshop, until everyone comes to their senses. Or at least until I can find somewhere safer for her.'

'You did the right thing. Mum would have done the same.'

'I know,' said Henry. 'I just wish you didn't have to hide.'

'Me too, but life goes on – and so does the fete! As much as I'd like to just hide away forever, I need to live my life. What have you always told me? If you're gonna be a bear...?'

Henry gave a small smile. 'Be a grizzly.'

They smiled.

'We'd better leave now before everyone's gone. I also told Cora we'd meet her in town in a few hours.'

'You're right, let's go.' He stood up and gave her a bear hug, his jaw wobbling a little. 'It'll be okay, one day, I promise. I hope you've been working on that right hook I taught you.' He sniffed.

Fei smiled. 'Every morning, since you got me those daggers.'

Then she felt her eyes begin to prickle and pulled away. She had never enjoyed crying. Things always had to be 'dealt with' when she cried – so she tried to avoid it.

They turned to see Mrs G standing in the doorway, beaming. Her years of beaming were apparent on her face, which gave her a wonderful warm peachy glow. Hercules jumped down off the chair and began meowing and pawing at her moth-eaten blue dressing gown, which matched her bright eyes. Pushing back her bushy white hair, she waved at Fei.

'Hello, dear,' she smiled.

'Hi, Mrs G.' Fei walked over and gave her a hug. 'It's nice to have you here,' she smiled.

Mrs G raised her shoulders joyfully.

'We're going into town for the fete. Would you like us to bring you anything?' Mrs G looked down at Hercules, who was entwined round her pale legs. She pointed at him and looked back at Fei. 'Treats,' she chuckled.

Fei smiled and nodded, and Hercules mewed with satisfaction. Having packed up what felt like the whole shop, they rushed off, the bell tinkling as they raced through with an excess of 'bits'. They headed straight for Clyde's stable, letting the front door slam on the hallway. Fei's daggers sitting on the hallway table.

With Clyde fed and watered, they harnessed him to the cart and made their way into the city centre, dodging more drunken people on the way – even some drunken guards, who were spilling wine down the front of their uniforms.

'That's comforting,' said Henry.

Fei pulled a face. 'Let's take a short cut.'

Henry nodded as another large, riotous group approached them, pointing at Clyde. They scurried down an empty road as a distant bang erupted, followed by another. Clyde did not enjoy loud noises, and he made his feelings known by stepping a little more heavily on the cobbles and snorting.

BANG, BANG, BANG.

Fireworks burst from the main road behind them.

'Gahh!' Fei jumped, their faces alight with pink and yellow flashes.

'I hate fireworks,' said Henry, stroking Clyde's nose.

'I can't imagine it'll go on for much longer, everyone's getting too drunk,' said Fei, forcing a smile at a group passing them, who patted Clyde's bottom.

He did not like this.

'C'mon, we'd better get a move on before everyone passes out.'

# CHAPTER THREE

Henry, Fei and Cora lived in the North sector of the city, not far, in fact, from the North gate. The North and South gates were the smaller of the four, the West gate being the main entrance to the city, and the East being where the Prime Minister and an assortment of other 'important' people lived.

Given it was the day it was, and the fact there were considerably more visitors this year, Valkyrios had not seen merriment like it in a long time, and the guards at the North gate were not about to miss out. They too had been drinking. Granted, not as much as everyone else.

But enough.

'This isn't right. Why do we have to stay here when everyone else is on one?' one North gate guard whined to the other, as he handed over a small bottle of whatever it was that had got them into their present state.

'I'm sick of this! We were on duty last year as well. No one even comes through this bloody gate,' agreed the other.

'They should just double-lock it. Besides, it's sunny as hell,' said the first guard, waving his bottle and sending more liquid flying. The other one nodded gloomily, watching festival goers skip past, flinging pints of ale over each other, one of them chomping on a juicy-looking chicken leg.

The guards' mouths watered.

'Chicken? I can't remember the last time I had a chicken leg,' said the first guard, drooling. 'That's it. C'mon, we're going. I tell you – no one's gonna notice.'

They nodded drunkenly at each other.

'Wait, lemme have a piss first,' said the second guard, unbuttoning his uniform trousers.

'Well, you'd best do it outside the gate. I'm not standing in your piss when we get back. Hurry up!'

'Really? Not sure how I feel about that Jack,' he objected.

'You haven't got a choice. I'm not standing in your piss, no matter how far gone I am! Just get on with it – besides, look up you plonker that sun is blinding.' Jack took another swig from the bottle and pointed up at the sky.

'I guess,' said the second guard stumbling towards the gate, his head spinning.

'Yeah, you guess now hurry up, Jerry. You got two minutes.'

Jerry swayed as he pulled the strap of his shotgun over his head, placed it on the ground and began to unlock the huge bolts attached to the North gate. He heaved it open and stepped out and round to the side of the wall.

Leaving the gate open.

A large grey cloud began to creep over them while Jerry stood humming and swaying, one hand against the wall, his head hanging down as he peed. The festival music had grown louder, and he was humming along.

The cloud rolled closer, a faint clicking sound emerged from its depths. Jerry turned and squinted behind him.

Silence.

He shrugged back round and continued to hum. The grey cloud slunk round him, making him cough. Wheezing and peeing, he looked up again.

'Hurry up, Jerry!' Jack shouted, taking another impatient swig.

Tok ... tok ... tok ...

Jerry frowned as he fumbled over his trouser zip. He then wafted his hands out in front of him, squinting at his blurry fingers.

'Jack?' he mumbled, as a firework popped in the sky above them. A dank smell swirled round his nostrils, turning his stomach. He clutched one hand to his mouth and used the other to steady himself against the wall, heaving.

'Jerry, I swear to God I'm gonna leave without you,' shouted Jack, as another firework shot up into the sky.

TOK!

Jerry's eyes widened in terror as he turned his head. He stood, frozen, staring at the huge skeletal body of a monstrous Tok.

Its empty black eyes stared down at him from its long, skull-like head. Its sinewy body swayed as the grey passed through its open, fanged mouth. The sparse patches of hair on its body twitching and smoking in the dappled sunlight.

It had long emaciated arms and legs, and display of battle scars, and Jerry stood, stunned to the spot, quivering in horror as the beast slumped onto all fours, sending the ground quaking. Its long, sharp yellowing claws dug into the dry ground as it gave a low, harrowing screech.

Jerry whimpered and fumbled for his gun, not taking his eyes off the beast as it skulked towards him, its unmistakable 'Tok' noise echoing from the flesh-covered hole in its throat that flapped open as it breathed.

'JERRY!' Jack shouted again.

Jerry's hands shook as he loaded his weapon and fired it frantically at the Tok.

Jack froze and turned his head from the neck of the empty bottle as the shot blasted behind him. 'Jerry?' his voice quivered, and he scrambled at his belt, grabbing his shotgun, which he clicked at the top. A tiny flame flickered from the end, and he aimed it at the open gate as the grey cloud rolled through. Sweat pouring from his brow as he edged forward.

The Tok screeched, heaving its body up onto its hind legs, puffed out its gaunt chest and brought its claw slashing down through Jerry's throat. His body flew through the air, blood spiralling behind him.

'J-Jerry, are you there?' Jack peered through the open gate, gasping and flapping away the grey.

He darted his gun around, aiming it at every bit of grey that moved as he slunk along the wall. More fireworks blasted from the festival ground behind.

A small crack sounded from within the cloud. Jack yelled and sent a long stream of hot yellow flames shooting from the end of the gun, waving it round. His teeth gritted as the flames sent the grey rolling away. A small, clear patch of ground opened up in front of him as the flames shrank back into the gun.

'Godammit, Jerry, where are you?' Jack whimpered, sweat cascading over his trembling cheeks.

He stopped and squinted as a dark, shiny mass on the ground slowly came into view. He edged closer, the dark mass growing wider as he leaned forward, the grey creeping further and further back.

Blood.

Jack felt his arms begin to shake, as he peered down at a finger. A hand. A uniform ...

Jerry's lifeless figure lay contorted on the ground, his throat torn to shreds.

'Jerry?' Jack winced.

Another crack came from within the cloud, and Jack swung round in panic.

'Who-who's out there? Sh-show yourself!'

Tok.

The noise shot through him. He pressed hard on the trigger of his gun, sending panicked flames illuminating the towers of grey as he screamed. The flames stopped, and he stared into the abyss, his heart pounding out of his chest.

Jack gasped.

TOK!

Jack gasped as the beast thrashed into his back and he dropped to the ground.

The Tok wheezed, its skin smoking, as it sniffed the guards' twisted bodies. It skulked towards the open gate, the grey tumbling through the doorway with it.

The Tok followed, and made its way through the shadows of the city.

\*\*\*

Henry, Fei and Clyde trudged along the cobbles towards the city centre. Fei found herself slowing as a dank smell wafted past them. She looked up and around.

*Strange.*

'What's up?' asked Henry.

'It's nothing,'

'You sure?'

'Yeah, just smelt something weird.'

'All kinds of smells today! Can't be stopping for every new one,' he chuckled.

'I know, c'mon,' she waved him forward.

As he walked off, Fei glanced back at the bleakness behind her. Clyde snorted, his ears pricked forward, as he too looked behind.

'You smelt it too, huh?' She patted his thick neck and tugged on his reins, following Henry.

It didn't take them long to set up their stall; they'd found a quiet spot, out of the sun, and they weren't selling much. It was still surprisingly hot though, and they found themselves standing under the shelter of the awning most of the time, watching as festival goers got drunker and more willing to spend copious amounts of money on pointless things. It certainly was a good day for people-watching.

'Fei?'

A sweet, quiet voice came from the side of the stall. Fei turned to see a young, slim, dark-skinned, nervous-looking girl smiling at her; a grinning little boy, balanced on her hip, was gripping the tight brown curls that had escaped from her black boater hat, which sat perfectly atop her pretty face.

Fei beamed.

'You didn't tell me you were coming!' Fei charged forward and bear-hugged them both. The little boy squealed with joy.

'Hi, Sam,' said Henry, glancing round from chatting with a customer.

'Hi! Well, I wasn't going to at first, but I couldn't have Ben miss this. Plus Mum heard there was a scarf stall out, so I had no choice really.' She smiled and Fei took Ben, bouncing him on her hip.

Sam straightened out her strikingly modern, green plaid pinafore, and re-floofed the ruffles on the white shirt she was wearing beneath it.

'I haven't seen you in ages.' Fei pulled a sad face.

Sam laughed. 'I know, I'm sorry. It's just, with everything happening at work, all the new people coming in, I haven't stopped.'

'New people? I didn't realise the Council was hiring?'

'They're not.' Sam nodded towards a group of stern-looking people who were walking through the square, peering at each stall. Fei squinted – they were not Kyriosy guards, who wore burgundy. These people were all in black and they were carrying much heavier weapons.

'Silgir! What are *they* doing here?' Cora joined them, her voice raised as she glared at the black-clad soldiers; Fei and Sam exchanged nervous looks.

'They've been sent here after reports of Mage smuggling within the city,' said Sam.

'Well, today would be the perfect day for it, I guess,' Fei sighed, sharing a sheepish look with Jamie

Sam sighed, 'I've been listening in at work, they haven't found anything yet, but I've been asking around and I've been told the new standard protocol is that they all carry an Eremis Pod now. You'll have to shift if they come over here, Fei. They'll clock you.'

Exasperated, Fei nodded. 'Great.'

'How the hell have they got hold of Pods? Those belong to the Sardan.' Cora stood rigid, scowling.

'Calm down, you're not a Sardan yet. No tear-ups today, please.' Fei jiggled Ben on her hip as he looked over at the children playing round a dying tree in the centre of the square.

Cora slumped back down into her chair to read her book. 'Bastards,' she muttered.

'She's not wrong. I daren't think how they got hold of those Pods,' said Fei, staring at the black uniforms.

'The same way they've stolen things from the Sardan since the dawn of time,' Sam sighed. 'The tip of a blade and many, many bullets.'

'Are there any Sardan left?'

'Honestly...I don't know.' They both looked round at Cora who was still reading her book.

'Should've guessed,' said Fei.

The wind picked up, and all the ladies in the square gripped their dainty little hats and shrilled in annoyance. The tree in the square began to sway, and the children laughed at their clothes flapping. Fei lifted her head, sniffing at the wind. There it was again. The same stagnant stench she had smelt earlier. Unsettlingly familiar.

Ben stretched his arms in the direction of the children playing. Fei handed him back to Sam, who popped him on the ground as he attempted to make a run for it.

Fei scanned the square uneasily.

'You okay?' Cora muttered from behind.

'Yeah, just cold,' said Fei as Ben began to wail and attempt to escape Sam's nervous grasp.

'Benny, you're too little. Please, c'mon!'

Fei reached for a shiny engine part and sent it spinning. Ben stared as the sun hit the shiny whizzing spindles of the engine piece, little pockets of light flying across his face and jacket. Reaching out for it, he smiled, and Fei herded him to the back of the stall.

'Easy as,' said Fei.

Sam sighed and rubbed her forehead. 'Thank you' she breathed, sinking on to a stool beside Cora.

What sounded like an argument made its way over to them from the other side of the square. It was Sam's mother – in a row with a vendor over a scarf.

'Oh God!' Sam's face dropped as she glanced over at the tussle.

'Do you want me to go?' said Henry.

'No, it's okay, thank you.' Sam's eyes darted between the approaching Silgir and Ben, who was still staring at the spinning engine piece.

'I'll watch him. You go.' Fei nudged her away.

'But they're not far.'

'It's fine, I'll push off. My dad and Cora will stay with him. Go!' Fei smiled.

Sam jogged over to the stall, glancing at the black uniforms every so often.

Fei watched as the Silgir prowled around the square, asking vendors for their licences and checking what they were selling. They frowned at the goods, clutching their rifles and sneering while passing drunken revellers gave them a wide berth. For a second, Fei was filled with an overwhelming desire to reveal herself to them. To mock them for their inability to spot her.

She smirked at the rebellious thought - but it was short lived.

A piercing scream permeated through the square and everyone's heads swung round. Fei felt her stomach drop and she grabbed Cora's arm. At the top of the square stood a Tok, plain as day, smoking in the sunlight. The biggest one she had ever seen. The bloodied body of a woman flopped in front of it.

'No,' whispered Henry.

Chaos erupted.

# CHAPTER FOUR

Screams rang out as the crowd tore through the stalls. The Kyriosy guards, in a daze, sprang into action and raced towards the Tok, shooting at it, fire blazing from their weapons.

It was no use.

The Tok ripped its way through them, screeching as it slashed at their bodies.

'The Silgir, they're running away,' said Cora. They watched as the Silgir slunk up an alley out of sight.

Fei patted her belt.

Empty.

'My daggers,' she whispered, her heart thumping violently as chilling wave of adrenaline pulsated through her.

'Fei ... Ben,' said Cora, staring at the crying children in the centre of the square. They watched as Ben wandered, bewildered, through the screaming frenzy.

Fei's heart lurched and Cora started tying her boots.

'Stay here,' said Fei, through gritted teeth.

'But ...'

'STAY HERE!'

Henry caught hold of Cora with one hand, and grabbed Fei's sleeve with the other.

'Fei, no, you can't!' His pleading eyes were wide with fear.

Fei gave a weak smile, turned and ran towards the Tok.

'FEINA!' Henry screamed, wrestling Cora.

Sam and her mother had been swept away by the frantic crowd, screaming and climbing over each other. Tears streamed down Sam's face as she struggled through the flailing bodies. Fei forced her way through, as the Tok made its way towards Ben, who was now standing alone, crying beneath the tree, while hysterical parents scooped away their children.

'BEN!' Fei cried, jumping up and around the crowd, the plinking music of the Ferris wheel barely audible above the screams. Fei's eyes darted around, her palms sweating as she dodged the onslaught.

*Weapon, please, weapon! Anything can be a weapon! ANYTHING!*

As the Tok finished off a couple of the braver Kyriosy guards, her eyes landed on an iron goods stall, a long fire poker gleaming at the front. She pelted forward, shoving the desperate festival goers aside.

The Tok had now set its sights on Ben. Fei skidded to a halt, frozen on the square. She closed her eyes for a moment and attempted to steady her pounding heart.

*You can do this, you can do this, you can do this.*

She opened her eyes to see tiny weeds curling around the toes of her boots. A blue flower pushed its way through, opening between her feet. She looked up and bolted towards the Tok.

The loathsome creature picked up speed as it leapt closer to Ben, jumping and flexing its claws. Screeching.

Fei sprinted forward and Sam turned to see the empty stall.

'BEN.' Tears poured down her cheeks as festival goers flew into her.

There he was, in the middle of the square, all on his own, the Tok closing in. Sam felt her heart fall into her stomach as the Tok leapt forward. 'BEN!' she screamed.

Fei smacked the Tok's arm with the poker. It let out a spine-chilling screech as it toppled to one side, scratching into the cobbles as it skidded. Sam blazed towards them through the crowd, forcing her way across the square, when she felt a panicker's arm slam into her head. The mania around her began to quieten as her head hit the cobbles; and her eyes closed.

*Oh God, Oh God, Oh God, OH GOD!*

Fei's body ached with terror.

She stared at the Tok, which was pulling itself off the ground. It opened its mouth, baring rows of sharp bloodied teeth. Fei's eyes darted between the Tok and the weeds squeezing their way through the cobbles, her heart numb as the Tok began to lunge towards them again.

She grabbed hold of Ben's collar. The Tok leapt, and – with a swift jerk – she shoved Ben out of the way. As the toddler rolled towards the crowd, Henry plunged forward and grabbed him. He squeezed Ben tight then gasped at the sight of the ground in front of him. The cobbles were covered in fresh green weeds, and Sam lay motionless on the other side of the square in a bed of blue flowers.

Cora skidded up next to Henry, pulling them both back. Ben was red-faced with shock. Cora looked to her sister, then to the hiding Silgir, who's eyes flicked between the fight and a contraption in their hands.

Fei swung at the Tok's face, her arms almost crumbling with the strain. It recovered almost instantly and swiped back, sending her soaring and slamming into the cobbles, then rolling winded into the side of the tree.

'NO!' screamed Henry.

'We have to do something!' Cora tore away from Henry.

'You're right, you're right. Oh, God, you're right.' Henry's voice shook. Cora bolted towards a Kyriosy guard, ripping the crossbow from his stiff arms as he cowered behind a stall.

Fei gasped. Her body was screaming for air as she crawled, wheezing, towards the poker that had landed a few metres away. The Tok charged and she crawled faster, blood trickling from her head.

*C'MON!*

The Tok leapt and she twisted round as it came thundering down. She forced her body to the side and shrieked as one of its long, thick claws tore into her leg. Blinded by a surge of adrenaline, she took a breath, jumped up and kicked it in the face.

The square had almost cleared, but a few stragglers from the Ferris wheel queue were still clambering to escape. Cora leapt over the barrier and through the metal carriages, shoving her way past.

The Tok stood, shaking its head as it regained its footing. Hands shaking, Fei lifted the metal poker and swiped again, slashing into its side.

The creature screeched, piercing through her ringing ears, she swung the poker again. Horror flooded through her as the Tok grabbed the poker, ripped it from her hands and sent it flying. Fei tumbled backwards, her muscles screaming with pain.

Cora peered through the sights of the crossbow. Watching as Fei crawled away from the Toks raised claw.

As she tapped the trigger, Cora's arrow soared towards the Tok and it gave a piercing screech as the arrow ripped through its arm. The Tok's skin continued to smoke in the sunlight and Fei watched its arm fly towards her again, hitting her in the stomach. She felt every cell in her body throb in agony as she plummeted to the ground, arrows whistling through the air.

She clawed along the cobbles, wrenching her useless body towards the tree, propping her head up against it. She had never felt so weak.

*I can't...*

Blood dripped from the Tok's jaws. Several more arrows flew into its side as it charged.

'FEI, GET UP!' Cora barked, racing towards her sister.

*I can't...*

On the other side of the square, Sam felt a foot kick into her stomach and she jerked awake as the last of the festival goers fled the square. She shakily lifted her head off the weeds, squinting into the square, only to discern Fei's body slumped against the tree trunk. And the Tok, skulking towards her.

Fei sat, her head bleeding and her arms limp by her side as she felt the last dregs of energy leave her. She looked up to see the branches of the tree above her beginning to sprout small green buds.

Heaving her head round towards Cora, she coughed, 'I'm sorry.'

'NO, FEI!' Sam screamed across the square.

'DON'T YOU DARE!' Cora bellowed, racing towards her.

Fei's eyes glazed milky white, and her sight left her. She could hear the Tok and its insidious clicking drawing closer. Clutching the weeds growing beneath her, she felt energy pulsate through her body and the ground began to hum.

All at once, huge tree roots exploded from the ground beneath the Tok, sending a shower of cobbles crashing to the ground, and blasting Cora backwards.

The roots wrapped round the Tok's neck and, with a sharp twist and an ear-splitting screech, it hung limp in the air.

Sam and Henry closed their eyes in despair as the roots slunk back into the ground, leaving the Tok's lifeless body sprawled across the mound of broken cobbles.

Fei opened her eyes but could see nothing but milky white. Blind and exhausted, she dropped her head back against the tree...

'NATHAIR,' came a shrill, accusing voice.

The word was like a punch in the side of her head, and she clenched her eyes shut as Cora skidded up beside her.

Fei felt a hand grab her arm.

Then another.

Still nothing but milky white.

Her ears rang, as she just about made out the blurry image of a growing crowd. The vague mumbles of an onslaught of abuse filled her head as she lay against the tree. The numb tapping of Cora's hand on her cheek.

'Fei ... FEI, you need to stand up, now, GET UP. We *have* to get you out of here.'

Fei felt Cora's strong little hands pull at her arm as Henry lifted her up and wrapped her arm over his shoulder; Cora ducked under her other arm.

'YOU BROUGHT THAT DEVIL HERE!' screamed a voice.

Fei winced as she wobbled to her feet, the gut wrenching feeling of both Henry and Cora shaking their heads.

'No, no, no. Please,' pleaded Henry.

'ARREST HER!' shouted another.

'Please, you don't understand. She was protecting you,' said Henry as the townsfolk began to close in. Fei winced at what she thought must be wall-shaped sweets flying into the side of her head.

'Dad, what do we do?' whispered Cora.

'You do nothing,' rasped Fei, the blurry figures coming into focus.

'PLEASE. I implore you. She was only protecting you!' repeated Henry.

'She is no danger to you, I promise,' said Sam, her voice shaking, while Ben howled and clutched at her leg.

'MAGE.'

'DEMON.'

'ARREST HER.'

'You need to go,' Fei wheezed to Cora.

'Don't be stupid, I'm not going anywhere,' Cora growled back.

'You *have* to!'

'Shut up, sister!'

'PLEASE, NO!' Henry's voice cracked, and the crowd began to cheer as regimented feet marched towards them. Fei's sight had returned enough for her to see six blurry burgundy jackets arrive in front of them.

'No, please, no. She meant no harm!' begged Henry.

'She is a friend of mine. I know her, she is no threat, I promise. Please, look, I work for the Council, I know these people!' said Sam.

'Feina Fourlise, you are under arrest for the practice of dark Nathair magic, under the account of multiple witnesses. Henry Fourlise, you are under arrest for sheltering enemies of the state.'

Henry shook his head.

'Cora Fourlise, you are also under arrest on suspicion of having inherited the Nathair magic. You will be investigated and must come with us.'

'NO!' Fei felt a harrowing emptiness flood through her. 'You can't, please!'

'What?' said Cora.

'No. No, please,' said Henry.

Sam shot a look at the Silgir; then, blocking Fei's view, she hugged her tight, whispering in her ear. 'Wherever they take you, don't make a fuss and don't use it again, do you hear? They'll be looking for any reason to punish you – or worse. Don't give them any excuse.'

'Sam, I...' Fei sniffed.

'You'll be okay, I promise.'

Fei watched as Sam's body was ripped away from her.

'SAM!' she screamed.

The guards sprang forward as Henry shot out his arm in protest, wrenching him away from the girls.

'Put him in the third one,' muttered a Silgir.

'DAD,' Fei felt her world spinning out of control, and she grabbed hold of Cora with all her remaining strength.

'Fei,' whispered Cora.

'It's okay, it's okay. They have nothing on you.'

'Take her,' said the same Silgir.

'No, no, please!' shouted Fei, clinging desperately to Cora's little green jacket.

The Silgir wrenched them apart while the crowd stood jeering. Fei looked down to see a square of torn jacket in her shaking hand.

'Get off me!' shouted Cora as she wrestled with the guards, kicking and scratching as they carried her away.

A particularly large Silgir bent down to Fei's eye level, holding a small yellow stone up to her ear, a devious smile crept across his face.

She could hear it vibrating.

'You so much as look at your sister, Mage, and she dies,' he muttered.

Fei sent a stream of spit pelting into his eye. Shocked by her own confidence, she trembled as a sharp weight struck into the back of her head and everything began to blur again. A shrill ringing blasted through her head, and she felt her body flop into the guard's arms, the blaring crowd fading away.

'Fei!' came a muffled shriek from Cora, who was writhing in the arms of the Silgir.

Fei watched as her sister was pushed into a large black carriage, a barred door slammed behind her.

The noise began to fade until there was only ringing. Piercing ringing.

She felt her feet being dragged along the cobbles towards another black carriage, her head flopped on one side, the mumbles of the cheering crowd dulling. Closing her eyes, she took in her last smell of the city as she was pushed into the carriage. The door locked behind her.

# CHAPTER FIVE

The pain in her head was staggering. Blinding. She forced open her eyes. All she could see was the blurry inside of a dark jail cell. The floor was cold and damp, and she really didn't want to know whatever is was that was dripping from the walls.

*Why, why, why, why?*

Moving her hand to the back of her head, she felt a clump of crusty blood in her hair, and a large agonising lump buried beneath her mass of matted curls. Hissing in pain she attempted to stand up, wobbling as she stumbled towards the cell door.

Sleep. One of the few things she knew for sure was that sleep would re-energise her. But she would have to sleep for a week to recover from what had happened in the square; agony pulsated through her body as she clung to the barred door.

'Cora?' she coughed.

'Try anything, Mage, and this bullet goes straight into her skull,' came the voice of a guard. She peered to her left to see the stony-faced guard standing outside the neighbouring cell, where Cora sat stoically in the corner.

'Are you okay?' asked Fei.

'Fine.' Cora looked unimpressed.

'Where's Dad?'

'Somewhere far away from you, Mage,' said the guard, a look of pure boredom on his face. 'No more talking.' He knocked on Cora's cell door with a baton, then stood staring at Fei, his hands crossed in front of him.

'Can you at least tell us how long we're going to be here?' asked Fei, her face pressed up between the cold bars of her cell. The guard gave her a slow, silent look, then removed the gun from his back, holding it in front of him.

Fei looked at Cora, who shrugged and dropped her head between her knees. It was bleak. So very bleak.

Dark, awful, horrible.

Cold.

It seemed so pointless – spending twenty-seven years hiding in the shadows, only to be thrust kicking and screaming into the light, before being thrown into a cell.

Fei had often imagined what it would be like, being out in the open – perhaps, with time and progression, people might have become more open minded.

*So naive.*

*Why did I run out there like that? Why?!*

Ben. Of course.

Her eyes glazed over. Rubbing her face, she let herself slide back down, on to the hard floor.

*If I could go back in time, I would do the same again.*
No change.
This had been coming for her, no matter what.
Destiny.
Horrible, annoying destiny.
*Urgh. I hate that word.*

What felt like hours went by; It was now dark outside and Fei watched through the tiny window as the sky filled with grey. The odd spot drifted in occasionally, making them all cough. Her trousers had now well and truly absorbed the stench of the cell floor. She sat on the cold cobbles, arms wrapped round her legs, her head on her knees.

Clunk!

The large wooden door at the end of the corridor creaked open. Fei lifted her head and clambered, wincing, to her feet. She heard footsteps, and voices whispering as she stood wide-eyed at the cell door, peering out.

Two heavily armed Silgir marched towards Cora and began unlocking her cell; she was stony-faced and bouncing in the corner, ready for a tear up.

'Hey, where are you taking her? HEY!' Fei shouted, her throat stinging.

They ignored her and proceeded to wrestle Cora to the ground, shackle her and lift her. They carried her wriggling body towards the open door at the end of the corridor.

'Get your hands off me, you scum!' Cora writhed as the guards carried her away.

'HEY!' Fei shouted again.

Three more Silgir walked towards her. They unlocked the cell and charged in, grabbing her arms, and shackling her wrists.

*Don't fuss, don't fuss, don't fuss.*

Fei stared ahead at the large, bleak door that Cora had disappeared through.

'Where are you taking us? Where's our father?' She felt herself being practically lifted off the ground, as the guards pulled her out.

'You know the deal, Mage,' a Silgir said quietly behind her.

Waves of adrenaline coursed through her as they walked through a maze of dark corridors. Her breath leaving her trembling body in short, sharp puffs.

Moans and pleas for release rebounded off the walls of the long corridors, lit only by large gas lanterns. Ahead, Fei could see a doorway to what looked like the outside. The corridor grew colder as they approached; two Kyriosy guards stood either side of it, huge shotguns in their hands.

Fei felt the cold night air claw at her face as the corridor led into a large courtyard. In the centre stood the tallest woman she had ever seen, her eyes fixed on them.

Fei stared into the woman's narrow eyes. The guard pushed the end of his shotgun into her back, shoving her forward down the steps.

The woman was wearing the finest Kyriosy armour, which had clearly seen years of use, as it was covered in scratches and scuff marks. Her fiery ginger hair had been looped up on her head, with a long shiny braid resting on her shoulder. She had a large, ornate riffle strapped to her back.

Fei and Cora arrived in front of her. She towered over them, her intense blue eyes settling on Fei.

'This is the one, Captain Scarthe.' The guards tapped Fei on the back of her head. Fei grimaced.

'I know,' said Captain Scarthe, raising a bushy ginger eyebrow. 'I will take it from here – she's been waiting long enough.'

The girls shifted on their feet.

'Are you sure you do not need further assistance with this one, Captain?' asked one of the guards.

The Captain gave him a piercing look, to which he swiftly nodded, pushed the pair forward, and headed back to the prison.

'Who are you? And where is our father?' demanded Cora. The Captain stood silent, ignoring Cora and continuing to stare at Fei.

'Did you hear me?' Cora's face crumpled in annoyance.

Captain Scarthe took one of the two pistols she had on her belt and pointed it at Cora. Fei felt small beads of sweat begin to form on her brow.

'I need not say it again Mage,' said the Captain. Fei gave a stiff nod, her face darkening.

'I shall instruct you on where to go.' Captain Scarthe nodded towards some large, metal double doors behind her.

The girls watched in confusion as the Captain indicated the opening doors, revealing the street behind them. Nervously they walked ahead, as the grinding sound of heavy metal hinges echoed round the courtyard. The Captain at their heels.

On the street sat another of the barred black carriages from the square, a guard standing beside it. He nodded and opened the carriage door. The girls stopped beside it, hesitating. It was dark and silent, and there was a chilling emptiness in the air.

'Inside!' barked the Captain.

'Where are you taking us?' asked Fei.

'Inside!' the Captain snarled again.

Fei clenched her jaw. The girls stepped in, and the Captain climbed in behind them. The girls on one side, the Captain opposite, still pointing her pistol at Cora.

The monotonous clopping of the horses' hooves sounded deafening in the silent early morning, and the Captain did not take her eyes off Fei for a second. They bumped and shook through the dark, empty city streets. The celebrations had well and truly ended and they watched as torn down banners and abandoned carts whizz past them. But as they continued, the streets grew cleaner and brighter, better lit by gas lamps and torches.

*We're going east.*

Fei watched, perplexed, as the buildings became grander, and the cars became shinier.

*Why the hell are we going east?*

They drew to a halt outside a building the girls had only ever seen at the top of government letters and photographs.

*It couldn't be.*

Fei rubbed her raw wrists as the carriage door swung open.

'Out!' The Captain waved her pistol at the door until they crept out, staring up at the large house.

Fei was mystified. She looked over at Cora, nodding up at the house. Cora shrugged, equally perplexed.

'Move.'

Cora felt a nudge in her back and began shuffling forward, Fei beside her.

The house was pristine. Its walls gleamed above an assortment of flickering gas lamps, without a speck of soot or dust to be seen. They edged down the concrete path, on either side of which were small beds of the most beautiful flowers. (Flowers like these didn't grow anywhere anymore.) Two guards stood on either side of the large black double doors at the end of the path. They nodded at the Captain.

As the doors opened, light radiated from inside the hallway, casting a yellow glow over their stunned faces, they stood gawping in the hallway. It was the most beautiful house they had ever seen, and the smell of freshly cooked biscuits hugged their faces.

The high ceiling was painted like the sky: clear blue with clouds and birds drifting across it. A wide staircase twisted its way up the building, carpeted in spotless white; they almost missed the two fluffy white cats sitting on it. As the girls gawped at the large gold chandelier and the mirrors in their filigree frames, the Captain nudged them down the marble hallway. The cats watched them closely as they walked towards another set of double doors, another set of guards waiting to allow them in.

The house was almost disturbingly pleasant.

The cats leapt down the stairs and ran ahead into the room they were walking towards. The guards at the door nodded at the Captain as they entered the room and closed the doors behind them.

The cats jumped up on to a vast green Chesterfield sofa facing a grand fireplace. All the curtains were closed, except for one window at the end of the beautiful room, where a small woman with shiny black hair sat on the windowsill, sipping tea from a pastel-blue teacup. The teacup matched perfectly with her long blue satin skirt, which was detailed with lace and a red sash round her waist. They stared open-mouthed at her as she gazed out of the window.

'I had hoped our first meeting would be under different circumstances,' said the woman.

The girl's faces were a picture of confusion.

'But it seems you are just too much like your mother.' The Prime Minister put down her cup and turned to look at the girls.

# CHAPTER SIX

For someone the Fourlise family had hated so bitterly, for so long, the Prime Minister had a remarkably kind face with soft and delicate features. Her warm smile sent small lines dancing round her brown eyes and crimson lips.

Fei gritted her teeth. 'Why are we here?' she asked sharply.

The woman stretched out her hand. 'Prime Minister Chéa Horne. So very pleased to meet you. How long I have waited for this moment!'

Fei frowned, keeping her hands firmly in her pockets, and turning away to look into the huge fire. Cora, too, looked away in protest. The Prime Minister nodded and smiled.

'Captain, please remove their restraints,' she instructed, sitting down on the Chesterfield while the cats rubbed against her, purring loudly.

The girls stood, perplexed, as the Captain unlocked their metal shackles. Rubbing their red wrists, they stared at Chéa.

'Okay, what the hell is going on?' demanded Fei.

'Please sit, girls.' Chéa gestured towards the equally large sofa opposite, as Cora crossed her arms in further protest. 'I must explain some things to you, and it may take some time.'

'You've a lot to answer for!' said Fei, her blood boiling as she slid onto the sofa.

'I'll stay standing, thanks,' Cora snapped.

'I knew your mother … very well,' said Chéa.

Fei's eyes widened and Cora's jaw dropped.

'You what…?' said Fei.

'We were great friends and I miss her terribly.' Chéa's eyes began to glisten a little, as Cora slid down next to Fei.

'What are you on about? *You're* the reason we just got beaten and dragged through the streets! Oh, and where might our father be?' said Fei, her fingers tightening into the chesterfield.

'Yes, I know, I'm so sorry. If there had been another way, I promise we would have taken it, but the risk has always been too great and not worth the chance. Your father is safe at home – with Mrs Goetz,' said Chéa, smiling weakly.

The girls sat dumbfounded.

'Girls, I'm not who you think I am. I'm a Sardan, I always have been.'

'You're a Sardan?' said Cora, leaning forward.

Fei interrupted. 'I don't understand, you hate Mage. That letter we all got … you can't be…and also we're just supposed to believe you?'

'I sent that letter as a ploy, to scare people off, discourage them from attacking magical folk.' Chéa unbuttoned her frilled sleeve and lifted it, revealing a small, blurry tattoo of the Sardan crest on her wrist.

The girls recognised the same blue smudge their mother had had.

Fei sat, shaking her head, as Cora reached forward to rub at the tattoo on Chéa's arm.

Smiling at the girls, the Prime Minister nodded at Captain Scarthe. As they peered round, the captain thrust her tattooed arm in their faces.

'Call me Berrie. Apologies for the head knock,' boomed the captain, smiling broadly. Fei rubbed the back of her head and gave a small nod.

'Why are we only finding this out now?' asked Fei.

'Your mother and I fought in the Crusades together. We fought against the Mage hunts, controlled and initiated by her. Ela.'

The girls' faces dropped. For years they had lived in the shadows, haunted by her existence. They felt a chill race up their spines.

'And we won, at least we thought we had, till she came back thirteen years ago.' Chéa looked at the girls.

'Why?' Fei's eye twitched.

'Because your mother had the one thing Ela needed, to do what she has now done.'

'The dagger,' Fei whispered, the lump in her throat returning.

Chéa nodded.

'Why did she need it?' asked Cora, looking pale.

'The dagger belonged to Ela's sister, Gyda. Hundreds of years ago, in a place called Parras, parallel to our world, Ela was born. Treasured by her creator, Vidras, she was much loved and grew up kind and caring, knowing that some day she would inherit the Earth, maintaining balance and harmony forever. Some years later, her sister, Gyda, arrived, whom she loved dearly. But, since Ela was the firstborn, she had to shoulder heavy responsibilities. Her freedom was limited, and she spent most of her life preparing to rule.

'Gyda, however, was granted a childhood of choice and excitement. Although Ela loved her sister deeply, she could not help but grow jealous. And her jealousy did not go unnoticed by Vidras. Years later, when Vidras was dying, he made a choice that would change the course of history. Vidras decided to split the power equally – between Ela, the Earth and Gyda. The energy Vidras sent to the Earth is as concentrated as that which lies in Ela. This energy created the Aon.'

The girls' eyes widened.

'The Aon?' repeated Cora. The Prime Minister held out a patient hand.

'When Vidras died, Ela fell into a very dark place. One night she could not contain her rage any longer, and she attacked their home with a group of loyal followers. She even ordered Gyda's assassination, in an attempt to reclaim the power she believed was her birth right.

'Gyda was woken and escaped into the night alone. Ela watched and followed her into the forest. Gyda ran deep into its heart, eventually dropping to her knees in despair – for she loved her sister deeply and could not believe Ela really wished to kill her.

Before she died, Gyda enchanted her dagger, allowing those who possessed it to find the heart of Vidras's, and thus the Aon's, power. She then strategically gifted her powers to the earth, creating warriors, protectors of the Earth and the forest – Nathair – who, over the years, would be born randomly, all over the world, so they could not be easily traced. After she had done this, she sent the dagger to Earth, where it has been protected and held close by Nathair and Sardan for generations.

'Ela then killed Gyda in cold blood, and in doing so she plummeted to Earth and was unable to return. Hungry to find the Nathair and the Aon, she searched for years for the dagger, mercilessly annihilating magical folk the world over, under the cover of political intent; polluting the minds of leaders - and she was very successful - leading to the rise of the Sardan, the only group of humans who have sworn to protect the forest and the magical folk even at the cost of their own lives.

After Ela took Gyda's dagger from your mother, she found the heart of the forest, took it, and poisoned it. Ever since, it has been impossible for the Aon to surface and, as far as we know, the Caraim were tortured so mercilessly that they were all but wiped out. We do not know how to find the dagger.'

'The Caraim?' echoed Cora.

The Minister held out another patient hand.

Fei's eyes widened. 'The grey?'

'Yes. It began the day she poisoned the heart of the forest. Once the grey has consumed the Earth, Ela will have taken enough of the earth's power to control our world for good. Thus, the line of Aon will die. The stronger the grey, the stronger the Tok – which is why one of them was able to come out in broad daylight today.

Ela has grown far more powerful than we ever imagined, and far quicker. We had hoped we would be able to do this without involving you; today has shown us this is not possible.'

Chéa smiled awkwardly at Fei, who sat staring at the floor.

'We?' asked Cora, puzzled.

'The Sardan. The few of us who are left have been protecting magical folk as best we can, and we will do so till the end. I was charged with protecting you, Fei, by your mother. So many Sardan have been killed over the years that the remaining Nathair and the Aon are our last hope. And to make our task more difficult, we don't even know the whereabouts of the Aon, or indeed who they are.'

Cora placed her hand on Fei's. It was hot and her heart was racing. Fei shot up and paced over to the large old bookcase in the corner, a hand on her sodden brow.

'What are you, like a double agent or something? How the hell am I supposed to believe all this? And what do you mean, the Aon are no more?! Have they ever even been real? And what the hell are the Caraim?' demanded Fei.

'I guess you could call me a double agent, and the Aon? Yes they are definitely real. I knew one a very long time ago, she was my friend when we were young. She was killed before the Aon had time to surface in her. I believe it transferred to another before she died, but we have no way of tracing its movements. It's like trying to find a needle in a haystack. Besides, its power may already have been poisoned.

'The Caraim were a group of incredibly powerful and benevolent witches, who tracked and protected the

Aon as they grew. It was a lot harder for us Sardan, being human, to locate their energy. But we know what you can do, Fei, and what the remaining few like you can do.' The Prime Minister got to her feet, clenching her hands together.

'This is too much! I don't know what you think I can possibly do to help. And there's no way in hell I'm getting her involved,' Fei replied, nodding in Cora's direction.

'Please believe me when I tell you we have done everything we can to keep you out of this, but we're simply not strong enough,' said Chéa, moving closer, fiddling with the buttons on her sleeve.

'And you really think I'm going to be better at this than hundreds of trained warriors? This has to be a joke.' Fei leaned her hands and forehead against the bookcase, her heart pounding. 'I know nothing,' she whimpered.

Chéa placed her hand on Fei's shoulder.

'You are stronger than you know. And if you are anything like your mother, I know you will not fail. Your home needs you – we need you,' she smiled.

Fei peeked at Chéa from beneath her arm; her mind was blank. She expected another wave of emptiness to pass through her but was greeted with numbness.

Expectation.

Visibility.

'In light of all this, what exactly is it you need her to do?' asked Cora.

'My daughter, Morie, lives in the city of Daramere, not far from here. Go to her. She is a Sardan, too, and has been tracking the remaining Nathair warriors for years. Together, you can find the last living Nathair, travel to the heart of the forest, and take back the power Ela has stolen from the Earth and the Aon. Only then will she be weak enough to be defeated.'

Fei looked at the Prime Minister. 'And how exactly are we meant to do that? Is there a manual? Instructions?'

Chéa looked defeated as Cora shuffled over to stand next to her sister.

'This is insane!' exploded Fei. 'This morning I was a mechanic, getting judged for having slightly dirty clothes. Now I'm part of a tiny group who are apparently the Earth's last chance of survival against a thousand-year-old tyrannical maniac who killed my mother!'

The fire blazed a little more fiercely. 'My entire life I've had to suppress and hide what I am – and I *have*. Happily, too. I can't just forget that!' The Prime Minister looked down.

'We *have* to go, Fei,' interrupted Cora, looking at her sister with a hopeful, weak smile, 'for Mum.' She felt her lip tremble and pinched at her hand. She *never* cried.

'For Mum?' retorted Fei. 'Mum's dead because of this – and there's no way I'm about to let that happen to you!'

Fei marched over to the double doors and started bashing her fists against the wood. 'Let me out. I'm serious!' she shouted. 'Tell them to let me out please!' She turned to look at Chéa, her cheeks glistening, as she drew her sooty sleeve across her nose.

'Fei, wait!' Cora called, as Chéa nodded at the guards to open the doors.

Fei rushed out, sniffing. Chéa and the Captain stood in the hallway and watched Fei jog down the path, followed by Cora.

'We can't just run away from this,' Cora bumped alongside her sister.

Fei silently turned away. It was the middle of the night and Cora watched helplessly as her sister disappeared into the darkness.

# CHAPTER SEVEN

A million thoughts flew in and out of Fei's head, each one more tormenting than the last, as her tears streamed. The icy chill blowing through the cold, dark, empty city blasted her face as she rushed along the streets.

*WHY! Why had no one prepared her for this?*

This sudden onslaught of recognition and expectation.

The cobbles under her feet blended into one, as the streets got dingier; she was almost home. Although she had taken multiple hits today, this latest revelation was hitting the hardest.

Occasionally shifting into a shadowy alleyway to avoid people, she finally reached her house. She stared at the black boards over the windows, and the two 'no entry' signs taped across the front door. A dictionary of abuse had been scrawled across the bricks.

She had thought about this day for a long time – most days, in fact. Imagined. Wondered.

She was no fool. She'd always known she would meet huge obstacles, but never like this. She clutched at her stomach, the pain rising as her body stiffened with every sniff back of a tear.

The 'Fourlise Motorcycles' sign creaked in the wind. After looking around, she ducked beneath the tape and crept into the house. A stream of adrenaline shot through her aching body as Jamie leapt out, squeezing his bear arms around her.

'Oh, thank God!' He pulled away and wrapped his calloused hands round her face.

'Ow, ow, ow.' Fei grimaced and slumped back onto the hallway bench, to see her daggers glinting on the hall table opposite. She huffed.

'I'm so sorry, Fei. Are you okay? Where's Cora?'

'I think the Captain is bringing her home.'

Fei rubbed at her tender arms. 'Dad, why didn't you tell me you knew about the Prime Minister, and that she and Mum were friends?' she asked.

Henry sat down on the bench next to her. 'I didn't want you to involved in that world. I worried it would lead to you being exposed and killed,' he said, picking at some dry mud on one of the coats beside him. 'I thought I'd be able to keep you safe.'

His eyes glistened.

Fei sighed, rubbing her forehead. 'You've always protected me. But there are some things you can't protect me from; and I need to know about those things, even if I wish I didn't.'

'I know. It's just that, after what happened to your mother, I couldn't bear the thought of losing you or your sister as well.'

'You won't lose us.'

'I bloody better not.' They chuckled.

'What did you talk about with the Prime Minister?' he asked. 'After Captain Scarthe smuggled me back here, I didn't hear anything, other than that you were going to be taken to her.'

'Oh, not much. Just that she and Mum were friends, that she is a Sardan, and that basically the malevolent god that is Ela killed Mum. You know ... fun stuff!'

'So not much then.'

They smiled, then found themselves wavering as the blackness of their usually colourful house dropped back into their reality.

'It's not easy to kill a god,' said Henry, staring down at the dusty floorboards.

'You don't say.'

'But your mother did it, with Chéa and...'

Fei cut in. 'How did she come back? How did she find her? I don't understand.'

'Like I said, it ain't easy. I just hope Chéa's got a plan.'

Fei stared at her daggers on the hall table. 'Yeah...'

'We'll have to move. The four of us. Chéa told me she would help us set up in another city. I'll start planning in the morning. But where to go?' said Henry, sighing at the prospect of having to move again.

Fei felt a twinge of curiosity intertwine with her pain.

'What about Daramere?'

'What? I mean, yeah, I suppose. It's certainly closer to Little Corby which is useful for the shop.' He nodded. 'But why Daramere?'

'No reason, just heard good things.'

A small puff of grey crept under the door, making them both cough. Then it clicked and Cora slunk in sheepishly, looking at them both, pointing and huffing at the tape she'd had to duck beneath, her gas mask strapped on tightly.

Fei and Henry waved at her as Hercules pottered down the stairs. Cora walked over and pulled off her gas mask, picked him up and buried her face in his ginger stripes.

Henry stood, kissed them both on the forehead and creaked up the stairs. 'You two get some sleep, we've got a lot of planning to do in the morning. And no going outside!'

They both forced a smile.

Fei was exhausted – her feet felt like lead weights. She picked up her daggers and heaved her tired body upstairs to bed, followed by Cora, who was cradling Hercules.

She let her body drop onto her bed, and stared numb, at the ceiling. She had finally been given the opportunity she'd spent her entire life wanting. And it terrified her.

'Fei?' Cora sat on the bed next to her, her face stoic, and Hercules purring loudly in her arms.

'I don't want to talk about it now, I'm so drained.' Fei used her remaining strength to wrench off her boots, and kick her daggers under the bed.

'Did you tell Dad?' asked Cora.

'No, don't tell him. Not yet at least. He won't take it well.'

Cora sat silent for a moment, stroking Hercules. 'We have to go.'

'I can't talk about this right now, it's too much, and I just don't feel I'm the one. I'm sorry sister, I can't.' Fei sank down into bed and thrust the covers over her face. Cora pushed herself up and shuffled to the doorway.

'No, you're right. You're not. Mum was, and she failed.' Cora snuggled into Hercules's warm tummy and walked with him to her room.

Fei squeezed her eyes shut as Cora settled into her bed next door, hearing the loose pole of the bed frame squeak as she nestled in.

Fei was desperate for sleep but, much to her annoyance, found herself wide awake in the middle of the night. Visions of failure tormented her as she tossed and turned for hours, but her bed felt uncharacteristically uncomfortable. The pressure she felt was immense, and her covers felt tonnes heavier.

Kicking them off, she flung her feet out into the cold air and held her aching head in her hands. She looked up at where a piece of tape had peeled off the window and the black board had fallen away a little. A small triangle of the street was illuminated beneath the streetlamps.

A grey cloud slunk past, obscuring the lamps and dimming the room further. She felt it, every cell in her body ached - both in exhaustion and for the challenge. The adventure. Embracing her 'Destiny'.

*Urgh.*

*Hate that word.*

She watched the grey cloud disappear into the night, drifting off to clog the lungs of another city.

Walking into the hall, she looked up at the small square door leading to the attic. She used to think that one day she might be tall enough to reach and open it, but, alas, she never grew quite high enough. But she'd always try, you know, just in case she happened to grow a bit.

She strained to reach it as usual, exasperated by the stubborn gap between her fingers and the door. Reaching for the wooden pole they kept nearby for her, she pushed the end against the corner of the door. It swivelled open, revealing the old wooden steps folded up just above it. She prodded again and stood back as the steps swung down.

A thick layer of dust had always lined the attic and was, incidentally, home to large family of spiders. She had informed Cora of this, which was why Cora had never been up there. Cora wasn't bothered by much, but spiders were definitely a 'no go'!

As she walked round the creaking attic, she heard Cora's wobbly bed pole squeaking downstairs. She worried that one day the floor would give way and she would plummet into her bed below, covered in bricks and dust.

Her eyes landed on a weathered blue box, with the letter 'D' scrawled on the lid. She crouched down beside it and brushed the top, coughing as a cloud of dust rose.

After their mother died, they had put all her special things in this box. Fei made a point of not looking in it too often; her chest hurt every time she did, and she didn't enjoy smiling and crying at the same time. Even looking at the box she felt a lump forming in her throat. She remembered far too much about her mother, and often wished she could forget it all – especially the smell of her perfume, mostly masked by the smell of wet dog.

*Gee!*

Fei tipped her head back as tears welled up in her eyes. How much her life had changed after that day! She missed them both so much, it hurt.

The box had gained a few holes in the corners over the years, which made removing the lid a little easier. As she placed it on the ground, memories washed over her. She pulled out some dusty black button-up walking boots. She remembered how she used to rummage around in her mother's cupboard as a child, and flop around the house in these boots. Sighing, she put them on one side.

A little straw boater hat, now covered in tiny holes, was squashed up between some old newspapers. Its top had caved in, she pushed it back up, only for it to pop back in again. She smiled and placed it on top of the boots.

The moonlight shone in through a circular window, which Henry had apparently decided not to bother boarding up.

*It was high enough not to worry about.*

The light had caught something poking out from under a book. Fei reached down, her fingers finding a cold piece of metal. She pulled her hand back and on it sat a small gold pin. It was considerably dented and scratched. Rubbing it with her fingers, she wiped off the dust.

There it was – the Sardan crest. A dagger inside a crown, with wings and a sun above the hilt. No matter how dented, it was definitely more impactful in pin form. Fei had always thought it was such a shame the tattoos had become so faded.

Fei sat back, holding the pin tightly. A tear made its way down her cheek and fell onto the boots, leaving a tiny black puddle. Wiping the boot and dusting them both properly, she pulled them onto her feet.

They were a little big. Which wasn't surprising. She had always been the small one in the family.

She walked over to an old, cracked mirror in the corner of the room, under a low ceiling beside the window. Crouching, she gazed at her reflection, the moonlight giving her face a pale glow. She had always thought Cora looked more like their mother than she did, but the resemblance was certainly there. Mostly in the hair.

She looked out of the window to see the only bushy tree in the street looking bushier than ever. Frankly, she thought, it was bizarre that no one had ever clocked her before - all the other trees in the street hadn't grown a decent leaf in years.

Another, slightly darker-looking grey cloud wafted by. Hiding the light of the moon, it crawled round the bushy tree, its leaves curling as it rolled through. She looked back at her reflection, now a little duller looking.

No matter how much it terrified her, she knew she had no choice. She had to go.

The gleam on the Sardan pin had vanished.

*I can't let them down. I can't let Cora down.*

*I can't let Mum down.*

She took a breath as she looked down at her mother's boots. She was filled with confidence and terror; it was exciting, but... Outlaw. That's what she was now, and she couldn't risk being out in daylight. She would have to leave tonight.

Click.

The sound of a door shutting downstairs made its way into the attic. Fei's brow furrowed. She walked over to the square door and peered down the steps below.

She felt the air leave her body.

# CHAPTER EIGHT

Two heads, shortly followed by another, snuck silently along the hallway. With huge, gleaming knives in their hands.

She drew back, cupping her hands tightly over her mouth. Her heart pounded. She looked around for anything she could use as a weapon.

Nothing.

*I can't believe this!*

Only old clothes and books. Her daggers were under her bed below. She looked again, to see the three strangers disappear beneath the first floor staircase. Silently removing her mother's boots, she tiptoed down. Sweat dripped from her forehead as she hugged the walls and peered into Cora's bedroom – there was the long, slim, comforting mound of her body still peacefully in her bed, with Hercules asleep next to her.

She peeked over the top of the stairs as the three figures separated, one heading in the direction of Henry's workshop.

*Mrs G!*

She didn't think it was possible her heart could thump any faster. She flew into her bedroom and stopped in shock – there were bed covers strewn across the floor and clothes hanging out of her chest of drawers. Baffled, she lifted her sheets to grab for her daggers beneath.

*What? No!*

Her stomach sank.

She patted desperately across the empty floorboards, only to pull back a dusty, empty hand.

*WHERE THE HELL ARE THEY?!*

The panicked ringing in her ears was deafening.

She spun round; still no one there. She darted into Cora's room, grabbing at the Cora-shaped mound.

Empty.

Cora gone – crossbow gone, chest of drawers open and ransacked. Hercules still sitting contentedly on her bed.

*WHAT? WHAT? WHAT? WHAT!*

Fei grabbed at her head, her shirt pooling with sweat as she heard a creak from downstairs. She peered round the bedroom door to see one of the intruders halfway up. Her muscles felt stiff with fear as her eyes darted round Cora's dark room. They fell on her bed, on the loose pole that sat on the end.

*Thank God she doesn't listen!*

She darted over and, as quietly as she could, began twisting out the pole. Her hands throbbing. Hercules watched from the bed, flicking his tail in curiosity. Fei's frantic gaze flicked between the door and her hands.

*Cora, where are you!*

She could hear the light creeks of the intruders' footsteps getting closer. Her clammy hands slipped on the metal, and the pole's familiar squeak rang out through the room.

Fei froze – as the intruders' feet stopped, turned and started making their way towards Cora's room. Feeling as if her heart was going to burst out of her chest, she pulled the pole from the bed and slipped across the room to hide beside the doorway.

She squeezed her hands over her mouth, as she heard the feet stop outside the door.

The armed hand of the intruder moved slowly into the darkened room, the light in the hallway glinting on his knife.

*Okay, do it. Just do it. Now. Just do it...Now. NOW!*

Fei jolted forward, bringing the pole crashing down on the intruder's arm; his dagger toppled to the ground as he groaned in pain.

She swung the pole back, smacking it into the back of his head, sending him thumping to the ground in a daze.

Lunging forward, she grabbed his knife. Pain swept through her body as the intruder spun round and kicked her in the stomach. She rolled across the floorboards wheezing, winded, as she spun to avoid his swiping arm.

She elbowed him in the stomach, which gave her a chance to hit him on the head with the pole again. There was a harrowing crack and he fell to the ground, motionless.

*Oh God. Oh God.*

*Oh God .*

*OH GOD.*

*What the hell is happening!*

Her mind flew a million miles an hour as horrific visions of Cora's dead body waiting for her at the bottom of the house pulsated through her blasting head. Gasping, and gripping her stomach, she stumbled as quietly as she could out of the door.

Then her heart stopped.

Another intruder stood at the bottom of the stairs, staring up at her.

Fei gasped, diving to the side as he grabbed his knife and flung it at her. Narrowly missing the side of her head, it lodged in her bedroom door.

She found herself back in Cora's room, scrambled up off the dark floor and slid into Cora's large wardrobe, carefully pulling the door shut behind her. She closed her eyes, focusing on her erratic breath.

*Please be okay, Cora.*

*Please be okay!*

*Oh God!*

The second intruder edged into the room, peering round the door. The hallway light began to flicker, obscuring the scene with intermittent darkness.

He walked round Cora's bed, getting ever closer to the wardrobe.

*Okay...*

Taking a quick breath, Fei kicked open the door, which slammed into him. The intruder fell back as Fei reached for Cora's dressing table mirror.

As he lunged at her, she smashed the mirror down on his head. It shattered, and she grabbed a dagger-like shard of glass. It sliced into her hand, as she rammed it into his neck.

Fei groaned in pain as the intruder flopped onto the floor. Wincing as the blood seeped down her arm, she pulled Cora's linen curtain, ripping a strip off the bottom and wrapping it tightly round her wound, before limping out of the room.

*So tired.*

But there was one more. And she hoped she wasn't too late. She flew down the stairs, pole at the ready, charging towards Henry's room.

*Please, please, please!*

She spun round the banisters into the hallway, Henry's open bedroom door only steps away; but before she could blink, an explosion of blinding white light blasted out of his room, sending her flying back into the wall.

Winded. She gasped for air. Shrill ringing filled her head as she attempted to steady herself, coughing as dust filled her lungs. She raised a hand to shield her eyes, looking to the slowly dimming light brimming from Henry's bedroom. Fei sat, open-mouthed.

Stunned.

*What the...?*

Refocusing, she squinted to see the third intruder collapsed on the floor opposite the doorway, blood smeared down the wall behind him.

Fei clambered to her feet, clutching at her arm as she staggered towards Henry's room.

'Dad?' she rasped, clawing at the doorway.

She peered in to see Mrs G standing over her father, who was lying in his bed fast asleep. The walls and ceiling were streaked with long, thin burn marks that stretched from the corner where Henry's bed was, towards the door. Mrs G turned to look at Fei, shaking.

'Mrs G! What – what happened!? Are you okay?' Fei hobbled towards her and grabbed hold of her shoulders. Mrs G just stared blankly past her.

'Mrs G!'

She gently shook Mrs G's head, her eyes focusing as she came to. Nodding, she held Fei's face in her hands.

'What's going on?' said Fei.

'Cora has gone, you must go too. I will look after your father,' she said softly. Fei stood stunned.

'There will be more, but you must go now, my dear,' she smiled.

For a moment Fei felt strangely calm as she nodded at Mrs G's stern but warm countenance.

'Yes. Yes I'll go. You'll look after him?' she whispered.

'You must, you must, and of course.' Mrs G nodded in the direction of the stairs, turned, and placed a hand on Henry's forehead.

'Will you be okay?' Fei stood for a moment, numb, as she took one last look at her father.

*Will I be okay?*

Mrs G gave her a small confident smile and nodded. Fei held up a weak hand in farewell and left.

*Please be okay.*

Every step, every touch – every smell – in the house she drank in, committing it to memory. Desperately absorbing as much as she could while it was possible, knowing she might never return. The annoying creak on the landing floorboards felt anything but annoying as she struggled to gather her thoughts.

*Supplies. What do I take?*

Dashing into the kitchen, she grabbed a bag from the counter, and started shovelling in everything she could get her hands on – including the emergency cash Henry kept in an old pasta jar on top of the cupboard. She stood for a moment, taking a last look. She would make sure she would see all this again.

Pulling open the front door, she inspected the porch for any more visitors. No one to be seen, just the long, bleak street.

*Will I ever come back?*

The tinkle of the Fourlise Motorcycles sign in the wind made her want to cry, but she didn't know what to feel anymore.

She ran to Clyde's stable and saddled him, leaning over every so often to feed him a treat. Grabbing the treat bag, she strapped it to the saddle, along with the supplies she had haphazardly thrown together, including money, a compass, some food, some clothes and her mother's Sardan pin.

She felt so gaunt, so tired. Her eyes bulged and her face was covered in small brown crusty spots of blood. There wasn't much she could cover it with, other than her hat and the collar of her jacket. She would just have to keep her head down and hope for the best.

She led Clyde out of his stable to the front of the house. Stopping, she looked up to see Mrs G, with Hercules in her arms, smiling from the attic window. Fei raised her hand and waved.

Mrs G waved back.

Through the winding, dark, cobbled streets, they jogged towards the North gate. The smell carried on the wind seemed different. Or perhaps she was just smelling it in a different way, a more inquisitive, assertive way. What could possibly lie ahead? Various scenarios played out in her mind as the buildings became scarcer.

Although terrified, and depleted of energy, she'd never felt more alive.

In the distance she could see the forest growing nearer, calling to her as it had always done. Only now could she hear what it had been telling her all these years.

As she approached the North gate, she saw that several more locks had been added, and a large sign had been nailed to the front:

## INCIDENT

*If you (or anyone you know) have any information on the events that occurred here, please contact your local authorities.*
*For your own safety, the Prime Minister advises you*
*NOT to leave the city walls.*
*You do so at your own peril.*

She sighed and swiftly unlocked all the bolts; each click sending a small surge of energy through her. A light flickered in a house opposite.

Clyde nudged her arm as she heaved the huge gate open and they both slid out, leaving their old life behind.

# CHAPTER NINE

They galloped into the night towards the forest. Fei looked back, as the city lights moved further and further away. She rode on, empty of emotion and expectation, not knowing what awaited her. She only knew that Cora had already gone to Daramere and was certain she couldn't be too far ahead.

They had almost reached the forest when Fei pulled back on Clyde's reins, sending him trotting lazily up Suga hill. He slowed and stopped at the top, sniffing at a tree trunk, his large round belly panting in and out.

She had never been this far from home. From here the city looked far smaller.

Clyde jumped and Fei swung round, clutching at her sore stomach as the faint sound of whistling arrows flew through the trees. Again, Fei felt her heart begin to race, and she grabbed hold of Clyde's reins. There was another faint whistling, this time followed by a roar of pain.

'C'mon.' Fei nudged Clyde's side, and they weaved through the darkness towards the commotion, the sound of shooting arrows and frantic running feet getting louder.

'Whoah,' Fei whispered.

Clyde stopped and she slid off his back, wincing. She hobbled forward. It was so dark; only the moonlight revealed the vague outlines of trees in front of her. Fei stopped, her eyes catching a tiny flickering white light ahead.

A torch!

Another arrow whistled through the darkness, and she heard an all-too-familiar argumentative voice.

'C'MON!' growled Cora's distinctive monotonous threats through gritted teeth, to what Fei could make out to be two figures stood either side of her, the same long knives in their hands as her previous intruders. A third lay dead on the ground, an arrow in his chest.

Cora darted between them, taking aim at one, as the other lunged at her, grabbing her from behind and pulling her into a choke hold as the other dashed over. Grabbing hold of her attacker's arms, Cora swung up her legs and kicked him hard in the face, the heels of her boots cracking his jaw.

'HEY!' Fei darted out, grabbing the torch that lay on the grass, her hands trembling. The assassin with the broken jaw turned and ran towards her, taking a swipe at her neck.

Fei felt her body screaming for rest as she attempted to dodge his flying blade as it sliced into her arm. Not too deep, but enough. She hissed in pain and swung the torch into his head, knocking him to the ground.

Cora watched as the blood pooled in her sister's clawed hand. She sent the heel of her boot crunching into her attacker's foot, then elbowed him in the stomach.

Fei bellowed 'Cora!' as she launched the torch at her sister.

Cora turned to see the torch flying towards her. She caught it and swung it into her attacker's jaw. He fell face down in the dirt.

The pair stood for a second, panting. Fei's face a sharp shade of burgundy, as she knelt to catch her breath. 'What the hell ... were you thinking?' she panted.

Cora jolted as the third, previously unconscious, attacker came to, and ran up behind Fei. Picking up her crossbow, Cora coolly planted an arrow in his forehead.

Fei slumped to the ground in exhaustion, her blood-soaked hand squeezing her throbbing arm.

'I knew you'd come,' said Cora, standing over Fei's limp body.

Fei shook her head. 'Yeah, well, there's better ways to go about these things...'

'I dunno you know, I reckon this was the only way.'

'I can't move... I've got bruises on top of bruises.'

'Don't be such a drama queen - Three little bad guys,' said Cora, stroking a bewildered Clyde, who had meandered over to join them.

'Umm actually, not just three. Six! I got surprise-attacked back at the house.'

Cora's face dropped and she twisted to look at Fei, ranting on the ground.

'Everyone's fine, don't worry,' said Fei, sensing Cora's concern. 'Yes, thank you, Fei. Also, you ran away in the middle of the night and took my daggers.'

No reply.

Fei felt her myriad of wounds take it in turn to sear with pain. She heaved herself up, grunting; there were too many aches to count now, they all seemed to meld into one. She tightened Clyde's girth, which made him snort but didn't annoy him enough to stop him eating the fresh patch of grass he'd found.

'You're not going back, are you?' asked Cora, peering round Clyde's huge neck.

'No, I'm not going back. Even if I wanted to, I can't. But you *have* to promise me never to run off like that again. You could have died. Someone is already after us, and I can't protect you if I don't know where you are.'

Cora looked guilty, a rare occurrence for her. 'I'm sorry, but we couldn't just sit and do nothing.'

'*I* can't sit and do nothing. *Me.* I know that now. You could've stayed safe at home with Dad. I should really send you back to him,' said Fei, hissing with pain as she rolled a small bandage from the saddle bag round her throbbing arm.

Cora shook her head.

Fei let her head tilt back, her thoughts unbearably heavy. 'But it's not safe for you there now. I wish you hadn't come; this was for me to do alone.'

'This isn't something you do alone, Sister.'

Fei pursed her lips as she tied a small knot in the bandage, then took hold of Cora's arm. 'Well, that's all the more reason for you never to run off again. You left me alone.'

'I won't, I promise.'

'Yeah, you promised last time.' Fei raised an eyebrow as Cora began to walk away, then turned to flash her a cheeky smile.

Fei shook her head and took out her compass. North was the direction they needed to go, and Cora was heading east.

Fei grinned. 'You don't even know where you're going, do you?'

'Daramere, obviously.'

'Right, well you're currently walking towards Corby. Daramere is that way.' Fei pointed north, and Cora gave a slow blink.

'I knew that. Just testing you.'

'Sure,' Fei laughed, lifting Clyde's reins then reaching down to pull Cora's spindly body up behind her.

The girls had in fact been to Daramere once before, a very long time ago. Cora was only about two, and Henry and Fei had never let her forget the time she'd helped herself to a packet of mints off a shelf in a shop. They had left without paying for them, not discovering them till they got home, wedged between the blankets in her buggy, which they had all found wildly funny.

Simpler times.

Daramere wasn't that far from Valkyrios, perhaps a two-day ride, but it felt much longer as they trudged through patches of dry grass dotted with leafless trees.

At least the journey gave Fei some time to recuperate; as Clyde clopped along, her bruises faded and her body strengthened. She had always found she healed faster outside – even if there was barely any green anymore. Twenty minutes' snoozing by a tree with Clyde and she would feel drastically re-energised.

Also, Fei need only sit in one spot for a moment to provide for Clyde's eternally rumbling stomach, so they didn't have to worry too much about him, but Fei had not left much room for food during their walk. Cora had brought barely anything and they were getting hungry.

Cora was not being unusually quiet. She had always been a deep thinker and Fei often wondered what her younger sister was thinking about. No doubt it was profound, especially now. Fei had always been jealous of Cora's sharp intelligence. When Fei thought back to when she was her age, she could only remember thinking about silly things, like how many freckles she had, and what shape it would make on her arm if she did a dot-to-dot with them.

Fei however, *was* being unusually quiet. But, to her dismay, she found herself thinking about neither profound nor menial things. Instead, she found herself trying *not* to think about what was to come. She thought it better to …

*Just go with it and to cross the various bridges when they presented themselves.*

Planning, she thought, would only lead to disappointment, and that was the last thing they needed.

So the two hardly spoke. Not out of choice; there was simply too much to talk about, and the thought of discussion was exhausting for them both. They would wait for less confusing times, if they ever came. She hoped that one day she would be able to think of such menial things as her freckles again.

Dodging patches of grey, they made their way through the last few trees to the furthest edge of the forest, before Daramere. It had been obvious they were closing in on a city, as the wilted trees had become even more coiled and lifeless.

'Fei, what do we do if we can't find Morie?'

Fei found herself zoning back to reality.

'Umm, no idea. For now, let's imagine she's waiting for us at the gates, open-armed, with a big roast lunch!' She gave Cora an encouraging smile.

They stood at the edge of the forest and looked down towards the vast gleaming city. Daramere had no wall – it was a much more relaxed place – but it did also have the highest rate of Tok-related deaths in the county.

'It's so much bigger than Valkyrios,' said Cora, sighing.

Fei closed her eyes and began to mutter under her breath as Clyde plodded forward.

'She's waiting for us at the gates, she's waiting for us at the gates, she's waiting for us at the gates...'

Cora smirked.

Having found a stable near the city entrance where they could pay to leave Clyde for the day, the girls strolled into the centre. The city was buzzing with visitors. The vendors and stalls that had been in Valkyrios a few days earlier had now set up in Daramere high street, and, much to their disappointment, Morie had not been waiting for them at the entrance to the city. There was no roast dinner either. So they switched to plan B, which at first consisted of quietly asking around, as they didn't want to alert any local authorities to their existence. Who knew what they might have heard about recent events in their neighbouring city, involving certain undesirables?

The streets were lined with sweet shops, bicycle shops, tobacco shops, wine and ale shops and book shops. Daramere was just as Fei remembered, although Laversham's Sweet Emporium seemed to be selling much smaller lollipops than the one her mum had bought her all those years ago. Far less pink in the swirls as well.

The cobbled streets were filled with the latest models of motor cars - this vendor they had not seen in Valkyrios. The girls watched as men stood lovingly wiping the gold rims of the cars, schmoozing onlookers, whilst young folk blazed down the road in the latest models, young men and women in the back, flinging wine out into the street, laughing.

It wasn't that rich a city, but it was famously frivolous. Younger men and women from Valkyrios would often drive to Daramere for the weekend for wild nights out. Vendors knew, if there was money to spend, Darameans were there to spend it. No matter how much trouble it got them into, which may have also added to the high Tok-related mortality rate. But Darameans could not have cared less. 'You only live once' was a much beloved moto in this city.

As they had noticed in Valkyrios, there were significantly fewer food stalls this year. They also noticed Green & Wood's tobacco house, which was famed all over the county, had a small sign in its window that read:

## GOING OUT OF BUSINESS
## EVERYTHING MUST GO

*Sparse times indeed.*

Despite the decrease in stalls this year, it had not in the slightest affected the number of people humming through the streets. However, it was clear that the older shops were far less popular than the newer, higher-tech shops.

The girls found themselves regularly hopping to avoid long skirts and carriages as they turned to walk towards Green and Wood's. They stood for a moment outside the shop, taking in the tobacco smell. It reminded them of their father, which made them each swallow down a lump in their throat.

'Where the hell do we start?' asked Cora, staring open-mouthed at the packed high street.

'I guess we just start asking around,' said Fei. They shared a pained look. 'You got a better idea?'

Cora shook her head and sighed. 'Guess we're starting here then.'

# CHAPTER TEN

They gazed through the glass windows of the tobacco shop, and smiled at the familiar tinkle of the doorbell hanging above the entrance as they shuffled through.

A large man stood behind the counter, with his back to them, peering down and shaking his head at what looked like a long sheet of receipts. The girls stared at his wide back.

'Hello?' said Fei.

The man spun round, flinging the receipts under the counter and raising his meaty arms in the air.

'Welcome, young ladies! I'm Mr Green. Not very often we have ladies in here!'

Mr Green was a round, pink man, with a belly clearly full of a barrel of Migson's genuine ale from across the street. Which his high-waisted, dark cotton trousers struggled to contain. He opened his arms wide, beaming through his great big bushy beard. It looked as if his braces strained every time he did this, which no doubt was multiple times a day.

The girls smiled awkwardly.

'What can I get for you? Perhaps a gift for your Pa?'

'Umm, sure, but actually we were hoping you might be able to help us find someone,' said Fei stepping forward.

'Find someone, eh? Picked a good day for it, haven't you, girls?' He bellowed with laughter, his face turning even pinker.

'Uh, ha, ha! Yes, indeed. Um, we're looking for someone called Morie Horne.'

Mr Green's face dropped and turned slightly mauve as he scanned the shop.

'The Moth?' he muttered under his breath.

The girls looked at him, perplexed.

'The Moth?' repeated Fei, bewildered, as Mr Green beckoned them closer.

'Yes, that's what she's known as here. You seem like nice girls – why on earth would you be looking for *her*?' His eyes darted between them and the shop door.

'Um, we need her help with uhh … with something.' The girls shifted their feet. 'Is there something we should know? I'm sorry to ask. It's just … we've only heard good things.'

They exchanged anxious looks as Mr Green hurried over to the shop door and swung the 'Open' sign to 'Closed'. He bustled back behind the counter and leaned in, gesturing for them to get closer.

'Last I heard, she was, you know, one of *them*,' said Mr Green in a low voice, his eyebrows raised. The girls narrowed their eyes.

'A Mage,' he half-whispered, half-mouthed, nodding confidentially, expecting an equal amount of shock in return.

The girls' hearts dropped as they drew back.

'Not the kind you want to get involved with, girls. Dangerous folk, those Mage. My cousin's husband's sister, Mary, swears it was a witch took her babe in the night, stole him right from the crib. Poor Mary. Nearly drove her mad, it did. Her husband, Daniel, had only just been released from prison as well.' Mr Green shook his head, tutting under his breath.

The girls gritted their teeth and Fei noticed the half-dead potted plant sitting in the corner by the cigars, looking a little more alive.

She nudged Cora.

'Thank you so much for your help,' said Fei, pasting on a fake smile. 'If I might ask, why do you call her the Moth?'

'Oh, you know, it's just a nickname we gave her; moths like to hang about in the darkness 'n' that. I saw her with my own eyes, in and out of the city at night-time on her own, doing God knows what. She's not someone you want to be involved with, I can tell you that. Lord knows what she's up to,' he finished, tutting again.

Fei gave another insincere smile and nodded at him. Cora did not smile.

'We'll be sure to keep our eyes open. But you don't happen to know where she's most often seen, do you? You know, so we can avoid it.' Said Fei.

'I've seen her most up near the library. You seem like nice girls, so be careful now. You don't want to get involved with any Mage.'

The girls marched out of the shop.

'Goodbye, Mr Green!' Fei called back, grimacing as she shut the door. 'Ignorant idiot!'

She charged down the main street, knocking the poufy satin sleeves of ladies who gasped and clutched their parasols as they got shoved into their suited husbands. Cora trotted alongside her.

Suddenly Fei froze – and gawped at a tall, muscular man dressed in cream breeches and a brown aviator's jacket. Goggles strapped to the top of his head, he was shaking the hands of the swooning women surrounding him. He grinned through a large handlebar moustache.

'Cora!' Fei pointed, grabbing her sisters arm, who turned to see the crowd of adoring ladies.

'What?'

'It's James D. Menillo.'

'Riiiight.'

Fei sighed. 'He's a triple Sky Chase Champion. You know, in Leos.'

'Sure.' She gave Fei a thumbs up.

Fei huffed and looked back to see him waving and blowing kisses, then disappearing into a tent at the back. They watched as two younger-looking women jumped around excitably, clutching at signed handkerchiefs. Finally, the women began to disperse, revealing a line of huge airship cockpits. One especially large one sat grandly in the middle.

'The Merenial,' whispered Fei, eyes sparkling. Cora groaned as Fei grabbed her arm and pulled her towards it, crashing through the remaining ladies. They came to a halt in front of it, and Fei crouched down in awe and began stroking its long burgundy doors.

'I can't believe it, I've only ever seen it in pictures. Dad's gonna lose his mind when he hears about this.'

'Oh yeah, you've got a picture of this in the uhhh...' Cora took a mouthful of candyfloss into her mouth from stall she'd swanned past and 'borrowed' a bag from.

'The workshop. That's right – we've been trying to figure out its build.'

'I'm assuming this is a really good one?'

'The best,' came a deep voice from above. They looked up and found themselves staring into James D. Menillo's olive-green eyes. He stood, smiling and posing as if he was at a photoshoot. His short chocolate-brown hair swooped perfectly over his chiselled face; his moustache twitching with the strain of maintaining his rather stomach churning smile. He had the faintest hint of a tan, except for a goggle-shaped white patch round his eyes, which made them look even larger and more sickeningly sparkly.

'Unbeaten,' said Fei, smiling and reaching out her hand. 'I'm a big fan.'

Cora grimaced as James laughed and took Fei's hand in his.

'Ah, what a joy it's been today, meeting my fans.' He proceeded to turn over her hand and reach into his pocket. 'Sounds as if you know a little about the race as well.' He lightly elbowed her arm, pulling out a pen.

*Surely that smile was starting to hurt?*

'Uhh, yeah, me and my father have been keen followers of the Sky Chase for as long as I can remember.' Fei gave an awkward smile as James began to scrawl his name across her hand.

Cora stood open-mouthed in disgust. The candyfloss dissolved on her tongue as she felt her stomach turn.

'And which ship do you like best, my dear?' James asked Fei, popping the pen back in his pocket, removing a glove and running a hand through his glossy hair.

Fei began. 'Well, I mean, the Merenial...'

James scoffed, cutting her off.

'Well, indeed, the Merenial is *the* best.' he mocked. 'But since you know more about the race than most...' He looked around and lowered his voice. 'I'll let you girls in on a little secret,' he smouldered, beckoning them closer.

Fei peered round at Cora and leant forward a little.

Cora did not move.

'There's a new one coming in soon, which is even better. And guess who might be captaining it in the next chase...?'

Fei forced a smile.

'You?'

'That's right!' he grinned. 'You're looking at the captain of the brand new...' He splayed out his hands in front of him, forming an arch, 'Millennial!'

Cora narrowed her eyes. 'But the millennium's not for another hundred years.'

James cleared his throat. 'Yes, indeed. But, you know, everyone's very, uhh, excited, aren't they?' He straightened his jacket, his mouth twitching as he turned his attention back to Fei.

They were interrupted by a shrill voice which came from a small, round man, who seemed to be James's tour manager. He was standing in the tent doorway, scowling at them. 'James! James! I say, we need you, for photos and what-not. You can come back out in a bit – we need you in here, now!'

'That sounds exciting. It was nice to meet you. Good luck in this year's race,' said Fei, who made eyes at Cora, who made eyes back.

'Wait.' James reached out for Fei's hand.

'James!' the tour manager squeaked a little louder.

'I don't even know your name. Perhaps you might come for a drink in my tent?' Fei recoiled, as James's smile widened even further, if that were possible.

'JAMES, I say!' The manager began to waddle over.

'Perhaps then, I can tell you a bit about my name, and the mysterious "D" in the middle.' He wiggled his eyebrows.

Cora heaved.

'I really should get going.' Fei grimaced.

'James, I must insist.' James's manager stood in front of him, his small potato-shaped body exuding an alarming amount of heat as he tapped his foot impatiently.

James released Fei's hand. 'I hope you'll be watching the race this year. Number eight, that'll be me. Yup.' And with a self-satisfied smile, he turned and marched back into the tent.

Fei blew out her cheeks – and made a loud heaving noise.

'Yeah,' Cora agreed, chucking another handful of candyfloss in her mouth.

'How very interesting you both are! Perhaps you should run along and see the other ship stalls here. I'm sure there are plenty of others that will appeal to you,' came the wry voice of the tour manager. He pursed his lips as he looked them both up and down, concentrating his gaze on their filthy boots, before slinking off after James.

Fei's smile faded as she looked down at her mottled trousers.

'Plonker,' muttered Cora. 'Library?'

'Library,' agreed Fei.

# CHAPTER ELEVEN

As they made their way further out of the centre and away from the market, the number of people began to decrease significantly; clearly, they thought, everyone had been made aware of where Morie, or 'Moth', lived.

After asking for directions, the huge grey structure of the library appeared. What was immediately apparent was how much dirtier it was compared to the majority of the buildings in the city. Fei remembered their mother telling her of how targeted Daramere had been during the crusades, how much of it had been destroyed. Its modernity had been the drawing point for all the youth in the area, and it seemed the library had been one of the lucky ones.

Daramere Library was one of the oldest libraries in the county. It looked rather like the gods' palace on Mount Olympus – clad in marble with fluted columns and enormous doors and windows.

The girls stood there, awestruck by its grandeur. Fei had always loved old architecture, and this building was most certainly old. It was so high, it had a flock of birds circling the roof, dodging the small grey wisps of cloud drifting around it.

'Reckon they have records of city inhabitants?' asked Fei, staring up.

'Probably. If she knows we're coming, where would she expect us to look for her?'

'God knows, but this is a good start.'

They nodded at each other and walked through the dauntingly large doors. It was the haystack of all haystacks, and finding this particular needle was going to be a task to say the least. Books lined the walls of the vast room, stacked precariously on top of one another, some book towers learning over just a little too far over for their comfort. The shelves seemed to go on for miles; and they had not comprehended quite how deep the library was.

'Like hell am I rooting through all these,' said Fei, staring into the book-lined abyss.

Cora nudged Fei's arm and pointed at a small toad-like man sitting behind a long wooden desk, with a gold and green banker's lamp shining on something. The huge desk made him look even smaller. A disdainful look swept across his face as they approached.

'This'll be fun,' said Cora.

'Hello,' said Fei, smiling.

He wore a tight blue pinstripe suit, and had an ill-coloured toupee balanced on his large, round skull. He looked them up and down over his spectacles, his lip curling.

'We were hoping you could help us find someone who lives here.' She tugged at her shirt, attempting to straighten it.

'Not from round here, I presume?' he croaked as he continued counting the pages of what looked like a large manuscript.

'Um, no. Do you have records of everyone who lives in the city?'

'No one looks at those anymore. Why do you need to consult our records?' He continued counting.

'We're looking for an old friend.'

The little man's grey moustache twitched, and he stopped counting to look them both up and down again. He stood and pointed up at the large iron clock hanging from the ceiling behind him. 'The library closes in half an hour. Follow me.'

He marched off, and the girls shuffled after him.

The library was full of beautiful dark wood panelling, and shelves holding dusty old books and globes. A vast chandelier hung from the painted ceiling, illuminating the green and red velvet sofas and chairs placed in front of fireplaces here and there. The different floors were connected by winding wooden staircases with ornately carved banisters.

Yet they saw only two or three people on their walk to Public Records. It seemed a great shame.

Eventually, the little man waddled down a darker aisle with a heavily bolted door at the end. The girls exchanged a look – this was the first door they had seen in the library.

'Ahem,' the little man coughed as they almost bumped into him. They looked down to see his disgruntled face, as he peered suspiciously at the bolted door, then back at them.

'Here you will find records of those who, over the last fifty years, have registered as residents of Daramere.

However, these records will not include those who live here, illegally,' he sneered.

The girls' hearts sank at the thought of fifty years' worth of files.

'The records are arranged alphabetically, and they shall remain so. Is that clear?'

They nodded.

'Is there anything more I can help you with?'

'Perhaps you could show us the section with the residents from the last ten years?' suggested Fei.

The little man huffed in annoyance and walked towards a ladder attached to the bookcase. He pulled it along with surprising ease and stared up at the wall of books. He swiftly, but not short of wheezes, made his way up the ladder. Stopping in the centre he moved his finger along the book spines and pulled out a slightly less dusty, but nonetheless, huge book.

A couple of aisles along, in a dimly lit section of the library, a girl stood rooting through a clinking bag. She was wearing wide cotton trousers, brown knee-high lace-up boots, a dishevelled white shirt, and a short greenish-brown jacket with some questionable maroon splatters across the sleeve.

Her hair was tied up under a black boater, from which a piece of netting hung down, covering half her face. A shiny black curl flopped over her nose as she rooted through the bag, watching for passers-by while she pulled out a quill. She quickly placed the pen back in the bag and continued rooting.

In her rummage, she found herself tuning in to the conversation a few aisles away, and she smirked. She had to agree with the small man – what *were* they doing looking for someone who moved here ten years ago? She pulled out what looked like a small screwdriver with a jagged tip. She would have to wait until the small man and the other two people had moved off. She stood in the shadows, waiting and listening, clutching the tool as she casually skimmed the books, her brow furrowed in curiosity as she listened.

'Who exactly *is* this friend of yours, who came here, perhaps (or perhaps not) ten years ago? The one you are only now attempting to locate?' the little man scoffed, a drop of spit escaping his mouth as he balanced on the ladder while flicking through the book.

The girl in the shadows sniggered.

Cora nudged Fei and shook her head slightly.
'A Miss M. Horne,' said Fei, her palms feeling a little clammy.

The girl-in-the-shadow's deep brown eyes widened, and she removed a book from the shelf next to her. She looked through, to see Fei and Cora peering up at the man.

The little man's lip curled. He stopped flicking through the book and slowly twisted on the ladder to glare down at them.
'You wouldn't happen to mean Morie Horne, would you?' he hissed.

Cora's eyes shifted to Fei.

'Um ... no.'

He pushed the book back onto the shelf and slunk back down the ladder.

'Is there a problem?' asked Fei, taking a step back.

The girl-in-the-shadows also took a step back, her heart racing, and bumped into an old woman behind her. She spun round, thrusting her arm behind her back, gripping the jagged-ended screwdriver tightly.

'Oh, I'm so sorry love, I didn't see you there.' The old lady beamed at the girl's shocked face. 'Are you okay, love?'

The girl nodded and looked at her bag. Bending down, she grabbed the handles and hurried towards the large double doors. The old lady watched, confused as the girl disappeared.

The little man pursed his lips. 'Oh no, dear. No problem for me at all. But there is only one Miss M. Horne regrettably residing in our city,' he said, with a malicious smile. 'And for anyone searching for the Moth, the problem lies most determinedly with them.'

They all scowled at each other.

'The library shuts in fifteen minutes, I suggest you wrap up your search.' He glared at the girls, then pushed past them, back to his desk.

Fei buried her head in her hands, then stared, infuriated, at the packed shelves.

'I told you not to say anything,' said Cora, raising an eyebrow.

'I wasn't exactly expecting her to be a celebrity now was I? I thought Sardan were meant to be sneaky,' whispered Fei, peering round the bookcase after the little man.

'They *are*. How the hell are we meant to find her in all this, in only fifteen minutes? There's no way we'll be allowed back in here tomorrow,' Cora replied under her breath, as she peered round the side of the bookcase to see the little man muttering to a guard, then turning to glance in their direction. 'Or perhaps even the city?' She looked at Fei, her voice rising in alarm.

'Goddammit. These people.' Fei edged round to the other side of the bookcase when the guard stopped her in her tracks.

'The library is closing, you must leave now,' his stern voice boomed as he pointed towards the double doors.

'Don't worry, we're leaving,' said Fei, as she grabbed at Cora's cuff.

They both shuffled past him, the guard staying close behind as they walked down the centre walkway of the library, past the few people still flicking through books who looked up at them with intrigue. The double doors were directly at the end and the girls watched as three more guards entered and began a hushed conversation with the little man.

Fei gave Cora a side-eye, and an almost imperceptible nod ahead.

Cora gave a subtle nod back.

They had no choice; they would have to make a dash for it.

The girls jumped as an ear-splittingly loud siren thundered through the library doors. The guard seemed unperturbed.

'What the hell's that?' asked Cora.

'It's the siren for the grey. A large cloud must have entered the city. Everyone must stay inside now,' said the guard, still walking forward, staring ahead.

'Stay inside? I thought you wanted us to leave?' said Cora uneasily, her hand shifting to her gas mask.

'You must stay inside,' said the guard, glaring at her.

Fei placed a hand on one of her daggers, tucked beneath her jacket. Cora clutched at the strap of her gas mask.

They were getting closer to the little man and the guards, as they made their way to the double doors.

They were going to be locked in.

Fei made sure Cora could see that she was ready as they neared the last bookcase before the long desk; the two guards were almost at the main doors. The third stood in front of the green lamp, watching them approach.

One step.

Fei flashed her eyes at the clock.

Two steps.

Cora nodded.

Three steps.

'Now,' Fei whispered.

# CHAPTER TWELVE

Fei lobbed a dagger at the glass covering of the clock, shattering it and sending pieces raining down on the guards, as Cora spun round and buried her fist into the gut of the guard behind them.

The two guards shot up, covered in shards of glass, and began charging towards them; the third lunging forward as the little man began to make a frantic phone call.

Fei hurled her second dagger at the lamp. It landed in the centre of its glass hood, which snapped, sending sparks and green glass chips flying into the little man. He squealed and dropped to the ground as the lamp flashed and smoked.

The third guard wailed in pain as glass splinters lodged in his hand and the side of his face. Fei scoped up her daggers, then readied herself; as the girls prepared to launch themselves at the two remaining guards who were frantically swatting at their eyes. Elbows out, they rammed full pelt into them.

Breathless, the guards flew back, slamming into the doors.

The girls winced at their now rather sensitive elbows and yanked their gas masks over their faces.

Fei stood catching her breath in the library doorway as Cora flew through the double doors. She watched as the guards attempted to get to their feet, while the little man shrilled down the phone, staring at her.

A sense of emptiness fell over her like a dark veil. Heart thumping, she turned to run after Cora.

The city had taken a bleak turn.

They darted down the hill, peering through their fogged-up masks to see a vast grey cloud slowly rolling down the high street as vendors raced to pack away their produce and seek shelter.

'We have to get Clyde and go. There'll be more of them!' said Fei, panting.

'We can't leave! What about Morie?' came Cora's muffled reply, gasping as they pelted along the high street.

'HEY, STOP!' the guards screamed, hysterically blowing their whistles as they careered after them. The girls whipped their heads round in panic.

'We haven't got time to think about that right now!' Fei shouted as they ran towards the cloud, past vomiting partiers.

It was as if someone had put a murky filter over the whole city. When combined with the condensation in their masks, it was impossibly hard to see.

'STOP NOW!' the guards bellowed again. They'd stopped blowing their whistles and had their masks fully on as they charged after them.

The girls glanced up as they ran past Green and Wood's Tobacco, Migson's Genuine Ale, and Laversham's Sweet Emporium. The vendors and customers stared back at them as they flew down the street. Fei watched the pink face of Mr Green shaking in disappointment.

Luckily Clyde was not too far away – but neither were the guards. Clyde whinnied at the girls through a large gas mask for horses that had been placed over his head by the stable owner.

Fei panted.

'How are you not dying?' she wheezed to Cora as she flung Clyde's saddle onto his back.

'No time!' said Cora, unbolting the stable door and jumping up behind Fei. Charging out, they galloped towards the main city entrance as the puzzled guards appeared from the cloud behind.

Tok. Tok. Tok.

They could hear the chilling sound as Clyde powered through the main city gates. Cora turned to see the guards slowing down and looking after them uneasily, as they disappeared into the grey cloud. The large city gates clanged shut behind them.

'Fei, we can't go back home!' Cora's muffled shout rang in Fei's ear as they galloped back towards the forest.

The leaves on the trees had already begun to curl.

'We can't stay here!' Fei shouted back.

Cora reached round and pulled on Clyde's reins. He did not appreciate this and slammed his hooves on the ground, skidding to a halt, snorting. Fei jumped off and began walking towards the forest.

'What are you doing?' shouted Cora, pulling off her mask.

They were in the middle of a doughnut of grey; darkness and obscurity surrounded them, except for a shaft of moonlight beaming down on the clearing.

Fei whipped round to see Cora looking baffled, glaring back at her.

'What we should've done ages ago – going back home to get help. I don't know how the Prime Minister ever thought we could do this alone.' Fei's eyes began to glisten. 'You shouldn't be here. Dad's all alone and you've been subjected to nothing but danger since we left.' She buried her face in her hands.

'You need me,' Cora mumbled.

'I need you to be safe!'

Tok.

The sound whistled through the grey, making their skin prickle. Fei shot up and whipped out her daggers, staring wide-eyed into the grey abyss.

'And this is anything but safe.'

Shuddering, she beckoned Cora, who slid off Clyde, unstrapped her crossbow from his saddle, and aimed it into the grey.

Tok. Tok. Tok.

'Get behind me.' Fei was glued to the spot, her hand shaking.

Tok. Tok. Tok. Tok. Tok.

The noises grew louder, closer, surrounding them. The sound of claws rasping into the dry ground ricocheted through the clearing.

'Jesus, how many are there?' whispered Cora, her voice uncharacteristically wobbly.

'Enough.'

A large antler appeared from the cloud, followed by the long skeletal snout of a mammoth Tok.

It towered over them; its jaw widened and the flapping bit of skin on its throat reverberated with its sickening noise. It stood staring at them with its black, soulless eyes.

'Oh God.' Fei shook.

Several more Toks slunk out, screeching.

'Sister, I think it might be time to, you know...' said Cora, staring at the multitude of bloodied jaws.

'I can't risk not being able to see you. Just aim for the head or heart.'

They stood back-to-back, rooted to the ground, as the first Tok raised its massive, clawed arm.

The girls jumped as strange noise whistled out from the grey.

A bark?

The Toks clawed the ground as they one by one, leapt towards the girls.

Cora shot at a smaller Tok, launching her arrow straight into its heart and sending it hurtling to the ground, as the swinging arm of another one flew towards her head which she sharply dipped under.

Fei watched in panic as the huge antlers of the first Tok thundered towards her. She dived under its legs, springing up and stabbing another smaller one in the gut. The first Tok watched her as it crept back into the shadows of the grey.

Cora shot at another, missing its heart by centimetres. Its jagged claws tore into the ground as it twisted and came careering back. Fei stood, frozen, watching as

Cora took aim at the approaching Tok, its erratic bounding clearing metres over the brittle ground.

Dumbfounded, the girls watched. As what looked like a large mossy-green doglike creature shot out of the grey and blasted the Tok into the cloud beside it. Disappearing. The sound of deep rumbling growls and ripping flying out.

They stood, transfixed, at the place where the dog had vanished.

'FEI.' Cora pointed past her sister, as the first Tok bound towards her.

Fei's body pulsated with adrenaline as the glint of a long, thin sword swooped out of the grey and sliced through the Tok's back. It plummeted forward onto the ground in front of them.

A small figure appeared from the cloud, bloodied sword in hand and black hair poking out around a gas mask. The girls stood open-mouthed as the figure leapt up onto the Tok's twitching body and drove a sword into its heart.

The dog once again flew out of the grey, cantering full pelt at another Tok. Its deer-like hooves drove into the ground as it ran. Fei stared at the dog in disbelief.

'Gee?'

The figure's head turned to watch as the dog rammed into the Tok, sending it shooting back into the grey. Once again, the ripping and growling noise made its way out of the swirling cloud; whilst, the figure sprang forward and sliced through the remaining beasts.

As the last Tok dropped to the ground, silence fell. Fei met her sister's eyes, to see her cool face drop.

'NO!' Cora swung up her crossbow, aiming behind Fei's head.

Fei turned to find the blade of the figure's bloody sword cast beneath her neck.

'Who are you?' The figure said in a low, muffled voice from behind the gas mask.

Fei raised her hands.

'Please. We don't want any trouble. We – we mean no harm,' she stammered, heart pounding.

The dog gave a thundering growl, steam billowing from its mouth.

'Who are *you*?' Cora spat.

'Why are you looking for Morie Horne?' demanded the figure, pressing the heavy sword harder against Fei's neck. Fei gasped, gritting her teeth as Cora tightened her grip on her crossbow.

Fei squinted at the figure, her heart slowing as she noticed the tufts of jet-black hair poking out of their mask.

'Cora, it's okay,' Fei said. 'We were sent to find her by Prime Minister Chéa. We need her help.'

The figure's stance softened, and Fei felt the sword slowly drop away. Peering at the small patch of lush grass beneath Fei's feet, the figure removed their gas mask.

A young woman, aged around thirty, with pale skin, messy black hair, dark brown eyes and a noticeable resemblance to the Prime Minister, stared back at them.

She gave a small smile.

'Well, I guess I've found *you*,' said Moth.

# CHAPTER THIRTEEN

The girls beamed and the Paodin began to wag its tail, its tongue flapping joyously.

'Morie?' Fei smiled.

'Call me Moth.'

Moth stepped forward to shake hands. Her grip was powerful, and her sleeve lifted a little to reveal a small tattoo – the same as the Prime Minister's and the Captain's.

Cora gave a wide toothy grin.

'You must be Feina Fourlise, and you must beee sister?' Moth nodded at Cora. Who nodded back.

'Cora. Nice to meet you. I'm just a standard human.'

'Snap,' Moth chuckled.

Cora grinned wider than Fei had ever seen.

'Yeah, she's a stowaway,' Fei half-smiled, half-huffed as the wagging Paodin began tiptoeing towards them. 'I can't believe you're actually here. Feels like it's been one task after the other so far. It's nice to have something go to plan.'

'Well, you didn't exactly make it hard for me to find you,' Moth laughed.

'Yeah, we've, um, been thrown in at the deep end, that's for sure. We'll try to thrash less in future!'

The Paodin nudged his nose into Moth's arm and stared at the girls. Fei squinted at its mossy-green face.

'Gee?' Fei reached forward.

'Surely not,' said Cora.

'This is Bisou, he's a good boy.' Moth smiled as Fei walked towards him, her eyes glowing. 'Did you have a Paodin?'

'A long time ago, she was called Gee. I'm sure Mum said she was the last one. Gee fought with her in the Crusades but died when I was thirteen. I've not seen one since. He looks just like her; just, green instead of grey.'

Fei beamed and Bisou swept his tongue across her cheek as she scratched behind his large fluffy ear. He closed his eyes and began beating his back leg on the floor.

'Paodin will never be extinct, but there is only ever one of them in the world at a time. It is, however, still unknown how they reproduce, since there is, only ever one.'

They all grinned. No matter the slight difference in appearance, Bisou smelt exactly the same as Gee, and a little also of Dhalia.

Bisou was a fair bit taller than Gee had been: his back came to around a metre high, and he was mossy green coloured. He had long, slim muscular legs with strong little black hooves like a deer, and a huge fluffy tail that he passionately wagged. His body was slim, like that of a greyhound or a cheetah, but his head was maned and proud like a wolf. He had a long, thin snout and small antlers. His right eye was glassy, like a crystal ball it glowed with smoky, ambery swirls. He was quite spectacular, but also remarkably doggy, which gave him a wonderfully endearing presence.

He dropped to the ground now, presenting his fluffy belly to the girls. His body wiggling with the exuberant wag of his tail. His tongue flopped out of his mouth in delight as they both knelt beside him, grinning and rubbing his soft tummy.

'You know, not causing a scene would be preferable for you both from now on. Or, in fact, not talking to too many people.' Moth raised an eyebrow. 'You won't get very far, blasting through cities the way you did today."

The girls sheepishly looked at Moth, causing Bisou to twist his head and stare at them and their momentary lapse of fussing.

'You know, there's another Nathair here, in Daramere? That's why I moved here. I've been watching over her.'

'There's one here?!'

'Mm-hm.'

'I've never met another one before.' Fei's face lit up.

*Not alone.*

'C'mon, we need to get back to my house. No doubt the Silgir have been summoned,' said Moth, scanning the swirling grey, and sheathing her sword.

'Chéa never told us there was one here,' said Cora.

Moth nodded. 'Only Sardan in the field know the location of the remaining Nathair. Since we live so remotely, we're less likely to be caught.'

'Thank you, Morie. You know...for looking after us. Feels different...It's nice.' Fei smiled, and Bisou huffed from behind, his belly still on display.

'Yeah, thank you,' said Cora, a little starstruck.

'You don't need to thank me, it's what I do. Just promise me you won't go blazing through a city like that again! And like I said, call me Moth.' She smiled back, beckoning Bisou to follow.

'Course, yeah. Sorry. Just gotta get out the brainspace that you actually like that name.' Fei nodded and smiled.

'So, you don't mind the name Moth?' asked Cora, her hand on Bisou's hot back as he sniffed her face.

'Well, yeah, moths hang around in the dark but they are also attracted to the light, something the genius members of this city didn't think about. I kinda liked it in the end, so it stuck. I'm taking power over the name I guess you could say.' She smiled.

They all chuckled and disappeared into the grey.

\*\*\*

'In broad daylight? A Tok?' said Moth, trying not to spill her tea.

'Mm-hm,' The girls nodded.

'It's happening so much faster than I thought it would.' Moth slumped down, rubbing her forehead; Bisou nudged her hand to pet him. The despair was palpable and, once again, the sickening, empty feeling dropped through Fei's stomach.

'How long do you think we have till the grey... gets... like, everywhere?' asked Cora.

Moth lived in a ten-by-ten metre room above a laundrette called Sally's. Sally was old and blind, and every night Moth visited her to drop off some food. Because of this, Sally let Moth use her loo and cleaned and pressed her clothes for her.

Moth smelt great.

Her room contained a gas cooker, an antique wardrobe, a coffee table covered in papers, a single roll-out bed, a cupboard, some cushions on the floor, a rather eerie-looking painting of a castle, and Bisou's bed. It wasn't much, but it was all she needed.

'I thought we'd have at least a year. But I imagine, now, it's probably more like six months.' Moth took a sip of tea and stared out of the window.

'Six months?' Fei's heart sank. 'So we have to find all the remaining Nathair, the dagger, the heart of the forest and the Aon, in six months?'

Cora sighed, placing her cup on the floor, as Moth gave them a weary smile.

'It just keeps getting better.' Fei shook her head.

'We knew this wasn't going to be easy,' said Cora.

'I know. It's just a lot to process in one go. And now I'm finding out I have to do this really hard thing even quicker than I originally thought.' Fei groaned. 'Where do we even start?'

Moth placed her teacup on the sill beside her. 'Well, at least I know how we can get the dagger, and where the two other Nathair are,' she said, giving them an encouraging look.

'No time to waste, I guess,' replied Fei.

'Where are they?' asked Cora, scratching Bisou's head. He had squeezed himself between the girls.

Moth glanced through the window at a large lit-up building down the road.

Showgirls stood at the entrance of a busy night club, swaying the long feathers attached to their backs, and shimmying in their short, beaded skirts. People were flooding in, dressed in extravagant dresses and suits, wobbling and spilling drinks on the cobbles. Spotlights beamed up into the night sky.

The girls pushed themselves up off the floor and shuffled over to watch the commotion.

Moth took another sip of her tea. 'After Ela poisoned the heart of the forest, she entrusted the dagger to a demon called Chichenache, a vile creature. He was a human who desired immortality. He sold his soul to Ela, so he can never die a natural death. He holds the dagger in Irinvale, a vast fort surrounded by guards and Tok. We will have to go there and take it from him. We've lost thousands of Sardan attempting to retrieve it. As for the Aon, the Caraim lost track of it over fifty years ago, and we lost track of the Caraim. No one has seen or heard of the Aon since. For all we know...'

'Yeah, your mum told us,' interrupted Cora. Her face getting an intense sniffing from Bisou.

'We can't rely on trying to find it.' Moth swirled her tea. 'Did my mother tell you about Abel?'

'Who's he?' Fei turned, narrowing her eyes.

'Abel was Ela's husband to be. When Ela fell, he went into a dark place, driven mad by her action; in anguish, he followed her, but he had nowhere near the amount of power Ela had, so he fell somewhere darker, Parras's parallel, imprisoned. In blind madness he has spent thousands of years consuming the souls of those who walk through the forest he resides in, growing madder but also more powerful. Abel was a good man, but he's now a different creature altogether. If Ela finds him and breaks him lose, the Aon will have nothing on their combined powers. Over the years, the Sardan have worked to keep the location of his prison a secret and there are few who still know the location, mostly witches and cunning men. We have to hope it will continue to stay hidden and that Ela hasn't gotten her claws into them.'

'Cunning men and witches? I'm assuming they got the same welcoming treatment as this one?' said Cora, pointing at Fei.

Moth nodded.

'How many Sardan are left?' asked Fei.

'Nowhere near as many as there used to be. Ela has killed a great many of us. We used to live in harmony with normal folk, but she has spent years poisoning the minds of world leaders against us. But those who survived are strong and ready to fight.'

'Here's hoping we'll be enough.' said Fei, picking at a chipped bit of windowpane.

'You will be,' Moth smiled. She pressed her fingertip into the chilled window pane at the gleaming building. 'Inamorata's, she works there – Nathair number two. Her name is Vanessa, Vanessa Marini.'

The girls looked at the dancing showgirls outside the club, while Bisou squeezed between them, wagging his tail.

'We know of three so far. One here, one in a city called Leos, and you, Fei,' said Moth. 'Starting with Vanessa, there's no time to waste. And I'm sorry Cora, you can't join us for this one.'

'What? Why not?' Cora looked betrayed.

'Someone your age will draw too much attention in a place like that.'

Cora huffed.

Fei gave her sister an amused look and Cora slunk back over to the cushion with Bisou. She sipped from her cup loudly while Bisou sniffed her face, sending ripples through her tea.

'I can't imagine they'll let us in looking like this.' Fei looked down at her dirty, dishevelled jacket.

'No, definitely not.' Moth scurried over to the wardrobe. It squeaked as she pulled it open, revealing a few clothes hanging up, and the rest in a heap at the bottom. She dug through the mound – scarves and shirts flew out, hitting the creepy painting of the castle behind her. Bisou got excited and began digging at the floorboards.

'Ah ha,' said Moth, muffled beneath the clothes.

Cora continued to sip her tea in a huff as Moth stretched her arm out of the wardrobe, two moth-eaten old dresses draped over it. She stood and held the two dresses stretched out in front of her; shaking off the dust, she coughed.

'These should do.'

Cora clenched her mouth in an attempt not to burst out laughing.

'And how old are these?' asked Fei, feeling the lace on one of the sleeves almost crumble between her fingers.

'They were my great-great-grandma's, sooo maybe fifty years old,' Moth grinned.

'Yeah, we won't stick out at all.'

'What do you mean? They're alright.' As Moth went to the window to get a better look at the showgirls, Fei caught Cora silently chuckling and Bisou wagging his tail.

'Have fun!' she spluttered.

'Uhh, hush you, or you'll take my place.' Said Fei under her breath.

Moth and Fei carefully put on the antique dresses, the frequent small ripping sounds causing them some anxiety. Cora inspected them for any new holes as they spun, creating a small tornado of dust.

Moth and Fei stood in front of the wardrobe mirror. They looked like a pair of cream cakes – slightly dusty, grey, deflated cream cakes.

'What beautiful cherubs you are!' Cora cupped Fei's cheeks.

Fei grimaced.

Moth pulled on her matching crumbling gloves and turned to the girls. 'Right, so all we need to do is get in and get out with Nessa as quickly as possible. She's very private, so she may not appreciate us being there.'

Moth beckoned Fei to the window and started heaving it up.

'In, out, quick, private. Righto.' Fei gave a tentative nod.

Cora snorted.

'Stay here and look after Cora, okay.' Moth kissed Bisou on the forehead, and he gave a small woof.

Fei faced Cora. 'Please don't leave the house. I'm sure we won't be long.'

'I won't! Don't worry, we're just gonna sit and wait till it all goes pear-shaped and you realise you need us.' Cora slumped onto the floor cushion and Bisou started sniffing her disgruntled face again.

'Oh, I almost forgot.' Moth shuffled back to the wardrobe, heaved open a small drawer at the bottom and reached in, pulling out two small black eye masks.

'You'll be going incognito tonight, my friend,' she said.

'Thrilling,' said Fei.

They each stretched a mask over their face, climbed out of the window and made their way to the club.

*** 

Fei and Moth watched from a dingy side street opposite Inamorata's, as the spotlights darted around, flashing across their faces. Two large, suited men with long black coats stood on either side of the main entrance. The showgirls danced, smiling and brushing their feathers on the cheeks of revellers as they went in.

Fei nodded at an approaching group. 'We can pretend we're with them. Don't want the guards to get too close a look at us,' she suggested.

'You're right, follow me.'

Moth darted back down the side street and further along the road, turning down a street parallel to the one they'd just been hiding in. They stopped in the shadows and watched as the drunken group wobbled closer.

The group staggered past and the two girls sneaked in at the back, laughing and swaying with the rest of them.

The bouncers grunted, opened the doors and the girls crept in as the music grew louder.

Inside, the club was a maelstrom of bright colours and tasselled red velvet curtains. The sound of pianos and trumpets blasted out as the curtain in front of them lifted to reveal a circular room full of people laughing, drinking and dancing. There was a half-moon shaped stage to the right, on which several showgirls danced in their beautifully embellished costumes, surrounded by blasting instruments.

Round, gold tables were placed sporadically around the room in front of the stage, seating drunk guests dressed in their finest suits with long silk dresses and top hats, watching and whistling at the girls dancing on the stage to the music. It was dimly lit and the only other exits Fei and Moth could see were a closed door at the opposite end of the room, and a stage door behind a curtain to the right.

They walked down the stairs, taking in the frivolity. A girl dressed in a similar costume to the girls out front stood holding a gold tray holding glasses of champagne. She was smiling and handing them out to the group. Moth nodded and took glasses for them both.

'Thank you.' They both smiled stiffly at the beaming girl.

The club had the distinct smell of tobacco - similar to that of Green and Wood's shop - mixed with wine. And sweat.

And the floor was just a little bit sticky.

'Is she one of these girls?' whispered Fei, as an older gentleman tipped his hat to her.

'No, we'll have to ask someone. I'm sure she's working here tonight, but she might be round the back.'

Fei nodded. 'Okay, so you ask that side of the room and I'll ask the girls round here. Meet in the middle, in ten?'

'Sure, just ... no taking the mask off.'

Fei gave her a thumbs-up and they separated.

Dodging flailing arms and feathered costumes, Moth and Fei manoeuvred themselves round the club. Of course, having seen practically all of the showgirls on the floor a second ago, naturally, they had now all dispersed.

# CHAPTER FOURTEEN

Cora sat on the windowsill, breathing hot air on one of the panes of glass and writing 'BORED' with her finger. The condensation crept over the glass and her eye caught some blurry flickering lights bobbing up and down in the street below. She leaned forward as the lights became clearer and the condensation disappeared.

Torches. Carried by, maybe, seven figures. Carrying heavy weapons. Dressed in black.

Cora shot up, her hands pressed against the glass, staring at the figures marching towards the club. Startled, Bisou whined and pattered over to her.

'Silgir,' Cora whispered.

The long ridge of fur along Bisou's back began to spike.

'We have to warn them, B.'

Bisou gave a woof, his ears pointed at the lights.

Cora took another look at the group; there was one figure at the front, far larger and more intimidating than the others. He was over six foot and had long slim, limbs. He was bald, with a brown handlebar moustache sitting central on his sallow angular face. He was forty perhaps? Very muscular and he walked tall, his face stoic with intent. His hands were gloved, unlike the others, and one of his hands rested on the hilt of a long sword, which poked out from under his more decorated black coat than the other Silgir.

His dark eyes scanned the streets as they turned the corner towards the club.

Cora grabbed her crossbow and their bags. Bisou whined and snorted, wagging his tail as he teetered on the spot by the window.

'C'mon.'

They flew down the shaky iron steps to the front of the house, where they hid in the darkness of an alleyway and watched as the gloved man stood chatting with the bouncers outside the club.

The tall man's face had not changed, severe and purposeful. The man and the bouncer nodded, and Cora saw him point for the other Silgir to enter through the main entrance, whilst he made his way round the back.

'He's gonna trap them. Bastard!'

Bisou gave another low woof.

Cora crouched, staring at the severe man as he disappeared behind the club.

'Come on, B,' Cora muttered, scowling. They darted through the shadows round the side of the club.

\*\*\*

'Excuse me, sorry, but do you know if Vanessa is working tonight?'' Fei asked a very merry-looking showgirl.

'No, sorry love, I don't!' she shouted over the blaring music.

A younger gentleman came up behind the showgirl and whisked her away in a dance, as she grinned and shouted. 'You should ask Mary!'

She pointed, mid-twirl at an older, cross-looking woman standing by the bar. Fei turned to see Moth approaching the woman.

Moth cleared her throat. 'Excuse me, you don't know if Vanessa is working tonight, do you?'

The woman stopped scolding one of the bar staff, looked Moth up and down, frowned, and tightened the bartender's tie, making him gasp a little. 'She'll be on in five minutes. Don't you go distracting her now. I won't have her starting late, as usual.' The woman bustled off.

Fei was standing in the centre of the room, bobbing her head to the music. She'd seen their interaction, and Moth pointed at the stage, then held up five fingers.

Fei nodded.

Moth looked past her and turned pale.

Fei felt her stomach drop as she watched Moth's eyes dart back to her. Fei turned.

As she peered behind her, her gaze met with the dark eyes of a tall, bald man, dressed all in black, staring back at her; his glare fixed as partygoers swirled past him. His mouth upturned to a menacing smile. Moth leapt over the staircase leading up to the bar and skidded beside her, grabbing onto her arm and staring in horror at the man, her eye twitching with venom.

'Moth, who is that?' said Fei.

'Harryn Yaeffe,' she whispered, her voice dripping with wrath. 'Leader of the Silgir, torturer, hunter. Murderer.' Moth's voice shook.

Fei had never seen a look of such pure hatred and she felt her palms begin to sweat. She turned to see Harryn powering towards them. They spun round, only to see six other Silgir closing in.

They were surrounded.

Fei and Moth stood back-to-back; Fei pulled out her daggers and Moth a small knife, the partygoers none the wiser as they danced past the Silgir. Harryn was bearing down on them, holding a knife in one hand, his stare fixed on them as he dodged flailing arms and glasses of wine.

'How the hell has he found us!?' Moth spat.

Fei looked round the room in a panic. Their two main exits were blocked by Silgir – but the stage exit was only blocked by dancers.

'The stage exit, we can get out that way,' said Fei, as the Silgir drew their swords, only a few steps away from them.

'On my count, drop to the floor, they're less likely to see us crawling in this crowd,' said Moth.

'Okay, okay.'

Harryn was getting closer by the second. The Silgir raised their swords, ready to swing.

'Now!'

Cora and Bisou had hurried behind the club, towards the rear entrance, and watched from behind a shrivelled tree as another group of Silgir, larger than the first, approached the front of the building. The rest of the Silgir stood waiting in regimented rows outside the club.

'We need to get in.' Cora stared at the back entrance as a group of showgirls in white satin dressing gowns appeared, lighting cigarettes and laughing.

An idea came to her. 'You're gonna have to give 'em a scare, B. Get 'em to go back inside, then I can get a foot in the door before it shuts.'

Bisou tilted his head and whimpered, staring up at her.

'You got a better idea?'

He snorted and walked, heavy-footed, towards the girls. Cora darted through the darkness and crept over to hide behind some large bins nearby.

Bisou approached the girls, who didn't notice him at first. He sat down looking sadly at them. Cora peered out and flapped her hand for him to get closer to them, imitating a growl. He watched Cora's animated face and whimpered. The girls' heads shot round.

They all screamed.

Bisou recoiled in shock, watching them scurry, shrieking, back into the club, feathers flying everywhere. Cora darted out and grabbed the door handle.

'Well, aren't you terrifying?!' she smiled at Bisou, who huffed in distaste, as they crept in through the back door.

Black.

The lights in the club went off and the music cut out. Fei and Moth dropped to the ground as 'oohs', followed by whistles and clapping, rang round the room.

'What the hell's going on?' Fei whispered.

'Nessa!'

Silence.

A spotlight beamed down onto the stage, highlighting the silhouette of a small curvaceous woman – one arm up, holding a fan, the other round her skirt, mirroring the crest of the fan.

More whistles and cheering sounded as some slower, more seductive, music began. They all stared as Nessa spun, springing open her fan to cover half her tanned face. She wore a long piece of sheer black fabric over her head that cascaded down, covering her long, dark, wavy hair.

She glided forward, barefoot, flitting the fan over her green eyes. She twisted with the music, spinning her flowing red skirt, which flew up to reveal her thighs, sending the crowd into a roaring frenzy. She continued dancing to the slow music in the spotlight, as the girls looked round for the Silgir.

Harryn had stopped moving when the music was switched off and was squinting at Nessa. The other Silgir had also stopped, and were staring, perplexed at Harrin's rigidity. Nessa danced to the centre of the stage. She bent forward into a bow and brought the fan fluttering back over her beautiful, freckled face, her bust pillowing over her white corset, the crowd yelling with excitement.

Harryn's face darkened as he spotted the girls. The glow from the stage landing on their terrified faces as they scrambled back to their feet.

He marched forward, the Silgir following suit.

Nessa watched Harryn from behind her fan, the spotlight glinting off the two gold cuffs she had strapped to her wrists.

The girls stood to the ready, Fei trembling and Moth charged with adrenaline as the Silgir closed in on them.

Harryn's lip curled as he reached for his sword.

Cora and Bisou skidded through the back door, searching the crowd as the club filled with light again, the music switching to something faster and more furious as Nessa sprang into the air.

The crowd lost their minds with glee. Drinks cascaded round the room and couples gyrated to the music. Nessa leapt from the stage, spinning and landing on the floor between Harryn and the girls, lifting the black veil away from her face.

She glared at Harryn.

Harryn froze.

'You,' he growled, as the music continued to blast.

'FEI!' Cora yelled, as she saw a Silgir race up behind her sister.

'Cora, get out of here!' Fei screamed.

Bisou lunged towards them.

'I want them alive!' bellowed Harryn, his face contorted with rage.

'Nessa, no!' Moth screamed.

Fei clutched at the sticky floorboards, her nails searing with pain as she scrambled back to stability, the foot of a party-goer slamming into her side.

Stunned, she watched as a dagger attached to a long piece of cord fly over her head, shoot through the Silgir's chest and fly out again. There was a small 'click' as the dagger reattached to one of Nessa's gold cuffs.

A long thick splatter of blood streamed across the faces of the drinkers and the showgirls. The screams began and the music stopped. Harryn stood, seething, and Nessa flung another of her daggers towards him.

He dropped to the floor as the blade whistled over his head, sending little droplets of blood splattering over his face.

Shrieks rang round the room as the guests clambered over each other to get out, clawing their way towards the doors.

Fei and Moth sprang into action as the Silgir charged, and Cora and Bisou hurtled down the stairs.

Harrin punched at Nessa's knee, crippling her, as her dagger returned to her cuff; she stared into Harrin's black eyes.

'Hola, old friend,' she said through gritted teeth, rolling away from his sword as he swung it down.

Moth and Fei swerved out of the way as Nessa spun between them. The shrill ringing of the club alarm began to pierce their ears, as the scary woman shrieked and flung herself behind the bar, sending champagne glasses crashing to the ground.

'Get down,' Nessa growled.

Fei, Moth and Cora dropped to the floor and Bisou leapt onto the stage, pulling a Silgir with him in his jaws.

They watched as Nessa twirled her daggers around her small body, sending them spinning through the chests of the Silgir. She clung to the cords and, using her elbows and neck, sent them ricocheting, like a Catherine wheel of death. The club lights bounced off the whirling knives and blood spiralled round the room.

Fei could hardly breathe, as she scanned the thrashing legs, desperately looking for Cora.

'Stay calm, not yet.' Moth grabbed Fei's arm.

'I have to do something,' said Fei.

'Not yet, we need to get out of here first!'

Cora crawled along the floor towards Bisou. He wagged his tail as she grabbed her crossbow and aimed at the tidal wave of Silgir piling into the club.

'Gotcha,' she muttered, sending her first arrow whistling across the room.

Fei and Moth crawled beneath the flying knives and arrows, watching as Harryn effortlessly dodged Nessa's daggers, the blade of his sword clanking against her knives as he sent them shooting away.

Fei and Moth sprang up and sliced at the backs of the last remaining Silgir.

'Cora!' Fei shouted across the room, as she watched her sister leap over tables and skid up next to them, followed shortly by Bisou.

The group watched as Nessa swung her knives faster at Harrin's stoic dodges. He thrust up his sword and caught one of the swings, sending the knife furiously wrapping round the blade.

He pulled her forward, dodging her other knife which was flying straight at him, and grabbed the cord attached to Nessa's wrist.

Fei lunged towards Nessa, stopping short when she saw another wave of Silgir piling through the back door.

Harryn began to drag Nessa towards him, his teeth gritted as she clawed her toes into the ground.

He stopped abruptly. 'Hello to you too,' he snarled, his stare burning into her face.

Nessa smiled and shot forward, bouncing off his chest. She flipped and kicked his chin. He went flying backwards, tumbling to the floor as the wave of Silgir closed in on them. Nessa scrambled to her feet and headed back for Harryn.

'NESSA, COME ON!' Moth bellowed, as Nessa glared into Harryn's dark eyes.

'I need to kill him!' Nessa growled, as the Silgir closed in.

'NESSA NOW. C'mon!'

Nessa roared, spat on the floor next to her, and darted over to the rest of the group as they disappeared through the stage door.

# CHAPTER FIFTEEN

Sharp, shrill ringing pierced through Harrin's ears as he clutched at his jaw. He hissed when his fingers passed over a large welt beginning to form on his chin.

Shifting onto all fours, he pushed down on the sticky club floor and tried to heave himself up. Blood rushing to his head as the muffled shouts of Silgir grew closer.

The dim club exploded with sudden brightness and Harryn flung up his arm to shield his eyes. Two Silgir dropped down next to him, thrusting their hands under his arms.

'Are you okay, sir?'

Harrin stood. However close to unconsciousness he had been, he still managed to direct a composed, but severe look at them. Removing their hands, they drew back.

'They went through the stage door,' Harryn snarled, straightening his uniform.

'Right, we shall go after them.'

'No. Half of you wait in here, the rest outside. Wait for my call.'

'Yes, sir,' the Silgir nervously saluted and nodded. 'You heard him, everyone outside. Quickly!' They hurried out.

Harryn curled his lip and looked over at one of the club bouncers.

'You!' he beckoned him over.

Harrin beckoned him over. The bouncer looked a little peaky and was consoling the scary woman. He handed the woman over to the other bouncer – who received her the way you might receive a screaming baby – and shuffled over, crunching across the broken glass scattered on the floor.

'Am I right in assuming there is another way out of this establishment, other than the two obvious ones? And, if so, where is it?' said Harryn, hands crossed, staring at the quivering bouncer.

'Umm, there's a hatch, sir, round the side of the building, about a hundred metres towards the forest, sir. On the floor by the shed, it's an old fire escape that leads to the dancers' dressing rooms.' Harryn gave a wry smile and nodded the pale bouncer away.

He felt a warm drip make its way down his face into his moustache. His lip twitched and he pulled a handkerchief from his pocket and dabbed at his forehead. Red blotches spread across the silk. Straightening his moustache, he placed the stained handkerchief back in his pocket and marched across the club to the back exit. He sheathed his sword and pulled out a pistol from the holster attached to his belt.

Nessa blasted open the club's kitchen door, which slammed against the wall as they rushed through, making all the pots in the room clang.

'How could you do this to me? I was so close to making a life here,' said Nessa, as some potatoes on the counter began to sprout leaves. 'You would not even let me kill that devil!' she bellowed.

'Nessa I'm so sorry, but things have changed, and we need you,' said Moth, hurrying to keep up with her.

Nessa stopped and spun round to face Moth.

'You need me? No, *I* needed *you* to let me live a normal life for once. To allow me to feel like I belong somewhere. I had that here, till you allowed them to bring these vipers into my home. Now I have no choice but to run. Again!' She turned, ripping the lace off her head, fury in her eyes.

Fei felt her stomach empty again. Finally, here she was: another one.

*Not alone.*

*But even she hates me.*

Fei followed Nessa as she stormed into her dressing room to grab a bag from under a large, moth-eaten chair, which she began to root through while flinging in other items.

'Look, we're so sorry to be doing this. Believe me, I didn't want this either. But despite being separated from our family and being attacked by just about everyone, I've never met anyone else like me before, and it's good to know I'm not alone,' said Fei.

Cora smiled, as Fei stared at the back of Nessa's shaking head. Her words had apparently fallen on deaf ears. Nessa abruptly zipped up her bag and turned to face Fei.

'You do not know me. At least you have a family — that devil killed mine. And I would rather have stayed alone, gracias,' Nessa hissed as she marched past Fei, knocking her shoulder.

'Guys, we need to leave, sharpish!' said Moth, who could hear thumping footsteps getting closer.

'Follow me.' Nessa disappeared down a narrow corridor.

'Come on, Fei.' Moth stood in the doorway, then ran after Nessa.

Fei stared at the tiny window at the top of Nessa's bleak room, when she felt a hand on her shoulder.

'Fei c'mon, we haven't got time to stare at things,' said Cora, urgency in her voice as shouts sounded from outside. Bisou licked Fei's hand, and she turned to followed Moth, Cora and Bisou trotting behind.

They crouched as they scurried through the narrow, brick corridor, following the light of Moth's torch. The passage was cold and smelt damp, as if water had once flowed through it.

'There it is,' said Nessa, pointing upwards. 'I will open it, check, and then we'll all make for the forest opposite. Do not stop for anything! Is that clear?'

The group nodded and Bisou gave a light woof.

'Maybe I should...' Moth began.

'Maybe you should just listen to me,' Nessa interrupted. Moth nodded.

Nessa reached for the hatch door. Weeds had wound through the latch. She struggled to open it, then peeked out through the tiny sliver of light that beamed through.

No one around.

Harryn stood in a mill shed nearby, his eyes trained on the trap door. His pistol poised and his breathing slow and focused. He was barely blinking.

Nessa pushed the door a little further, peering round, her eyes landing on the mill shed.

Harryn darted behind a beam.

The coast still looked clear. Nessa thrust open the door with all her might, sending it slamming down onto the ground.

'Vamos! Go now!' whispered Nessa.

Bisou and Cora climbed out of the hatch and began to run as fast as they could towards the forest, about a hundred metres away. Bisou charged off ahead, scanning for approaching Silgir; Cora followed, watching as the glow from torches began to flicker to the right. The Silgir were getting closer – they would soon be turning the corner.

Harryn watched as Moth climbed out.

'You go next, I'll watch behind you,' said Fei.

'I do not take orders from you,' Nessa snapped back.

Fei swallowed and climbed out of the hatch. Moth stood at the top looking round, her arm stretched down to help Fei out. Nessa leapt through and lowered the hatch door.

She froze as a loud click sounded behind her.

Fei turned, mid-run, to see Harryn with his pistol pointed at Nessa's head.

'Nessa!' Fei screamed.

Moth, Cora and Bisou skidded to a stop, as the Silgir began to run round the corner.

'Don't move,' sneered Harryn. 'Hands where I can see them.' Nessa turned, as Fei began to fly back.

'Not another step, Mage.' Harryn raised his pistol a little higher and glared at Fei who stood rigid in the grass.

'Any last words?' he seethed.

'I would do it again if I could,' said Nessa.

Harryn's lip twitched.

Fei was unarmed, and the Silgir were virtually upon them. She had no choice – and turned her head away.

Harryn narrowed his eyes at Fei.

Her sight left her, and the grey surroundings shifting to milky white as she felt energy from the ground pulsate up and through her.

'FEI!' Cora bellowed, seeing her sister motionless, staring white-eyed at the approaching Silgir, a small tornado of grey encircling her. Cora grabbed her crossbow and fell onto one knee, aiming at the soldiers. Bisou lowered his head, his mouth smoking as he growled. Moth pulled a knife from beneath her skirt and bounded towards Nessa and Harryn.

'You will die like your scum Mage parents,' Harryn growled as he pressed the trigger.

Moth flung her knife at Harryn and a thundering tree root shot through the ground, blasting the pistol out of his hand and sending him flying backwards. Moth, too, found herself soaring back into the dry ground.

As the bullet shot through Nessa's arm, she crumpled in pain, blades of grass bursting up through the earth around her.

Harryn desperately clambered to dodge the erupting tree roots. He unsheathed his sword and leapt, ducked and twisted, slicing through them as they tore through the ground towards him.

Moth ran towards Nessa as Harryn found an opening and lunged forward, kicking Nessa's stomach. She groaned in pain, her blood dripping onto the petals of fast-blooming flowers.

A root smacked into Harryn's face and he roared, grabbing hold of Nessa's neck and squeezing, lifting her off the ground as the roots began to weaken.

Fei was still lying on the ground. She felt her head fog, and her legs crumble; pain shot through her head as the tree roots sank back into the ground.

'I should've tried harder to kill you the first time – you're like a cockroach,' said Harryn to Nessa's purpling face.

Moth peeled her eyes open to see the blurred shadows of Harryn and Nessa. Adrenaline coursed through her as she scrambled to reach Harryn's pistol in the grass.

'You always were pathetic,' Nessa wheezed. 'And you still are,' she gasped, her lips turning blue as she clawed at Harryn's hands.

Harryn's face dropped as Nessa's dagger sprang from her cuff, slicing through his cheek. They fell away from each other, Nessa gasping for air, half-conscious; Harryn howling and clasping his bleeding face.

Moth crawled to Nessa and flung her sound arm over her shoulders, dragging her to her feet as she wheezed, blood streaming from her arm.

'Fei!' shouted Cora, her eyes darting between the approaching Silgir and her dazed sister. 'Follow my voice!'

Bisou inhaled, then released a thundering stream of flames, sending a wall of fire flashing along in front of them, separating them from the soldiers.

Cora gasped, flinging her hand up over her eyes. The heat was immense and the forest behind them lit up in a menagerie of dancing colours as the flames coursed from his mouth.

Snorting, Bisou cut the stream of fire, coughed, then raced towards Fei, who wobbled to her feet, sweating. Moth and Nessa weren't far behind her.

Harryn writhing on the grass behind them.

Bisou grabbed Fei's sleeve in his mouth and began pulling her towards Cora and the forest. She ran with him, her arm over his back, stumbling blindly, Nessa wheezing behind her. She looked around at the vague yellow and red flashes, moved her fingers to her mouth and blew a sharp, shrill whistle. Clyde, who had been waiting patiently behind Moth's house, shot up his ears and began thundering towards the whistle.

Two Silgir ran to Harryn, who was kneeling on the grass, clutching the gash across his face. His gloves were drenched in blood and he was pulsating with wrath.

'Are you okay, sir?' one of them asked tentatively.

Harryn moved his hands away from his bleeding face.

'Set the city alight,' he muttered.

'I'm sorry, sir?' asked the soldier.

He turned to reveal a long, red slash along the side of his cheek and head, blood coursing through his – now crimson – collar.

'SET THE GODDAM CITY ALIGHT!' he roared.

# CHAPTER SIXTEEN

The Silgir lieutenant pointed to the flaming torches on the walls around the club. The soldiers all grabbed at the ones they could reach and began smashing them through the windows.

Fei, Cora, Moth, Nessa and Bisou hobbled through the forest; Bisou's wall of flames slowly twisted and disappeared into the wind as Clyde charged towards them.

Having dragged themselves up a small hill to get to a thicket, Fei and Nessa slumped to the ground, Bisou and Moth panted, and Cora stood silently, watching Daramere burn.

Nessa pushed herself up, tears streaming from her bloodshot eyes. The group sank to the ground as screams echoed from the city. Fei and Cora watched in horror, as terrified families ran from the flames.

Bisou lay with his head in his paws while the group stood there, silent. Fei clenched her jaw.

Harryn pulled himself towards a well near the club. The flames towered above, making him sweat as he crouched beside the bricks. The blood dripping from his face and hands sent small ripples through the water, distorting the image. His lip twitched and he stared back at his mutilated reflection.

Removing one of his black leather gloves, he revealed a badly burnt hand. He pulled off his other glove, which had hidden the same forked scarring around his strong fist. Then he reached into the water, closing his eyes and bracing himself.

He splashed water over his face and grimaced, panting from the heat of the fire, as remembered images flashed through his head...

*He was looking up at a burning building, his hands alight.*

He fell back, eyes shut, as blood continued to stream down his cheek.

Another flash.

*He was staring down a flight of stairs from behind a banister, watching as a young woman answered the door to a large house. She opened it; a tall, dark figure stood in front of her, a gun in their hand. The bullet flew into the woman's chest, and her lifeless body stared up at Harryn as the dark figure stepped through the doorway.*

Harryn clenched his jaw and sat forward, clutching at his head.

Another flash.

*A man ran in to find the woman's body on the floor. Devastated, he turned, only to be shot down by the same dark figure.*

*Harryn ran in terror up the stairs, stopping outside the attic room at the top. Flinging open the door, he peered down at two terrified figures on the floor. He plunged a knife into their hearts, then turned to see a girl with long dark hair crying in the doorway. He watched, horrified, as she smashed a gas lamp on the wooden floorboards of the room, then locked the door behind her. Trapping him.*

*He smashed his way out of the house through roaring flames and falling beams, his hands burning as he stumbled out, and screamed into the night sky.*

Harrin opened his eyes.

He stared at the Silgir marching through the city, torches in hand. The heat of the fire angered his already burnt face as he clutched his head. He pulled out the spotted white handkerchief from his pocket and tied it round his head, grimacing as the crimson clouds crept further across the sky.

The Silgir troops were standing outside the city, watching as the city walls crumbled and the people of Daramere fled. One Silgir stood to attention as he saw Harryn striding towards them, the handkerchief strapped diagonally across his face, a small pool of red clouding in the middle.

The other Silgir followed suit and arranged themselves in a line.

'Sir, we have set alight all four corners of the city, as you commanded. It should be ash by morning.'

Harryn stared at him with dark bloodshot eyes.

'Sir?'

Harryn climbed onto his horse, spurring it towards the crowd of city-dwellers sobbing by the trees, while their houses burnt to the ground.

Figures emerged from the smoke, coughing as they stumbled towards the forest; cars raced out, sending spirals of smoke and grey flying into those behind them; horses too leapt out of the thick air and raced for the cover of the trees, as the flames ripped through the city.

Harryn ground his teeth, glaring at the weeping people of Daramere.

'Let this be a lesson to you all. From now on, any cities found to be harbouring Mage will be burnt to the ground. If you allow them to twist your minds, as it will be you, who will suffer the consequences,' he boomed, looking again towards the hill.

He rode towards his first-in-command, a stout, stern, thick-necked man, whose face always wobbled when Harryn was near.

'See to it that this message is spread.'

'Yes, sir,' he stared down his nose in disgust at the mass of new refugees.

Thus the Silgir left the broken citizens of Daramere crying, amid the ashes of their lives.


'We have to help them.' Fei stepped forward, her voice shaking as she watched the library building topple to the ground. She felt a hand grab her arm, pulling her back.

'There's nothing else we can do for them. Going down there will only slow us down, and we can't afford that. Not now,' said Moth.

Fei shook her head, sick to her stomach. 'We can't do this alone.' The lump in her throat made it hard to speak, and tears clouded her already hazy vision.

Moth nodded.

'Is there anyone else who can help?' said Fei.

'Yes.' Moth's voice had grown quiet. 'But I have to go alone, there's no time for you to go off track now.'

Cora frowned. 'Alone?'

'We're not going without you. We stay together,' said Fei.

'No, you need to carry on and find the other one, before they do.' The smell of burning turned Moth's stomach. 'This can never happen again.'

Guilt filled every cell in her body as she picked up one of the bags Cora had brought for her. She stepped behind a tree trunk and began to change her clothes.

'This wasn't your fault,' said Cora.

'Then whose fault was it?'

'Ela's,' said Fei, looking up at the large ash cloud that had begun to intertwine with the grey.

Moth stepped out from behind the tree.

'There is only one way this will all end. You're right – we need more help, and I will go to Brunas Peak to get it.'

'What's in Brunas Peak?' asked Cora.

'It's where I was born. They are good people. I'm sure some, if not all, of them will help us. I'll find you.' As she began to walk away, her bag hoisted over her back, she shook a small yellow stone at them.

'Moth, please don't leave us. We don't even know where the last Nathair is,' said Fei.

'Leos,' wheezed Nessa under her breath, picking at a purple flower that had sprouted in front of her.

They turned to Nessa, who was slowly and shakily getting to her feet. Her cheeks glistened with tears and her shirt was soaked with blood.

'I have to go. Bisou will look after you all,' said Moth.

Bisou woofed and stood next to Cora. She tickled his ear.

'If I leave now, we have a better chance of winning this war. Stay together, protect each other. You three are all we have left.'

Fei hugged Moth tight.

Moth bent to kiss Bisou's head, as he wagged his tail.

She turned to Fei.

'His name is Alfie Albonas, the third one. He's not hard to miss,' she said with a weary smile. 'Find him at Peaches in Leos, and I'll find you.'

Fei nodded. Moth smiled and disappeared into the darkness.

Nessa winced as she twisted a bandage around her arm.

'Here, lemme me help you.' Fei reached over to Nessa.

'I'm fine.'

'Please, look I can –'

'I said I'm fine!' Nessa snapped, glaring at Fei.

'Look, there's not enough "sorrys" in the world for dragging you into this, but we had no choice. Right now, we have absolutely zero chance of defeating an entire army. We need you, and we need the others; otherwise what happened in Daramere will just keep happening. I can't live with that. And I reckon you can't either.'

Fei's eyes glistened, as Nessa continued to wrap up her arm, her jaw firmly clenched.

'This is the first I've truly seen of all this, the first time I've had so many people looking to me for answers, and I have none.' Her voice began to shake. 'So we'd really appreciate it if you could help us try to beat whatever is coming for us. Otherwise this has all been for nothing.'

Fei stood, patted Clyde's thick neck, picked up their bags and started walking.

Nessa fought back tears, her hands shaking as she attempted to clip the bandage together – unsuccessfully. The end of it sprang away and began unravelling onto the ground. She buried her face in her hands, then looked over to where her house had once stood. Now a crumpled heap of scorched bricks and ash. Five years of rebuilding, gone in a flash. Painfully familiar.

There would be no going back.

She dropped her hands and saw her bag had been placed next to her. She returned to her bandage and calmly clipped the ends together. Opening the bag, she pulled out a jacket, some furry brown button-up boots her father had made for her, a long dark-grey skirt, a long-sleeved button-up shirt and a black bow and a scarf. She pulled on the clothes, careful not to knock her injured arm. Fastening the jacket buttons, she stood for a second and watched the burning city.

The flames were still raging, and she found herself tensing as a memory darted through her mind.

*Two lifeless bodies in a dark room, sprawled in a pool of blood; a tall young man standing over them, with a knife in his hand. He turned to see her. She grabbed the gas lamp on the wall and threw it into the room, watching it explode on the floor as the man ran towards her, terror in his eyes. She shut the door and locked it.*

Nessa looked down at her feet to see bluebells begin to push their way out through the thicket. She took a last look at the burning city she had tried to call home. Glowing orange in the centre, she could still feel its heat on her face. She picked up her bag and followed the others.

# CHAPTER SEVENTEEN

Three days they walked – and Leos was still many miles away. After the second day, they retired to wearing their gas masks most of the time, as the grey had become much more frequent. They trudged past countless abandoned towns. Fei was in front, leading Clyde, who was carrying their bags; Cora and Bisou in the middle; and Nessa at the back.

Despite remaining close to local towns, they didn't see a single person, which wasn't that surprising really. The grey usually stayed close to cities, surrounding them, making the rest of the world seem unreachable. They walked on, unable to see more than thirty metres ahead, breathing a sigh of relief when a forest appeared, dispersing the grey somewhat.

For the last hour or so, Fei had found herself at arm's length with Clyde, pulling him along until he stopped, stomping his feet a little more forcefully into the ground. Without noticing, they had walked into the largest forest on their journey so far. They had got so used to wearing their fogged-up masks, they hadn't noticed the grey disappearing a while back.

Fei looked into Clyde's tired eyes and stroked his nose.

'We're gonna rest here for the night,' she said, unstrapping his girth and pulling off the bags.

'We shouldn't be stopping in the middle of the night.' Nessa marched towards Fei and Cora, pulling off her mask. Red imprints covered her face. 'It's too risky.'

'Clyde needs to rest, and to be honest, so do we all. We can take it in turns to keep watch.'

'You should not have brought him. The less bodies, the better,' Nessa grumbled and slumped to the ground, taking a swig from her flask as Fei began pulling out blankets.

Fei raised an eyebrow. 'Well, you're more than welcome to carry the food and provisions for him, but he's going nowhere. He's old, he needs to rest.'

Nessa pursed her lips.

Cora lay on the ground and looked at the stars between the swaying branches of the mottled trees above them. Fei sat down beside Clyde and placed her hands on the earth, closing her eyes. A loud ringing resonated through her ears as grass began sprouting through the cracks and grew into a small, lush patch.

Clyde's ears pricked up as he stretched his tired neck down and began munching. Bisou also began hungrily ripping at the grass. Fei and Cora exchanged looks of surprise and shuffled over to let them eat in peace.

Fei sat next to Cora and bit into a slightly stale piece of bread, while Nessa sat staring into the darkness.

'You've met before, haven't you?' said Fei.

Nessa frowned.

'You and Harryn… What happened?'

Nessa was silent, and began fiddling with her flask.

'Moth knew him too. D'you know what happened between them?' asked Cora.

Nessa blinked. 'About ten years ago she infiltrated his ranks, disguised as a Silgir. She got into his tent, meaning to steal his plans – the army's movements, what they knew. He caught her and imprisoned her there. For days he starved her, attempting to find out where the Sardan were based and their identities, but she would not give them up. One day he decided to drag her out into the middle of the soldiers, strap her to a post and whip her till she succumbed. She would not. He whipped her for hours. Till on the verge of death, Bisou came, and he saved her. They have been inseparable since. And since Harryn has a particularly strong hatred for me as well, she decided to align herself with me. Share the load I guess.' Nessa fiddled a little more aggressively with her flask as she continued. 'I never wanted anyone to have to watch me, look after me. I just wanted to live a simple, normal life, away from this. I should have known the moment I shut that door and locked it behind me that would never happen.' Her lip trembled.

'Locked what door?' asked Fei.

'It does not matter. I am going to sleep.' Nessa wiped away a tear and grabbed one of the blankets from the pile by the fire. She tossed it over herself and snuggled up next to a tree, turning away from Cora and Fei.

'We should probably try and get some sleep too,' said Cora, reaching for two other blankets. 'I'll take first watch.'

'Are you sure?' said Fei, yawning.

'Yeah, I'm not tired yet.'

'Okay, well, just wake me up when, I dunno, it's been a few hours.' Fei reached over and grabbed Cora's crossbow, planting it in Cora's lap. 'Anything moves, you wake me up straight away.' She looked at Bisou through heavy eyes. 'Don't let her wander off.' He woofed and nuzzled up next to the fire.

Fei lay back and looked up at the stars, which were glistening in the reflected moonlight. She turned to see Clyde, legs tucked in, eyes shut, and his lower lip wiggling with his snores, nestled in the patch of grass he'd eaten. She smiled and let her eyes close.

Fei felt her shoulder being nudged. Then a tongue made its way across her face. She heaved her eyes open – Clyde had rolled and was now lying on his side, right next to her. He was boiling, and Fei was dripping with sweat. She looked up to see both Cora and Bisou staring at her.

'It's your turn. I'm tired as hell – Bisou wouldn't stop making me throw sticks for him.'

Fei groaned and pushed herself up. Cora was already making herself comfortable under a blanket, Bisou crawling in behind her.

She got to her feet, panting from Clyde's hot body, fanned herself and walked away from the fire. There was a small wind tunnel between some trees and Fei closed her eyes as the cool air washed over her.

Cora was out like a light and immediately started snoring. Despite her snores, it was deliciously quiet, still and clear.

Then a soft ringing made its way through her head and the damp smell she had become so accustomed to faded away.

She narrowed her eyes.

*What on earth...?*

In the distance she could see a small, round, white, glowing object, which appeared to be hovering. She squinted at it, open-mouthed. The white ball of light drifted to the left and right, floating in mid-air.

She took a step forward and moved her hand down to her belt to grab one of her daggers. *Just in case.*

The light moved a little closer and she pulled out the dagger, holding it in front of her face.

*Okay...*

Her eyes bulged and her heart began to race.

Glancing back at the camp, she took another step.

The light did not move.

She stared, fascinated, at its glow on the trees and felt nothing but warmth. It seemed to shine brighter, the closer she got; and the closer she got, the happier she felt. The ball hovered in front of her face, its light radiating over her. The forest was silent.

'Hello?' she whispered.

It did not move.

*What the hell is it? God, Cora's gonna kill me for this.*

She raised an arm and reached forward. Just as she was about to touch it, the ball floated away, bobbing gently from side to side.

'Hey, hey, wait.' She took another quick look at the others sleeping behind her, then stepped after it, following it through the trees, as it floated away.

*Just for a bit.*

The glowing ball continued to glide forward. Patches of grey rolled towards it, only to be swiftly dispersed by its light. Fei was mesmerised and checked behind her to see their flickering campfire getting smaller and smaller. She would only follow it a little further.

*Perhaps it was here to help? It bloody better be.*

*Dammit.*

As she walked through the trees, the sun began to appear above the horizon, its light mixing with what Fei thought must be that of a forest wisp.

*I'm sure of it. Don't remember ever hearing stories of them being bad either... yeah... yeah, I'm sure... I'm sure.*

The ball was now creating a gold haze that bounced off the bark of the withered trees. The light illuminated a field up ahead, full of half-dead wheat. The trees ended and Fei felt the dry wheat tips brush against her hands as she continued to gaze at the glowing wisp.

'Where are you taking me?'

The wisp stopped, then continued through the field. Fei watched as clouds of grey passed ahead.

She stopped, 'I'm sorry, but I can't stray too far from the others. What do you want?'

The wheat began to plume beneath her fingers. The sunlight, which had peeked through the grey, bounced off the shiny kernels.

The wisp stopped again.

Floating a little closer to her face, its glow brightened. Shielding her eyes, she squinted as the ringing in her ears grew louder.

'Sorry.'

Fei's stomach dropped as the word uttered from the whisp, before vanishing. Her eyes adjusted as the ringing stopped, and she stared across the field. The passing cloud of grey revealed a creature stood in the centre, its head hung down.

Fei craned her head forward.

The creature was tall, with thick arms and legs that looked as if they were made of bark; small weeds and leaves poked out of cracks in its body. Fei stared. She had been told of the forest dryads before, but she'd heard that they were deeply secretive creatures.

*Something's wrong.*

'Hello?' Her voice shook as she stepped towards it.

Two deep-green glistening eyes moved up to meet her gaze, while weed-filled hair hung over its cracked face. Fei took another step closer and, as she did, the dryad's mouth turned up into a sinister smile.

Fei gasped as the dryad flung up its arm, its twigged fingers splaying out in front of it, suspending her above the ground, frozen into a floating crucifix. Gasping for air, she watched as the Dryad made its way towards her.

Her limbs seared with pain as she felt her body pulled outwards. Her arms trembled with tension as short, sharp breaths blasted from her chest.

*STUPID, STUPID, STUPID!*

She stared, terrified, into its glaring eyes. A myriad of emotions flew through her as she thought of the others, oblivious by the campfire.

Unable to scream, she felt herself floating down towards the dryad. Trembling.

Their eyes fixed on each other as she floated level with it's stare. A large grey cloud emerging from over a hill behind it.

Fei clenched her jaw, sweat shooting down her back as she realised that the usual weight of her gas mask was absent from her belt. Her arms growing numb. The dryad turned to see the approaching cloud, then looked back at Fei's stiff, floating body.

'My second greatest achievement,' its low, soft voice hissed into Fei's ears.

'Who are you?' she strained. Her head frozen forward, she moved her eyes to meet the dryad's.

'Do you not know me, Feina Fourlise? I know you.' The dryad stepped closer to her. 'I know you, and your mother, very well.'

Fei paled. 'Ela,' she whispered, the pounding of her heart shaking her entire body. 'You're a dryad?'

The creature gave a wry smile, tipping its head to one side.

'No dear child. I have, as you might say, 'possessed it' and how very kind it was of you to present yourself to me like this,' she jeered.

'You killed my mother!' Fei shouted.

The creature's face dropped. 'Oh no, child. *You* killed your mother.'

Fei felt as if her heart had stopped. 'What are you talking about?'

'Your mother was human. When she went into hiding for all those years it was impossible for me to find her... until *your* powers fully surfaced thirteen years ago. I felt your energy, thinking it was her, communicating for the first time in years with her little Sardan friends. And I tracked you to your sweet little house in the forest.'

Fei grew hot with rage.

'You'll see her soon, I promise.'

The creature gave another twisted smile and Fei felt herself getting gradually lower, until they were face-to-face. Meanwhile, the grey cloud was rolling closer and closer.

'Fei!' Cora shot up, out of her blanket.

A dream.

She sighed and rubbed her forehead, placing her hand down beside her. The other blankets were cold and empty.

*Not a dream.*

'Fei!' She jumped up and Bisou barked, sniffing round the camp. Cora grabbed her crossbow and scanned the trees.

*Gone.*

'Fei, where the hell are you?!'

Bisou bounded forward and sniffed between some trees. Lifting his head, he whimpered and trembled, pricking up his ears as he stared into the forest. Then he sat down, licked his lips, and gave a loud bark.

'What is it, B?'

He jumped up, pointing his nose towards the trees, whining.

Nessa was still sound asleep; Cora ran over, grabbed her foot, and shook it hard. Nessa turned over, one of her daggers clicking out as she grabbed at Cora's shirt, her eyes wide.

'What are you doing?' she hissed.

'It's Fei, she's gone!' Cora stood up, holding her crossbow.

'What do you mean "gone"?' Nessa stood up, glaring at her, and scanning the camp. 'She better not have wandered off; I swear to God!'

She threw on her jacket and looked over to see Cora staring at a thin grassy path that led through the trees; and Nessa watched, as Cora and Bisou shot down it.

'Cora, wait!' Nessa hopped forward after them, pulling on her boots.

'You're pathetic,' said Fei, her teeth clenched.

'And why might that be?'

'Killing your sister because Vidras didn't love you enough – it's pathetic.' Fei spat.

'You know nothing of my past.' The creature stepped closer to Fei, its mouth twitching.

'I know enough, and only a coward would kill their sister for the sake of power. We will find you and kill you for what you have done to us.'

The creature's face emptied of emotion, the grey behind almost upon them. 'With thousands of us, and only four of you, I very much doubt that.'

Fei's brow furrowed.

*Four?*

'Oh dear, you thought I didn't know about each one of you? Such a child!'

Her heart continued to pound out of her chest as she watched the Dryad drift back. The grey cloud surrounding them as Fei felt her lungs tightening.

'Why don't you just kill me now and get it over with?' she seethed, her outstretched arms throbbing.

'Believe me, I would love nothing more, but sadly dryads are too pure to take another soul. *This* vessel only works for torment. But I see you now, Fourlise. So arrogant, just like your dead mother.'

'Then come find me yourself, coward.'

'I need not do anything – you are so feeble after all.'

Fei's jaw twitched as the grey crept towards her and began to spiral round her feet. She wheezed as it rolled up to her shoulders, then took one last breath as her eyes clouded over.

'Too easy,' the creature scoffed.

An arrow whistled through the air, landing in the creatures shoulder. It shrieked as another whistled past its head.

Fei's sight returned and she began frantically coughing, gasping, as the grey began to fill her lungs.

The creature yanked the arrow from its arm and sent it flying back through the grey. A bark resonated through the cloud and Fei watched, wheezing, as two daggers shot through, twisting themselves round the Dryads stiff body and securing themselves into the ground behind.

Fei felt herself almost drowning.

Bisou and Cora leapt through, masks on, and the creature writhed on the floor screeching.

Nessa skidded through the wheat, holding tight to the cords of her daggers, wrestling with the thrashing creature.

'What is wrong with it!?' she shouted, pulling at its heaving body.

'El... It's El...' Fei strained through hoarse gasps.

Cora hurtled towards Fei and, unstrapping her own mask, pulled it over Fei's head as Bisou's mouth began to smoke. He barked, and a huge blast of fire rolled from his open jaws, consuming the writhing creature. Nessa flew backwards, her daggers returning to her cuffs as she stared at the flames exploding from Bisou's mouth.

Fei dropped to the ground, limp and gasping for air, as the grey shot out and away from them.

Cora cradled her head as the fire revealed the dryad lying motionless on the ground.

Bisou's fire was cold but bright. Closing his mouth, he shook his head, snorting and sneezing as he trotted over to the creature, and sniffed it.

Nessa sat back, her mouth wide as she stared at Bisou sitting next to the dryad wagging his tail. She stood, and edged towards its softly breathing body.

# CHAPTER EIGHTEEN

The grey dispersed; Fei leaned forward onto her palms, tears streaming down her face. 'It was Ela – she possessed it.'

'Was Ela? What do you mean?' said Cora.

Nessa pushed the dryad's shoulder flat against the newly growing wheat stems. Its eyes were closed and its breathing was light.

'It is lucky to be alive,' said Nessa.

The dryad glowed, as the colours washed back into its earthy skin. Nessa stared at it in wonderment. Bisou whined, his head on his paws and his tail gently wagging.

'Fei, what's wrong?' said Cora, taking in Fei's flushed cheeks and swollen eyes.

'If – if I wasn't what I am, Mum would still be alive,' she said.

Cora drew back, shaking her head. 'What are you talking about?'

Nessa crouched down beside Fei, her face firm.

'Mum wasn't a Nathair, she was a Sardan. That's why she was able to stay hidden for years – until I was born. Thirteen years it took for my abilities to surface, which is when Ela felt it, and found us.' She looked down at the ground, numb. 'Mum's dead cos of me.'

Cora shook her head again. 'Don't be stupid, Mum's dead because Ela's alive.' she pressed, pushing Fei to sit up and look at her.

Nessa's face sobered. 'I used to think that as well. My parents, they meant everything to me.' She took a staggered breath. 'It was Harryn who killed them.'

Fei and Cora blinked.

Nessa's eyes started to fill. 'Believe it or not, Harryn's parents were two of the kindest people you could ever meet. Kind enough to protect a Nathair, his wife, and their daughter during the Crusades. Somehow it got out that we were hiding there. So one night, someone sent people round to kill Harryn's parents. He watched them die. In a rage, he went up to my parents who were hiding in the attic and killed them. I came home to find him, standing over them, covered in their blood. I threw a gas lamp in the room, locked the door behind me and ran. It haunts me to this day that I am no better than him, killing out of rage. Do not let this shake you, you have come too far. It was not your fault; Ela would have found her eventually.'

Fei felt warmth radiate through her body as Nessa – for the first time – smiled at her.

'It's hard to believe that everything that has happened so far is real. I can't imagine ever having a normal life again.' Fei sniffed and dragged her dirty sleeve over her wet face.

Nessa nodded.

'Guys, I hate to break it to you, but neither of you were ever *really* normal,' said Cora.

'Yeah well, only *you* knew that,' said Fei, a small smile breaking through her tears, as Nessa reached down to help her up.

Nessa smiled. 'Regardless of what happened to your mother, and no matter the consequences, she would not have wanted you to be anything other than your true self. I am sure you must know this.'

'I do. I just can't help feeling guilty.'

'Well, you are an annoying but decent human being. I would be concerned if you didn't.'

They laughed.

Fei coughed and, as she began walking towards the dryad's limp body, Ela's words flashed through her head and she stopped in her tracks.

'Four,' she said, her eyes wide.

'Four?' Nessa scrunched her face.

'She said there were *four.*'

Cora stood, hands on hips, her eyes narrowed. '*Who* said there were four? What are you on about?'

'Ela. When she was in the dryad, she said "with thousands of us and only four of you". She must have meant four Nathair.'

'I'm confused,' said Nessa, also clamping her hands to her hips.

'She told me she can feel the energy of a Nathair, so she must know that there are three of us ... but she said "four".'

Nessa pursed her lips. 'You do realise she probably meant Moth and Cora, you know, the group we are currently in.'

'She doesn't know Moth's with us, or Cora either. She must've sensed us two Nathairs here, and she won't have been able to sense anything from Cora...Sorry sister.'

'Cheers,' said Cora.

'So, to her, there were only two here. But she said four.'

Cora's mouth hung open.

'There must be one more than Moth thought.'

Bisou, sensing their excitement, was still staring at the dryad. But he began to wag his tail with more vigour and whimper a little louder.

Nessa's mouth also hung open in amazement. 'Dios mío.'

'How come Moth hasn't been able to find them?' said Fei.

'Pobre alma.' Nessa shook her head. 'I am not sure, but if I were to guess, Sardan would not be able to feel the energy of a Nathair as strongly as Ela would. I have heard of this happening before, in the past, especially during the Crusades. This Nathair must really reject what they are. They must have suppressed it so much – almost to the point where it barely exists within them anymore; living a half-life.'

The trio quietened and Bisou stopped wagging his tail.

'I can understand that,' said Fei.

Nessa nodded.

The dryad gave a sharp cough and started wheezing as it attempted to push itself up.

The three drew their weapons.

'Don't try anything,' Cora barked, her crossbow aimed at its forehead.

The dryad took a long, laboured breath and studied the four of them. The girls squinted at the dryad over their weapons, as Bisou sniffed its hand and sat down next to it, making his approval known.

'Who are you?' asked Fei.

The dryad cowered. 'She has left me. My name is Raomeya, you may call me Rao, and I am so very sorry.' Rao sniffed, hanging her head in shame, her weedy hair flopping over her face. Bisou tiptoed next to her and nuzzled her arm. They exchanged a smile and Bisou returned to stand next to Cora.

'Rao? It's okay, we're friends.' Fei lowered her daggers and stepped towards her smiling.

'Are you alright?' asked Nessa.

'I don't remember much, other than it hurt – a lot.' Rao's eyes glistened and she clutched her torso. 'I was with my family, in the forest, tending to the trees. Then suddenly there was blackness, dreadful, empty blackness. I thought I had died, but I kept getting flashes, images of you three. Then I knew I'd been taken. I tried so hard to take myself away, to be somewhere else, but the pain kept bringing me back. I just hope my family are okay. I must go to them.'

As Rao attempted to stand, her legs buckled, and Nessa and Cora thrust their hands under her arms, as Bisou pushed her legs from behind, and Fei held her hands.

'I'm sure they're fine. I imagine she only needed one vessel,' said Fei, squeezing her rough, bark-covered palms.

'I hope so.'

'Rao, can I ask you a question?'

'Of course.'

'Do you know who the four Nathair are?'

Rao smiled as small buds began to bloom along her arm.

'I feel it within you. And you,' she said, looking at Fei and Nessa. 'But I do not know the other two. I draw my energy from the Earth, but it is weak now. I am so weak. It was so easy for her to take me.'

Rao gave a faint smile. 'I must go now; I've been away from my home long enough. Pydomun may be able to help you with your question. Thank you for releasing me, my friends.'

Bisou woofed.

'Goodbye.'

Rao gave one last smile as she stretched her tall, majestic body, which twisted and glowed with small leaves and pink flowers. Raising a twigged hand, she waved and disappeared through the wheat field towards the forest.

'Pydomun?' repeated Cora.

Nessa gulped. 'Witch Wood. It is west of here, if we leave now, we – '

'There isn't enough time. We know for sure that one of them is in Leos, thanks to Moth. And we need to find Alfie now, before Harryn does. Once we've found him, we'll find the fourth, wherever they are,' said Fei.

Nessa nodded.

Cora gave a proud smile. 'Well, we'd best get a move on. Let's hope no one's made off with Clyde while we've been gone,' she said, marching off with Bisou.

'I'd like to see em try,' scoffed Fei.

'I would not be so confident. That horse will follow anyone who offers him food,' said Nessa, following Cora.

'True.'

Fei stood there for a moment, facing the morning sun. The warmth hugged her face as she felt in her pocket for her mother's pin. Pulling it out, she held it in her hand, squinting as the sun reflected tiny beams of light into her eyes. She clutched it tight and fought back the lump that seemed to be a perpetual presence in her throat.

'Oi, what you doing?' Cora shouted from the edge of the forest, shielding her eyes.

'I'm coming!'

She opened her hand to see the imprint of the pin on her palm. Carefully placing it back in her pocket, she followed the others.

Another four days passed as they continued their passage towards Leos. Once again, the group found themselves tied to their gas masks, which Clyde despised. On around day two, when they navigated their way through a particularly dense patch of grey, it occurred to Fei how difficult she was finding it to remain optimistic that the events to come would unfold in their favour. Or, how they would unfold at all, she just could not predict it. Which annoyed her greatly as she was very much one for preparation and planning; spontaneity terrified her, and so far, spontaneous was all this trip had been.

The land began to elevate as they got closer to Leos, and the group found their thighs aching as they climbed for what felt like forever across acres of dull countryside, although it was growing far greener and brighter than from where they had come. Fields stretched for miles – and for the first time they could see further than 100 feet in front of them - their eyes singing with relief at the view.

Arriving at the top of a hill, their eyes sang with relief at the view. They saw what looked like the remains of a mill. The big mill wheel was half broken, its spokes sticking up awkwardly next to the staggered brickwork of a small ruined house next to it. The river had long since dried up and there were long, deep cracks stretching across the entire valley floor.

'Let's go down, have a look. Never know what we might find,' said Fei, holding Clyde's rope as he plodded behind her.

Cora nodded.

'It is unlikely there will be anything there, scavengers have just about covered the country. Alimañas,' lamented Nessa, shaking her head as she navigated the steep decline.

Cora and Bisou blazed past her, shrieking with glee as they sped up towards the bottom. Nessa landed on her behind with a huff.

As they approached the mill, which looked ten times larger now they were nearer it, a feeling of anxiety pulsed through them. They had seen the devastation of their own homes and cities but had never seen how far it had stretched - they knew, but it seeing it was a whole different experience, and it jarred them. The water supply had completely dried up, which would have been the source for the local villages, and the mill house looked to have been burnt in some places.

'I wonder who lived here,' said Fei, wincing at the scorch marks, and crouching to investigate a crack in the ground as the mill wheel creaked in the wind. She placed her hands on the ground and closed her eyes. Her ears pierced with a shrill ring as water began seeping back into the ground, till eventually the ground shone and a small gleaming puddle appeared beneath her hands. Clyde and Bisou bent their necks to drink.

Fei stood, a little off balance, as silence fell. Cora met her sister's eyes, then pointed at her ears. Fei nodded, wiped her wet hands on her legs and joined the others, touching the weathered brick around the broken front door as she navigated through the ruins.

Cora and Nessa dodged the broken turrets and potholes, then stopped at what looked like a disused well. Fei laughed as they peered down and called 'Helloooo', grinning at the echoes that bounced up from the shaft.

Cora took a step towards the broken mill wheel and heard a small crunch beneath her boot. Bending down, she brushed away some of the dust and dirt, revealing what looked like a shiny stone. She dug some more. Bisou spotted this and began digging next to her.

It was a yellow stone that looked remarkably like the one Moth had.

'Guys!' Cora shouted, staring at the stone, and rubbing off its crust of dry mud. Fei was still wandering through the ruins, oblivious, so Nessa tugged at her shirt and pointed at Cora.

They all stared at the stone, transfixed as small yellow dots reflected on the floor as it vibrated. Bisou pounced on as many yellow dots as he could.

'An Eremis Pod. Someone must have buried it during the raids,' said Nessa.

Fei nodded, her hearing still compromised.

'I wonder if they were Sardan?' wondered Cora, as she peered round the decrepit mill, lifting the Pod higher.

'Very possibly. About five years ago there was a sharp increase in Sardan deaths. Moth had to go into hiding. I didn't see her for six months,' said Nessa, shaking her head. 'This has Silgir written all over it.'

Light beamed through the yellow stone, and both Nessa and Cora raised their hands to their eyes. Fei squinted at the dingy glow of the sun as she stepped forward towards a broken window.

She could see a large shadow in the sky, and her face lit up as the grey cloud rolled away, revealing a floating orb. 'An airship! Look.'

Nessa and Cora peered upwards, as two more gleaming balloons whizzed round, beside the first one.

As the grey passed, the glinting city on top of Solas Mountain appeared; the vibrant green and gold could be seen from where they stood. Their stomachs growled and their feet ached for relief from the endless walking.

'Leos?' asked Cora.

'La ciudad de oro.'

The girls peered at Nessa. 'The city of gold,' she translated with a chuckle.

Fei scrunched her face. 'Hang on, what's the date today?'

'Umm, May twenty-seventh, I think,' said Cora.

'May twenty-seventh! The race is in three days, I can't believe it!'

Cora laughed, as they looked up to see the clouds rolling away, revealing more of the luminous city.

Fei let out a breath. 'Right, well, if we're gonna climb all those steps we should eat something first.'

'All those steps?' repeated Cora, looking confused as she stumbled over a crumbling wall.

Nessa grimaced and patted her on the back.

Fei gave a knowing grin. 'Didn't Dad ever tell you? The creator of Leos built the city on top of Solas Mountain, and put about a thousand steps between it and the ground, to exhaust any intentions of attack from neighbouring cities. It's a thriving city to say the least!'

Fei reached into her bag for a loaf of bread and tore off hunks for herself, Nessa and Cora.

'Sí, nobody likes stairs,' Nessa sighed.

Cora's lip curled as she watched the airships whizz above the city. She groaned and took a bite of her bread.

'Yeah, and no one in Leos likes anything obviously magical either, they may just be the worst for it, lucky for us. Which means I'm sorry, B, but you're gonna have to stay down here.'

Bisou woofed as Cora frowned and scratched his head.

'Clyde can't climb the steps; will you look after him for us?' said Cora.

Bisou leapt up and woofed again, wagging his tail and clicking his hooves on the ground. Then he and Clyde trotted into the beginnings of a shrivelled forest by the dried-up riverbed, while Fei, Cora and Nessa flung their bags over their shoulders and began the final climb to the city.

# CHAPTER NINETEEN

Sweat dripped down their backs, soaking their shirts. Cora was in a foul mood and regularly snapped at the others. With Nessa marching in front, Fei lagging in the middle and Cora bringing up the rear, they climbed… and they climbed… The sun beat down on them and the mill eventually disappeared beneath the clouds.

Finally, they were greeted by the glorious sight of the huge golden gates to the city, decorated with gleaming twisted vines and flowers. They imagined this might be how it would feel to arrive at the pearly gates after death. Pure relief.

'Is this real?' asked Cora, her face gleaming as she stared at the enormous entrance, bustling with activity.

'No wonder they've never been attacked,' gasped Fei, bent over and leaning on her knees, as she took the last swig of water from her flask.

Nessa rolled her eyes. 'I hope no one chases us out of here.'

It was beautiful.

The city gleamed with rich life and vitality. The light bounced off the gilded buildings and ships that glided above the vast streets. Couples lavished with lace and satin laughed and smiled as they walked through the wide cobbled paths, which, unlike Valkyrios, looked like they were fairly regularly washed. And flowers! Flowers of all colours lined the roads beneath large spotless buildings.

Not a speck of soot or grey in sight, or, for that matter, furious coughing fits.

It was almost too good to be true: the clothes, the motorcars, the food, the smells, the colours, the animals. Like nothing they had seen for years; and for Cora, ever. Not a single person carried a gas mask or any form of weaponry. Only baskets of food and shopping bags.

It was bizarre.

Nessa tutted. 'Tontas.'

The smell of freshly baked bread wafted into their nostrils as they stared down the main street. A bakery door was wide open, and a plump woman stood in the doorway, cooing at a baby boy who was holding a breadstick. The woman's hair was coiled into the shape of a bread bun and was a similar rich brown colour.

Fei's eyes widened at the sight of a cheesemonger; she began to salivate as she stared up at the delicate gold writing on the sign and a milkman strode out to his cart which was harnessed to a small milky-white horse.

'Well, I know where I'm going,' said Fei, staring into the cheese shop.

'I think maybe Peaches first,' said Nessa.

Fei pulled a face. 'You're right... Alfie.' She sighed as the cheesemonger took a delivery of large round cheeses.

It felt as if they had travelled back in time: Leos seemed untouched by what was happening elsewhere. The city appeared prosperous and ripe with opportunity; vendors plodded along the streets with carts full of food. The further into the city they got, the more out of place they felt. As they walked along the street, extravagantly dressed couples looked them up and down. A few even gave them a wide berth.

'We need to find Peaches sharpish before we get arrested for dressing badly.' Fei smiled awkwardly at a passing couple, who looked down their noses at the bedraggled trio.

'There!' Cora pointed across the street at a tiny boutique – peach coloured, of course – with the word 'Peaches' painted above the glass windows in beautiful italic gold script. It was tucked between a barber's shop and a general supplies store.

The neighbouring buildings loomed over Peaches in an almost predatory manner, but the little boutique still looked very inviting.

'C'mon, let's go in,' said Fei, feeling uneasy as a policeman on the other side of the street stared at her.

Cora frowned. 'I don't think we look rich enough.'

They hurried over to Peaches, turning their backs to the policeman. Three mannequins stood in the window, dressed in unusual, brightly coloured outfits that seemed more than a little ahead of their time. There wasn't a bustier in sight and the hats were large and fantastical. The three girls were spellbound by the unique designs but eventually pushed open the little glass door, adorned with a painted peach tree, and walked in.

It was empty, and Fei could not understand why. The clothes were...

'Beautiful,' breathed Cora, caressing the fabric draped on a mannequin and reaching wide-eyed for a long black angular skirt. Something none of them had ever seen before.

Fei smiled at Cora's entranced expression.

'Hello?' called Nessa, gazing round a clothes rack.

There was a desk with a metal till on top, also embellished with delicate peach blossoms. Peaches was nothing if not consistent.

A head covered in tight black curls popped out from the small hallway behind the counter. The man smiled and waved; his mouth full of food. He dipped away, wiped his mouth then strolled out, buttoning up his waistcoat.

He was what you might describe as average height for a man; average build and looks, but a very kind face.

And his outfit.

The girls stood, mesmerized at just how wonderful he looked. He had on the most beautiful burgundy velvet jacket with matching turned-up velvet trousers, both fit him immaculately. The colour complimenting his dark skin perfectly, and the silk lining again, adorned with peaches to match the pin on his lapel.

His jacket sat atop a fantastically pleated white shirt, strapped in by the black braces Cora had been admiring. The burgundy brought out his beautiful hazel eyes, which for a moment were covered as he lifted a black bowler hat onto his head, a pheasant feather sticking out of the band.

'I do apologise, ladies, I was just finishing my lunch.' He beamed at them and made his way to the till. 'My name is Byrdy, how can I help you?'

'Byrdy? That's an interesting name,' said Fei, smiling.

'Yup, Byrdy Beattie. When I was a baby, there was a bird that would always sit outside my window. My parents were lazy, so there you go,' he chuckled.

'Well, my name is Feina Fourlise. This is my sister, Cora, and our friend –'

'Vanessa Marini.' Nessa stepped forward to shake his hand.

Byrdy nodded as he looked the girls up and down. 'Well, it's lovely to meet you all. Only just arrived, I assume?' He smiled, raising an eyebrow at their somewhat shabby appearance.

'How can you tell?' Fei laughed as they examined each other's outfits – it was a miracle they hadn't already fallen apart.

'Well, you've come to the right place.' Byrdy clapped his hands together as he glided round the desk and circled Nessa, logging her measurements and trotting off to one of the racks. 'Might I say, what a beautiful figure you have,' he smiled, twiddling his fingers across the hangers.

'Thank you, I am a dancer,' said Nessa, her cheeks flushing.

'Wonderful! So are we wanting more decorative attire or more functional?' he asked, heaving some dresses along the rail.

'Umm, functional, if possible. This isn't our last stop,' said Fei, exchanging a hesitant look with Cora.

'Understandable, but then what have you climbed the treacherous steps of Leos for?' he laughed.

'We're looking for an old friend.'

'How exciting! Who? I might know them.'

'Alfie Albonas,' Fei muttered.

Byrdy blinked – and clutched at a large fluffy coat, as his legs wobbled under him.

'Byrdy?' said Cora, breaking the silence.

'I knew you'd come for him one day,' He muttered, looking down at the pile of clothes in his arms.

'Moth sent us. We need him,' said Fei.

Byrdy turned to look at a small potted tree in the corner. 'I haven't seen life in that tree in weeks.'

They all looked at the peach tree in the corner, which had started blossoming.

'What do you mean "weeks"?' asked Nessa.

'Exactly six weeks and three days ago was the last time I ate a peach from that tree.' He sniffed, as a tear dropped onto the clothes in his arms.

The girls gulped.

'Byrdy, what happened six weeks and three days ago?' said Fei.

'He was taken from me, dragged away like a dog. I didn't even get to say goodbye!'

Byrdy's breathing shuddered, as he began sniffing.

'Who was?' said Cora.

Nessa marched over to the shop door, pushed the lock across, and spun the sign round to 'Closed'.

'Maldita sea! *Who* was dragged away?!'

'Alfie.'

Fei sighed. Byrdy hung his head, his lip wobbling as more tears ran down his cheeks. Nessa buried her face in her hands, rubbing her forehead.

'I'm sure we can get him back. Where is he?' asked Fei, reaching for his shoulder.

'You won't be able to get to him.'

'Why not?' asked Cora, handing him her handkerchief, with a small blue 'D' embroidered in the corner.

'He's in jail – for life.' He sobbed and buried his face in the handkerchief, sniffing as he dropped the clothes on the counter.

'What do you mean? Why is he in jail?' asked Fei.

'How did Moth not know about this?' wondered Cora.

Nessa's eyes widened. 'Moth said the last time she spoke to him was – '

'Seven weeks ago,' Byrdy completed her sentence. 'She couldn't contact him too often for fear that someone would catch on. We only spoke to her maybe every two months.' He hung his head.

The group exchanged looks of dismay.

'How the hell are we supposed to get him out of jail – just the three of us?' demanded Nessa, pacing the room, her face reddening.

'Byrdy, what was Alfie arrested for? It must have been bad if he was given a life sentence,' said Fei, moving in front of the desk.

Byrdy sniffed. 'You've really never been here before, have you? Solas Mountain is home to the last remaining Roc population.' He looked at their perplexed faces. 'The super endangered massive eagles?'

The group nodded.

'Their territory is cornered off, for their "safety", and Alfie, being Alfie, decided to investigate their territory one day, as he didn't believe it was being protected. I begged him not to. It's risky enough living with another man, but being what he is, AND breaking the law, you can expect that this city was gonna find a way to lock him up for good. And that's what they did. And they won't even let me see him.' Byrdy sobbed some more into the handkerchief.

'Do they know what he is?' said Cora.

'Nathair, you mean? No, I don't think so. The silver lining is that there is absolutely no semblance of life in those prison cells, so it would be hard to catch.

The group nodded again at the tiny victory.

'His bail has been set at twenty-five thousand pela, and I don't remember the last time the shop made any decent profit. I'll be saving for the rest of my life.' Byrdy's eyes glazed over again, the handkerchief hanging limp in his hand.

'There's gotta be a way we can get him out.' Fei walked over to the glass door and stood watching the setting sun.

'Well, unless you've got the money, I'd say things are looking pretty bleak,' lamented Byrdy as Cora rubbed his back and Nessa huffed.

A large silhouette of an airship migrated slowly across the glowing sky, casting a shadow over Fei's face. Her eyes lit up and she spun round to face the others. 'The race! There's a fifty-thousand pela prize that goes to the winner, no?'

'And where the hell are we gonna get a working airship in forty-eight hours, and someone who can fly it well enough to win?' demanded Nessa.

Byrdy cocked his head and narrowed his eyes.

'Byrdy? Anywhere we might find a ship? Or at least hire one?' she asked, stepping towards him.

'Even if you *could* find one, the entrance fee is five thousand pela, and entries close in twelve hours,' he pointed out. Fei hung her head. 'But I guess there is somewhere you could try.' He slowly stood up. 'Can you drive an airship?'

Three expectant pairs of eyes were trained on Fei. 'Um, well, I drove one once, and I've watched a lot of races. I suppose I can try... What other choice do we have?' Fei swallowed the nervous lump in her throat.

Nessa slumped onto the stool, rubbing her face in exasperation. 'We also do not have anywhere near that entrance fee.'

Byrdy pulled out a rusty tin, with a painted fish on the lid, from beneath a pile of books.

'You can have this. It would take the rest of my life to save up the amount needed for his release, so you may as well have a try with the race. You've come this far and that can't have been easy. Three thousand, four hundred and twenty pela. It's not all of it, but it's a good start,' he said, opening the lid and sighing as he scooped up the crinkled notes and presented them to Fei.

'Byrdy, are you sure?' asked Cora.

He looked at the tree in the corner, which now had a plump peach hanging from one of its branches. Walking over and picking it, he said, 'I've got nothing left to lose.'

'Thank you!' the trio chorused.

Fei took the notes and tucked them into her inside jacket pocket.

'Anyway, no use me standing here crying when there's a plan afoot,' Byrdy sniffed, raising a fist into the air. 'You girls better pick out some clothes to wear – you'll never be allowed into the race in that kit.'

They nodded. They really were in quite a state.

Cora and Nessa began flicking through outfits on the racks while Byrdy sank down on the stool behind the till, spinning the peach in his hands; Fei rested her elbows on the desk.

'So, how long have you and Alfie been ... "business partners"?' she asked smiling as Byrdy smirked and began fiddling with a stray piece of thread on the counter.

'About three years now. We met in a place called Gallereas, a village at the bottom of this mountain.' Byrdy's face saddened. 'You might have noticed it on your way here.'

Fei frowned. 'I don't think we did... All we saw was a...'

Byrdy met her eyes. Blinking back tears, he fiddled with the thread again.

'...a mill,' she finished, her eyes wide.

'Gallereas, in our language, means "water bearer". When they came, Alfie and I managed to escape. Leos only took in a few refugees – mostly the ones with desirable skills. Luckily for us, Alfie has a degree in animal conservation and biodiversity and I can make a pretty decent outfit, so we were allowed in. Sort of.'

'Sort of?'

'We may have been allowed into the city but we're still classed as refugees. We'll never be allowed into polite society. Most of the residents didn't want us here in the first place. "Disruption of the delicate balance of elitism you might say".' Byrdy sighed.

Fei laughed bitterly. 'If it's any consolation, it's happening everywhere. Believe me, I couldn't have felt less wanted where I'm from, and they didn't even know what I really am. There's nothing quite like being an undesirable!'

'Yup,' Byrdy agreed.

'I can't help but wonder, even if we *do* manage to beat this, will anything change?' Fei stared at her fidgeting hands. The lump was creeping up her throat again.

Byrdy gently pulled her hands apart and placed the fuzzy peach inside. 'The juice is worth the squeeze. Perseverance is everything.'

They smiled at each other.

'You were talking about somewhere we could try to find an airship, Byrdy?' said Nessa, heaving some clothes onto the counter.

Cora followed, with an even larger pile.

Byrdy laughed at the mountain of garments they'd presented him.

'There's a bar not far from here, called Wranglers. It's a well-known hangout for drivers. I can't think of anywhere else you might find someone who can point you in the right direction.'

Fei nodded. 'Wranglers, it is.'

'Asi que, we go to Wranglers, find an airship, maybe even a driver, enter the race, and come back here.'

Byrdy looked glum. 'I would love you all to stay here with me, but it's too risky. Since Alfie was taken, the authorities have been watching this shop closely.

I couldn't live with myself if you were found here. But I'll send you off with some food, and whilst you're out I'll clean and fix your clothes. They'll be here waiting for you tomorrow, after you've won.'

He smiled nervously, pulled the little peach pin off his lapel, and placed it in Fei's hands. 'Please save my Alfie, he's all I have.' His eyes glistened again, and Fei clutched his hands tightly in hers.

She hugged him. 'Thank you Byrdy. We'll do our best, I promise.'

Cora and Nessa returned from the changing rooms in their new outfits, both looking fantastic. Cora wore a long, loose, white skirt, covered in a black polka-dot voile fabric, held up by polka-dot braces, over a ruffled, medieval-style sleeved black shirt. A small black bowler hat with a green feather was perched on her long, wavy auburn hair.

Nessa wore an off-the-shoulder knee-length violet dress, covered in little white stars. It was nipped in at the waist, with puffed sleeves, and a boater was balanced atop her waterfall of glossy, thick, dark hair.

'Try to avoid being seen. I'll keep the shop closed. Come round the back when you return tomorrow. You both look amazing,' Byrdy gave them a nervous smile.

As they left through the back door, they hugged Byrdy goodbye and headed for Wranglers.

# CHAPTER TWENTY

How could there be such a dingy old bar in this city of gold and wonder? The three stood outside for a moment and stared up at the building which stood in a dark alleyway in the heart of the city. It had promise of past popularity. Or indeed was it its unique appearance that made it so popular amongst drivers? Whatever the explanation, the girls had not felt this comfortable in quite a while.

The closer they got towards it, the more distinctive they found it: most of the buildings they had seen had been a variety of shades of white, or light brick. Wranglers was put together with jet-black wooden beams, stretched high between its neighbouring buildings. It was shaped like a slice of sponge cake, with the front door at the point where one would naturally take their first bite. A gentle glow peaked through the condensation on the windows, various illegible words scrawled into the damp pane, dripping onto the windowsill.

The front door became larger as they made their approach. As dusty as it was, the brass metalwork above the front door was beautiful; it twisted and swirled, like waves; meeting in the middle where chipped, scratched gold letters spelt out the name 'WRANGLERS'.

They stopped beneath the glow of the lantern above the door and stared up at the sign. A large, impressively drunk, older man weaved passed them, humming, and proceeded to urinate against the wall of the courtyard in front.

'Okay.' Fei scrunched up her nose, turning towards the other two, as Nessa scoffed and reached for the door handle.

'Wait. So how old are you again?' Fei asked Cora sternly.

Nessa pursed her lips and let the door wiggle back into place.

'Do you really think I've forgotten in the last five minutes?' said Cora, unamused.

'Humour me,'

'I'm eighteen,' said Cora, huffing.

'And you remember the year you were born?'

'Yup.'

Cora pulled sharply at the door handle, followed by Nessa, who raised an eyebrow at Fei as she passed.

They needn't have worried about standing out for being too young. They stood out anyway – because they were the only women in the place.

There were a few men at the bar, some sitting at the tables and a few playing snooker. Silence fell, as every set of eyes in the room focused on the trio as they piled through the door.

Fei smiled awkwardly.

The main bar was positioned in the middle of the room. Long, brown leather sofas stretched to the back, where two snooker tables, covered in stains and cigarette burns, stood. The men sitting at the tables closer to the front door scoffed and continued to puff on their cigarettes.

There was one man who looked as if he was around their age, sitting on one of the tall wooden stools at the bar. He had mousy brown hair, was slight in build and wearing noticeably tatty clothes. His eyes narrowed as he looked up from his half pint and squinted over his hunched shoulder to see the girls, standing in the doorway.

'Ow old are you?' the large, bearded barman boomed across the room, pointing at Cora.

'I'm – '

'She's twenty-one, yes, twenty-one' interrupted Fei. Nessa and Cora tilted their heads at her in confused discomfort.

'Hmm,' the barman snorted. He continued to dry a glass while chatting to an older man, who wore a weathered aviator's jacket. The rest of the room followed suit and continued with their conversations.

'Look, a driver,' said Fei under her breath, staring at the man chatting with the barman.

'Dónde?'

'Obviously the one in the jacket, over there.'

'You are assuming every driver in the world wears those jackets,' said Nessa.

'C'mon though ... they do,' said Fei, raising an eyebrow and moving towards the bar.

The younger, mousy man continued to watch them until Nessa glared at him, which made him hunch his back and look down at his drink.

His pocket began to buzz. His face paled as he reached inside his inner pocket and pulled out a small yellow stone, holding it under the table. It was buzzing so hard it almost bounced out of his hands. His breathing quickened. As subtly as he could, he looked at the girls as they strolled past, and pulled his cap a little further over his eyes. He discreetly placed the stone back in his pocket and sipped his drink quietly.

'Twenty-one?' whispered Cora through gritted teeth.

'I'm sorry, I panicked.'

'Well, you need to calm down sharpish, otherwise someone will clock us,' said Cora.

'Quiet, both of you,' whispered Nessa as they slid onto the clammy bar stools.

'What can I get you?' asked the barman, flinging a rag over his shoulder and resting his hairy sausage-like fingers on the bar in front of them.

Fei opened her mouth to speak.

'Three white wines, please,' interrupted Nessa.

The barman nodded. Nessa smiled at Fei and Cora.

'I like white wine; I haven't had one since the club.'

Fei and Cora nodded as the barman arrived with three glasses, put them down on the bar, and began to pour.

'You wouldn't know where we could get a ship, would you?' asked Fei.

'A ship? As in, an airship?' The barman's eyes flashed in judgement as he poured.

'Umm, yes, an airship.'

Nessa narrowed her eyes.

The mousy man blinked. He was listening intently, the stone in his pocket vibrating wildly.

'And what would you be needing a ship for?' asked the barman.

'To go hiking,' said Cora.

Nessa gave her a sharp kick in the leg as the barman looked at her, unamused.

'I want to enter the race,' said Fei.

The mousy man's eyes widened.

The barman pushed the three glasses towards them, making sure Cora's glass arrived especially abruptly in front of her.

'You might have started your search earlier – just about every ship in the city will be in use over the next three days. You'll be hard pressed to find one now,' he said turning away.

'Yes, I realise that, but I thought you might know someone who could point us in the right direction.'

'I don't think there's anyone here who can help you.'

Fei pursed her lips. 'Please! Is there nowhere around here that might have one free?' she said a little louder.

The mousy man looked over at them.

'You might try another city,' said the barman, turning away to serve someone else.

The spectators sniggered and Fei looked around to see them all shaking their heads as they continued with their conversations.

The lump was there again, crawling up her throat, making her eyes sting with humiliation. The mousy man found himself breathing a little quicker as he grasped his jacket pocket.

Fei shot up and pushed her chair back with a loud scraping sound. Once again, heads swung in her direction as she stormed towards the door. Nessa knocked back her wine and she and Cora hurried after her.

'Good luck!' The barman said, laughing.

The mousy man looked around the room at the shaking heads, laid a mottled note on the bar, buttoned up his jacket and left, slipping through the front door into the darkness.

He pushed up his collar and crept after them.

'Fei, wait, where are you going?' Cora called.

'Another bar. There must be someone who's willing to help us. I'll search all night if I have to.'

She marched forward.

'At least slow down, we cannot afford to draw attention,' said Nessa, grabbing her arm.

Fei stopped and stared back at her; the mousy man dodged behind a shop, his eyes shadowed by the peak of his cap.

'I've never tried so hard in my life not to feel disheartened. But they're making it impossible.' Fei shook her head in frustration.

Cora checked around and pulled them into an alley.

The mousy man tilted his head, listening.

'It's like trying to save someone from drowning and them slapping your hand away.' She made off down the dark alley towards a well-lit street at the end. 'It's just so crushing.'

The bare branches of a bare tree forked over the top of a street lantern that shone down on the shiny wet cobbles. Cora pulled Fei's arm, stopping under the tree to look at her.

'Right, repeat after me: *I am not alone. I am not alone. I am not alone.*' Cora closed her eyes and swung her arm like a conductor.

Fei smiled and chorused back, then slid down the wall to sit on the ground. 'I hope one day they'll all get it.'

'If they don't, are you gonna go home?' Cora crouched down beside her.

Fei snorted. 'Bit late now,' she sighed. 'It would just be nice not to feel so unwanted.'

'Yeah, well don't hold your breath, Nathair. No one likes you.'

'Nice!'

Fei rested her head against the brick, laughing. She clutched at her thighs, which were still burning a little from the trek up the steps.

'Come on, you plonker, stop whinging.' Cora reached for her hand and pulled her sister up.

Nessa stood staring down the alleyway. Her eyes narrowed.

The tree began to blossom and small pink petals floated down onto them.

The mousy man was wedged behind an alcove, in the darkness, his face scrunched in fear.

'Maybe we should move away from this tree,' said Fei, pulling a face.

'Too late,' Nessa whispered.

Fei and Cora turned to see Nessa staring past them at the street they had come from.

'What is it?' whispered Fei.

'Tranquila. We are being followed.'

Cora and Fei froze. The blossom tree swayed, sending pink petals spiralling to the ground.

'We keep moving,' Nessa hissed.

The hairs on their arms stood on end as they shuffled along.

'Did you see who it was?' asked Fei faintly.

Nessa shook her head.

The mousy man slipped around the corner, staying in the shadows, and skipping past the street lantern. Nessa moved her head ever so slightly to the left as he darted into an alcove. His heart was pounding. He covered his mouth, closed his eyes and waited, listening to their receding footsteps.

As the tapping of their feet on the cobbles grew fainter, he took a breath, opened his eyes and stepped into the light.

He froze, as Nessa stared back at him. Her hands clutched around the hilts of her knives. The mousey man gasped as Nessa sent the cords of her knives whirling around him. She yanked hard and sent him spinning into the ground.

Fei and Cora sprinted down the alley, skidding beside his immobilised, winded body. They leaned over him as Nessa loosened a cord, only to send it flying, and tightening around his neck. His eyes bulged with panic as he gasped for air.

'Who are you? And why are you following us?' spat Nessa, holding the cords tight.

'Please, my name is Baylor. I can help you,' he wheezed, pulling at the cords.

'I saw him watching us at the bar,' said Nessa.

Fei exchanged puzzled glances with Cora and Nessa. 'Why follow us, Baylor? If your intention is to help, why not just approach us?' she said, crouching beside him.

His face was bright red as he rasped, 'I ain't seen a Nathair in years, I had to be sure.'

They stood, perplexed, as he coughed; Nessa made a gap in the rope around his neck, releasing his hands enough to wiggle at the cord. When his sleeve slipped up to reveal a small 'S' tattoo on his wrist, her blood boiled. 'Silgir!'

She wrenched down on the cord, slamming his face into the cobbles. He gave a loud grating wheeze – and Cora and Fei whipped out their weapons.

'You think you can pull a fast one on us, Silgir? No verás la mañana!'

Cora's face was a picture of anger as she took great pleasure in watching Baylor's face purpling.

'No, please. I mean you... I'm a de...'

Fei gritted her teeth as she bent beside him, her knife at his neck. 'What are you playing at?' she spat into his bloodshot eyes.

He pulled up his other sleeve, his hand shaking, this time revealing a 'D' branded on his arm.

'A deserter!' chorused Fei and Cora, their eyes and stance softening.

'How can we be sure he did not do this to himself?' demanded Nessa.

'Believe me, no one would do this to themselves,' said Fei, staring at his limp body.

'What do you mean?'

'Runner, he was called. He used to work outside the Wall back home. He was a deserter.'

'I've not heard of him,' said Cora.

'Exactly. Three years after he ran, we found him beaten to death in the forest. Believe me, it's no life.'

A tear dripped down Baylor's swollen cheek.

Nessa growled and released the cord from round his neck. He gasped, coughing and spluttering. And they watched as he pushed himself onto his hands, heaving himself up against the cold brick wall, gulping the cold night air.

'Ex-Silgir. Three years, I served. Till I couldn't take it no more. I ran away four years ago. They found me, captured me, branded me, and sold me off.' He continued to gasp for air as he rubbed the red marks on his neck. His mousy hair flopped over his pale pink face.

They stared at him.

He reached for his tatty tweed cap, which had fallen off, and popped it back on his head. His thin black braces had sewing and scorch marks all over them; frays curled from the elastic, which seemed to ping out even further when he straightened them over his yellowing shirt, which sat beneath a smudged black jacket that stretched tight over his sinewy torso.

As he moved to rest his arms on his knees, his equally grubby black trousers rode up to reveal his feet, sockless, in some tired old black leather shoes, the seams withering away at the toe.

'Who are you?' said Fei.

'Baylor ... Baylor Doone, pleasure.'

# CHAPTER TWENTY-ONE

Baylor tipped his cap and rooted round in his pocket for a cigarette. Once he'd lit it, he took a deep drag and closed his eyes, wisps of smoke drifting up to the lantern.

'You mentioned something about being able to help us. What exactly did you mean?' asked Fei, as Cora fanned away the smoke in distaste.

Nessa glared at him; her hands still gripped firmly around her knives.

'I 'ave a ship,' he said, bringing the cigarette to his lips again.

'*You* have a ship?' said Nessa.

He nodded and plucked up the courage to look at them.

'Y se supone que debemos confiar en este ex extraño de Silgir!' Nessa protested, clearly doubting his claim.

Fei sighed. 'I don't see what other options we have right now.'

Baylor shifted his weight, blinking at Nessa who crossed her arms frowning.

Fei turned back to a sheepish-looking Baylor. 'Where is this ship of yours?'

'In my workshop. Well, it's not *my* workshop, but I work there.' He took another drag on his cigarette, which glowed and sizzled, burning his fingers. Hissing in pain, he dropped the cigarette on the ground.

Nessa narrowed her eyes. 'I thought you said you were a slave?'

Baylor hunched over and wrung his hands. 'I was, till they found out I was a better than average engineer and figured they could make more out o' me if I worked in the factory. So now I get paid. It's hardly anything, and I'm basically still a slave, but at least now I have a semblance of dignity.'

He wobbled to his feet. The girls took a step back.

He was tall but the years had not been kind to him. Although his features were soft and pleasant enough, he was thin and his cheeks sallow. Like Wranglers bar, he had clearly seen better days.

'Please, you 'ave to believe me, because I need your help.'

The girls shared an apprehensive look.

'You need *our* help?' said Fei.

'My wife, my beloved, she was a witch. Is a witch. We fell in love when I had just been drafted into the Silgir – by force, I might add. Those of us in the poorer villages really 'ad no choice but to join. When they found out what my wife was, we ran away, but I was caught and sold into slavery, and she vanished. The last thing she said to me was that she would find me. That was four years ago, and I ain't seen or heard from her since.' His eyes were glazed, and he looked desolate.

'Does your ship work?' asked Fei.

'It should do.'

'Your wife. Was she a good witch?' said Cora.

Baylor nodded. 'Most witches *are*. It's just them Silgir spreading lies about them all being devil worshippers. She was a healer, a wise woman. But what they don't understand they fear, attack and kill. There's no room for compromise or understanding.'

Fei, Cora and Nessa turned away and stepped out of earshot; Baylor pulled a flask from his trouser pocket and took a long swig.

'I do not trust him. Once a Silgir, always a Silgir, alimañas,' Nessa pronounced, spitting on the floor.

Baylor gulped.

Fei rubbed her forehead wearily. 'What choice do we have? The race is in twelve hours, and we have half a crew and no ship. If the worst comes to the worst, I can fly it alone, but we need a ship.'

'How do we know he is not just gonna take us to this ship and have all his little Silgir buddies pop out and arrest us?' asked Nessa.

Cora nodded. 'I have to agree with her.'

Fei hung her head. 'We can't know - we haven't known, and we still have no idea what awaits us. So, we either carry on as we have so far, with our eyes open, ready for whatever thrusts itself in our path; or we give up. How else are we meant to get Alfie? We *need* him.'

Nessa sighed, and Cora smiled.

'So whaddya say, guys? We doin' this?' Fei raised her eyebrows. 'Nessa?'

'Maldita sea, somos idiotas, bien! Bien!'

Fei nodded in mild agreement then turned to Cora and gave her a questioning thumbs up.

Cora nodded. 'Let's do it.'

Fei turned to Baylor. 'Take us to your ship, and we'll help you find your wife.'

Baylor looked up, and his sallow face glowed. 'Thanks,' he blinked as grateful tears began to form in his eyes.

'If she really is a witch, she may well be in Pydomun, which we need to visit anyway,' said Cora.

Baylor nodded, straightened his dishevelled jacket, and pointed in the direction they had come.

'Down 'ere,' he smiled.

Nessa narrowed her eyes and indicated that he should walk in front of her. As she followed him, she kept her hands firmly on her knives.

\*\*\*

Baylor unlocked the heavy metal door to the factory, and they all shuffled in. It was huge, and dark, and it smelt of oil. A smell that filled Fei and Cora with warm thoughts of home. Engine parts lay on worktops, glinting in the moonlight that streamed in through the enormous windows. Half-built motorcars were surrounded by screwdrivers, wrenches and other tools; oily rags hung over chairs, ready to be used the next day. There were pots of open polish – Fei shook her head at the waste. That would never happen in her father's workshop.

A low growl rumbled through the darkness, followed by the pattering of paws. The girls froze as the growl became a series of soft barks, and a stout, toothy silver bull terrier appeared in front of them, snarling.

Fei stretched an arm out in front of Cora as they held their breath and started moving backwards slowly.

'Buen chico,' shuddered Nessa.

'Jarvis. Hey, buddy!' Baylor beamed, knelt down in front of the grumbling mass of muscles, and scratched his head; Jarvis flopped onto the floor, presenting his belly.

The girls let out a sigh of relief as Baylor patted the dog's stomach, cooing, 'I gotta go, buddy. Stay. Good boy.'

'Don't worry about 'im – 'e's a soft arse. This way,' he said quietly, beckoning them towards a door in a particularly dark spot on the left side of the room.

They exhaled and shuffled after him, gripping their weapons tighter as they crept forward.

The old lock clunked as Baylor pulled the key away and heaved it open. A 'No Entry' sign flapped as he stumbled over the doorway. 'Every time,' he chuckled.

The three girls inched their way through, one after another.

And gasped.

There it was. Floating in front of them.

The most beautiful airship they had ever seen.

'Ta-dah!' Baylor smiled nervously.

The large white balloon that sat above the main carriage was rather the shape of a melon - if you pinched it at both ends and pulled it out a bit. Ropes lined the side of it, equidistant from each other. The carriage below was tucked under the balloon, It, too, was long and thin - perfectly streamlined - and a pleasing mix of colours. The main structure of the carriage was deep blue and the metal framework was brass. All of which had been carved with the most intricate filigree pattern work.

At the top of the balloon, Baylor had attached a flagpole: a long, thin white flag flopped over the side, joined by a long mast at the front.

On the side of the carriage there was what looked like a large fin, its lining not yet sewn together. Clearly the job was in hand, as a sewing kit had been left beside it.

It was simply stunning.

The girls stood, in awe at the craftsmanship. Even Fei had not seen anything like it in the many shows she had been to with her father.

'Do you like it?' said Baylor to their blank faces.

'It's ... incredible,' said Fei, touching the outstretched fin.

Baylor smiled and touched the soft linen of the balloon. 'So, why are you entering the race? Seems a bit risky, if you're trying to stay hidden?'

Fei looked up, checking in with Cora and Nessa.

Cora twined one of the ropes between her fingers, before explaining, 'Another Nathair has been imprisoned here – we need the race winnings to bail him out.'

Fei nodded.

'Another Nathair, here? I 'adn't even 'eard of *one* still existing before tonight, let alone three.'

'Well, that's no surprise,' answered Fei, 'considering we're the only ones left. That's why we need Alfie. Without him, we don't stand a chance; the grey is growing so much faster now.'

Baylor clutched the door of the carriage, his eyes wide with anxiety. 'My wife. Does this affect her?'

'It affects all of us,' said Fei.

Baylor buried his face in his hands. 'What do we do?'

'Well, I know we'll have a better chance of winning if you drive.' Fei looked at Baylor hopefully.

'I *can't* drive. If I'm found out, I'll lose my job.'

'You said yourself, you're not a slave anymore – and anyone can enter if they have the money. We have the money; you have the talent. If *I* drive, we will definitely lose, and this will all have been for nothing.'

'You don't understand, there is a hierarchy and I'm right at the bottom.' Baylor rubbed the brand on his arm, which had suddenly begun to itch.

'If you are at the bottom, we are not even on the ladder,' said Nessa.

'This is the only way we can get out with Alfie and help your wife,' said Fei. 'Besides, there's no point having a job if there's no place left to work in.'

Baylor blinked as he placed a hand on the balloon; the cool linen was taut under his weathered fingertips. A warm breeze crept under the large door, into the workshop, as he stared at his battered shoes. 'I built it to escape. I've been waiting for the perfect time to slip away unnoticed. There's been plenty of perfect days, yet I'm still 'ere.' He glanced soberly at Fei. 'I'll think about it.'

Fei smiled. 'Of course.'

He bent to pick up a spanner. 'Besides, there's a few things that need finishing first. Prepare yourselves for a long night.' He placed the spanner in Fei's hand.

'Tell us what we need to do,' she replied, rolling up her sleeves.

***

It was indeed a long night, but the work wasn't difficult. Baylor knew the ship inside and out; he knew exactly what needed to be done, where, and how long it would take. They took a few breaks, creeping into the main workshop and stealing the odd biscuit from the store cupboard.

No one would notice, they hoped.

Unless, of course, they followed the trail of crumbs that led to a small pile in Jarvis's bed.

While Nessa and Cora carried on sewing some of the seat covers, Baylor and Fei sat down beside the fin, waxing its long brown leather panels.

'What's her name, your wife?'

'Yana,' he said, taking a puff of a cigarette he'd found in the workshop.

'Got a picture of her?'

Baylor stood and jumped up into the cockpit of the ship. After briefly rummaging around, he returned with a crumpled piece of paper. Swinging back over, he landed gently on the floor beside Fei, and handed her the photo.

Fei smiled. 'She's beautiful.'

A young woman with pale skin and amber eyes stared out of the picture, her long auburn hair draped over her shoulders. Fei handed it back to Baylor, who sat staring at it, his cigarette hanging from his mouth.

'Four years. I wonder if she still looks like this.'

'Course she will.'

'I remember it so clearly, the day we were separated. A part of me died that day, and so did my faith in humanity.'

Fei looked down. 'I can understand that. My faith in humanity isn't too strong these days either. But there are certain humans who remind you why you need to keep going, and let you know that there are still good, honest people who care deeply about you. You have to remember that; otherwise you just end up sad, bitter, scared and lonely. Believe me, if it weren't for Cora, Nessa, Bisou and Moth, I wouldn't be here.'

'Bisou and Moth?' A wax drip had begun pooling on Baylor's trousers.

'You'll meet them soon, I'm sure,' she smiled.

As she stared past him, at a faded poster of the Merenial on the wall, he turned to follow her gaze. 'Lucky that thing ain't gonna be joining us tomorrow,' he said, shaking his head, as he moved onto another panel.

'Yeah, lucky its driver won't be in it either.' Fei rolled her eyes.

'James D. Menillo? What you got against 'im? 'e's a great driver! The best, in fact.' He chuckled and nudged Fei's arm.

Fei mimed being sick and they laughed.

'Yeah, I've heard. I had a friend who was a big fan. Safe to say her opinion changed dramatically, once she met him!'

'Shocker,' Fei scoffed. 'But, seriously, tell me how you've been able to build this? If you're at the bottom of the ladder, surely a ship like this is a no-no?'

'When you're good at something, there's always someone out there who's ready to take advantage of your skills for their own gain. They've allowed me to work on a design of my own, in exchange for my many years of obedient service.' Baylor shook his head. 'If we do well tomorrow, you can be sure I'll never see it again.' He squinted at a section of the wing that still needed sewing.

'Why don't you come with us afterwards?' Fei asked. 'We need all the help we can get.'

As Baylor looked into her hopeful eyes, a blue flower pushed its way through a crack in the concrete where she sat.

He smiled. 'I know there's nothing left for me 'ere. I've known it for years, but what if we're not enough to beat 'em?'

'All I can say is, you're not alone in feeling that way, believe me,' Fei chuckled. 'But we're stronger together.'

'You're quite somethin, you know that?'

Fei shook her head and raised her eyebrows at the ship.

'*You're* quite somethin, did *you* know that?'

Baylor gave a small smile and fiddled with his cap. 'So… I've had a think.' He turned to her.

'And?'

'I'll do it. What 'ave I got left to lose, eh?'

Fei beamed and hugged him. 'Thank you, Bay.'

'And thank *you*, Fei.'

They laughed – and things seemed a little more hopeful.

*** 

It was a sleepless night for all four of them, but they'd done it. The work was finished. As the sun rose, beams of light burst through the windows, bouncing off the ship's glistening metalwork.

'Right, so run the plan past me again,' Fei said to Cora and Nessa.

'Dios mío.'

'Seriously? Because it's not like we haven't been through it a million times now,' said Cora, shortly.

Nessa stared at Fei, equally exasperated.

'Cora, please!'

Cora rolled her eyes. 'Enter the race. Go to the stadium. Meet you there in three hours.'

'Where's "there"?'

'Drivers' ring. Happy?'

'Yes.' Fei grinned and Baylor chuckled behind her. 'Entries close in two hours, so you'd better get going. Be safe.'

Cora and Nessa climbed through the door and Fei admired the ship, floating in the vast room. Then she looked anxious. 'I never asked you how we would get it out of here?'

'Ahh!' Baylor raised a finger and disappeared behind the ship.

There was a loud clunk, followed by a low rattle. Sunlight streamed in as he heaved open the vast metal door on one side of the workshop. A gust of wind blew through, and the flag began to flap.

Fei glowed; if she'd ever seen a beacon of hope, this was it.

Baylor looked at her, then the ship, and smiled. 'Shall we?'

Fei nodded. In the bright sunlight, the ship was. Breath-taking.

# CHAPTER TWENTY-TWO

'Right...Okay.' Sitting in the cockpit, Baylor stared out of the workshop door. Large sweat patches formed under his armpits in the glaring sun.

'Right.' He pulled his goggles down, examined the gear stick, and began touching everything, nodding, and quietly reciting where each instrument was, and what it did.

'All good?' asked Fei, from the passenger seat, behind Baylor's nodding head.

'Uh, yep, yep. Just, uh, re-familiarising myself.'

His heart began to pound and Fei trembled with excitement; her hands gripped the leather seats, thoughts of home rushing through her mind.

*The name.*

'Bay, I almost forgot, what's the ship's name?'

Baylor looked across the cockpit at an engraving in the brass rim of the dashboard, and his pounding heart slowed. 'Catica.' He rubbed his finger across the engraving.

'Catica...' echoed Fei. 'I love it.'

Baylor swallowed, his forehead clammy as he reached down, flipped switches, turned a few dials, then pressed down on a large brass lever on his left.

The whole carriage vibrated as cogs began whirring in the engine. Fei felt her heart skip a beat and she grinned as the soft clicks and whirs ricocheted round the room. She clasped her seat belt straps.

The propellers whizzed until they became a blur on either side, and they looked back to see puffs of smoke wafting away.

Baylor pushed on the globe-shaped gear stick, and the engine began to hum. 'Here we go,' he shouted.

Fei held her breath, with a mixture of elation and terror, as Baylor pushed forward on the yoke. The ship jerked a little, then hovered forward. They crept through the door of the workshop, the sun beaming down on them.

Fei looked behind, to the rear of the ship; it was out of the workshop. She gave Baylor a thumbs-up, he gripped tight onto the yoke and pulled up, pointing Catica skyward.

Their eyes sparkled as the wind rushed past, and Fei felt herself being blasted against the seat. She was grinning from ear to ear as they flew. Higher and higher they rose, over the glittering buildings of Leos city, towards the clouds. Fei was gawping in wonder. The city was growing smaller and smaller; the people disappearing.

*Free.*

Baylor's hands ached with tension as he continued to push Catica up, his eyes wide. Until they crested on top of a sea of fluffy white cloud, and bobbed through. They gazed down at the glorious colours below – the peaks of lush green hills and snow-topped mountains.

Silence.

'WOOOOOO. YES!' Baylor smacked his hands down on the dashboard and thrust his fist into the air.

Fei jumped.

'YES, YES. You bloody beauty, ha-ha-ha.'

Fei laughed as Baylor kissed the dashboard, then stood, beaming, arms outstretched. Fei also stood, taking in the crisp, clean air of the mountains. She could smell the morning dew, the grass, the rain, the snow. Lifting her goggles, she squinted into the sunrise ahead. It had been years since the sun had warmed her skin.

*Imprisoned for so long.*

She sniffed and felt a tug on her arm.

'Fei, you okay?'

Opening her eyes to see Baylor, she wiped her nose with her sleeve.

Baylor laughed. 'Good to know I'm not the only one who does that. You ready?'

'As I'll ever be… Where exactly do we need to be heading?'

Baylor studied the compass he'd welded to the inside of the cockpit door. 'Umm,' he pointed to the side. 'That way.'

'With all this cloud, are we gonna see it?'

'Believe me, it's 'ard to miss.'

'Alrighty then, Captain. Let's go and win some cash.'

'Hell, yeah!'

Catica gave a loud whir, and they veered off towards the stadium.

\*\*\*

They hadn't been flying long when Baylor pointed down, and Fei saw other ships floating through the clouds and disappearing towards a single destination.

'There it is!' he shouted.

Fei peered over the side of the carriage, and heard the crowd roaring, cheering and clapping below. After years of hearing about the race and its grandeur, the reality put all the descriptions to shame. As they floated down, the true vastness of the stadium became clear.

Smaller, red, hot-air balloons, joined together with white ropes, bobbed around the mountaintops, marking a clear path: each red balloon had a number, from one to one hundred. Fei knew exactly how these balloons worked. Inside the basket under each one sat a person with a white flag. When the last ship in the race had flown past their balloon, they would thrust out their flag. This way, race commentators knew whether any ships had crashed or deflated.

For years, Fei had desperately wanted to be a Leos flagger. When she was little, her father often found her sitting in the driver's seat of one of the cars in his workshop, flapping his white handkerchief from the window.

The main viewing area was in the centre of the mountain peaks and was packed to the rafters. Over which hung a humongous metal net sprawled high above the audience, to prevent crushing via any stray falling parts, or, indeed, any falling ships.

Hovering above the net were around fifty enormous balloons, all impressively embellished with gold. An assortment of flags flapped from their silk-lined baskets, in which sat gloriously dressed men and women, sipping champagne, and laughing together, the women under lace parasols. These were coveted seats indeed.

Fei saw the occupants feeding each other strawberries and clinking their glasses as once again, Baylor's hand popped out in front of her.

'Driver's wing, that's where we need to go!' he shouted, pointing to their left.

Ships swirled down towards a vast, empty field that had been sectioned off into white-painted squares. Figures stood guiding the ships in to land, using white and red paddles.

Baylor steadied Catica. 'I hope they've registered us, because we'll be asked for our names when we land.'

'Fingers crossed.'

They peered at the waving red and white dots, as they joined the other ships spiralling down.

As they descended, shouts and cheers ricocheted through the stadium. All they could see were tiny dots, excitedly waving their arms and screaming at the smaller races taking place before the main event.

'Well, we definitely got here in good time,' Baylor said as they hovered towards a flapping race worker, who signalled them into their square. The squares continued on for what looked like miles behind them in the blindingly green field.

'I'm surprised were are one of the first,' said Fei, pushing up her goggles and examining the other ships.

'They'll be here soon – probably all drunk!' Baylor replied.

'Can't complain bout that.' Fei smirked.

A rather sharp-looking woman, in a black blazer and scrupulously pressed flying trousers, approached them, carrying a clipboard. A small boy, wearing a blue and white stripped blazer and a black cap, trotted along beside her as she scribbled. The boy was dragging a basket containing a small pot of paste, some sheets of paper and a thick paintbrush.

The signaller with the red and white paddles nodded at the woman as she approached Fei and Baylor, then marched over to direct the next ship as it came in to land.

The woman didn't look up, just continued scribbling on her clipboard,

Fei and Baylor exchanged anxious looks.

'Name?' the woman barked eventually, as the small boy skipped up beside her.

'Uh, Baylor Doone, Ma'am.' Baylor gave an awkward smile and removed his cap as the woman furiously flicked through sheets of paper.

They began to sweat.

The boy squinted off at the stream of ships coming in to land. The sharp woman was taking an alarmingly long time to find their names.

Fei attempted to flatten her jacket, while rubbing at a small black smudge on her trousers. Finally, the woman gave a sharp nod, her lips pursed as she scanned their faces.

'Number eleven,' she said, looking down at the boy, who was still gazing at the ships.

She tapped him on the back of the head with her pencil.

'Number eleven!'

He swung round and scrambled in the basket, pulling out four white squares with the number eleven painted on them.

The woman pointed at the pair with her pencil. The boy scurried over to Baylor, handed him two of the squares, then rushed to the front of the ship, dodging a spinning propeller, and pasted one of the squares on the front. The fourth square he pasted on the back.

'The race starts in an hour. Wait here. You'll be called forward when it's time.'

Fei and Baylor nodded as the woman and the boy marched off to the next arrival.

'Just in time! I think we were right at the end of the list,' said Baylor, passing Fei one of the numbers and four safety pins.

Fei felt the paper between her fingers. The black number smudged a little beneath her warm touch.

She smiled as she proudly pinned the number to her chest. She'd seen pictures of numbers like this in the newspaper each year. It was hard to believe she was wearing one herself, at last.

'I wonder where they are,' Fei said, watching friends and family members approach various ships in front of them.

'Even if they are 'ere, it'll take 'em a while to get through that crowd.' Baylor shook his head at the mass of people standing behind the drivers' ring gates, waving bits of paper and pens at the drivers.

Fei sighed. 'I'm gonna take a look around, suss out the competition.'

'Cool, I'm gonna do some last-minute tweaking – I keep worrying that bits of the ship will drop off halfway through the race!' Baylor pulled a spanner from his trousers.

Fei laughed. 'I won't be long; if you need me, just like, scream or something,' she grinned.

'Will do.'

# CHAPTER TWENTY-THREE

Fei meandered through the field; she could hear the comforting whoosh of propellers as she admired the other entries. The larger, grander ships were surrounded by women in satin dresses, with smashed champagne glasses scattered on the ground.

The smaller, less glitzy ships were far more interesting, and significantly less suffocated by onlookers. The designs were exquisite. There was a purple ship with white trim and a cream balloon, the carriage rather fish-like in shape, with long, flapping gold flags. And a green ship with a light brown balloon, light wood trim and white flags. She particularly admired a slate-grey ship, with light trim and a white balloon. Something about it reminded her of Clyde. *The large balloon, perhaps?*

Fei smiled to herself as a louder, deeper rumble whirred from behind her, followed by shrieks of joy. She turned, craning her neck round the smaller balloons, and walked towards the commotion, where a significantly larger, white balloon bobbed above the rest.

She stopped in her tracks as she turned the corner. Camera flashes illuminated the colossal carriage of a double-decker ship hovering beneath two massive white balloons, encased in thick gold trim.

A tall man with a camera dashed towards her, planting the lens in her face, to which she could not hide the distaste on her face. At the same time, a smaller, rounder man waddled up, holding a notepad and pen.

'Driver number eleven, how do you feel about being up against the great Millennial this year?' he asked loudly, as the draft from a nearby propeller almost lifted off his bowler hat.

Fei stood there, dumbfounded.

'Umm, sorry, no comment,' she mumbled, pushing past him to get a better look.

She sighed as she stared at the near perfect craftsmanship of the vast ship.

'Beautiful, isn't she?' came a deep voice from behind.

Fei grimaced.

She turned, lifting her hand to shield her eyes from the sun, to see the silhouette of a tall, muscular man in an aviator's jacket.

James D. Menillo pulled the cap from his head and wistfully shook his silky brown locks in the wind, his eyes closed as he ran his fingers over his head, smoothing down his 'cap hair'. He turned his sparkling green eyes upon her and gave that familiar sickening smile.

His moustache twitched as he reached out a hand. Fei, still blinded by the sun, squinted at his glowing head.

'James, James D. Menillo. Pleasure.'

Fei forced a smile as she shook his hand. 'We've met.'

James raised an eyebrow. 'Gosh. You're not that filly from Grabascus, are you?' he chortled.

Fei sighed and shook her head. 'No James,' she replied, arms crossed.

'Thank God. That was a near bloody miss I dare say!' he said, waving at some passers-by. 'What's your name then? What brings you to our "little" gathering.' He gave a throaty laugh as he finished the glass of champagne he'd taken from a passing tray.

'Feina Fourlise, I'm a driver. Well, co-driver.' James nodded.

Fei pursed her lips. 'That's our ship, over there,' she said, pointing at Catica.

They turned to see Baylor, standing waist-deep in one side of Catica's carriage.

James smirked. 'Bit scrawny, isn't he? Sure he's up to the challenge? It's a long race.'

He wiggled his eyebrows, which turned Fei's stomach – she inhaled back a thundering insult. 'We'll manage, thanks.'

James blinked as Fei pushed past him, to which he shot out a gloved hand and squeezed her arm. 'Hey, hey. Do let me know if you fancy a ride with a real ... "ship",' he grinned.

'If I sustain multiple head injuries during the race, I'll let you know,' Fei pulled herself away from his clammy palm and marched back towards Baylor.

James inhaled sharply as he walked back towards the Millennial.

\*\*\*

'Excuse me! Sorry, excuse me.'

Nessa and Cora squeezed through the mass of black suits, large skirts, and oversized hats. Cora had lost count of how many times she'd had champagne spilled on her coat. Their badge passes became more and more stained, and she stopped for a second, her frustration mounting. The noise was deafening and she could barely hear herself think.

'Right, I need to stop. This is insane.'

Nessa nodded, equally frustrated.

Cora climbed a step leading to a packed bar. She held her hand to her eyes in the blinding sun and scanned the crowd.

'Can you see them?' asked Nessa, dodging some large, feathered hats and spitting as they brushed past her mouth.

'No, and I swear that usher who gave us directions was drunk. Where the hell has he sent us?'

'Lord knows, but this is a nightmare. voy a perder la cabeza en un minuto.' Another stream of champagne flew Nessa's way and she growled.

Cora stopped to see some airships slowly descending. 'There!' she pointed.

Nessa tiptoed to see over all the hats and heads. 'Come on!' She pulled on Cora's coat sleeve, and they set off again, jostling through the crowd, towards the drivers' ring.

The excitement was building. People were waving wads of cash at the bookies, who stood booming in front of their boxes (already rammed with money) and numerous blackboards, on which they were furiously rubbing out and rewriting odds as the bets flew in.

Cora and Nessa arrived at a gate to the drivers' ring, where the ground was vibrating from the ships' engines. A tall man stood in front of them. Dressed all in black.

Nessa glared at him, as he watched them approach.

'Silgir,' she hissed to Cora. 'Alimañas, they are everywhere.'

Cora gripped Nessa's arm as he raised his palm for them to stop.

He raised his hand for them to stop. 'Identification,' he said, in a low, stern voice.

'Friends and family.'

As they showed him their badges, Nessa tried hard not to scowl. He examined them, nodded, and opened the gate.

They rushed through, and the Silgir turned to watch them as they left.

'Cucaracha.'

'Never mind him,' Cora said, urging her forward. 'He couldn't even feel his Pod over the ship vibrations. We need to find Fei and Baylor!'

They marched up to a woman, who was flicking through a list on a clipboard, her lacquered grey coiffure standing strong in the thundering propeller winds.

'Uh, Baylor Doone?' asked Cora.

The woman raised a finger, not looking up from her flicking, while the girls stood awkwardly in front of her.

'Number eleven,' she barked, pointing right but not looking up. A small boy in a striped suit, with a basket on wheels, stared blankly at them.

'Thank you.'

They rushed off, swerving through groups of merry celebrators who were having their pictures taken with ships and drivers.

'Six, seven...'

Cora almost heaved as she saw James posing for pictures with a mass of women around him. Nessa scrunched her face.

'Friend of yours?'

'Nope. Nine, ten, eleven. *There* they are!'

They traipsed through the field, heading for the blue and brass beacon.

Fei and Baylor had stepped out of the ship, Baylor having his last cigarette before the race. Fei rotated, scanning the field. She spotted two small figures, who waved as they approached.

Fei beamed. 'Cora!'

They hugged.

'I can't believe we're actually here! This is so exciting,' said Fei, grinning.

'Yes, very exciting, but don't lose sight of why we're here. You've got half an hour,' Cora reminded her.

'And in fifteen minutes we'll be directed to the starting line,' Baylor said, as he ambled over to join them.

They jumped at the sound of a loud engine thundering behind them.

A ship parked nearby.

There it was. Long, sleek and daunting. Its long burgundy carriage nestled under its beautifully streamlined cream balloon. Its long, black flag flapped in the Leos sunshine, while its copper propellers sat snug behind two large black fins.

'No,' gasped Baylor, unfolding his arms to gawp.

'Qué, what is it?'

'Great,' said Fei, burying her face in her hands.

'Hey, that's the one on your bedroom wall, right?' said Cora pointing. Her face dropped, 'Oh.'

'The Merenial,' mumbled Fei, through her fingers.

'It must be hired. How the hell did they get hold of one when it's not even in circulation yet?' said Baylor, still gawping.

'If James D. Menillo can bring a prototype, someone can bring the Merenial.'

'You don't mean..?' said Baylor, glancing nervously over towards the Millennial, which was towering above the rest of the ships.

Fei nodded. 'And it won't have been cheap, hiring the Millennial.'

'So, this is the really good one?' said Cora.

'The best, I think...' said Fei, looking anxious as she saw James kissing the side of the Millennial, more camera flashes exploding in front of him.

'Unbeaten,' groaned Baylor.

'Urgh,' groaned Fei.

'All drivers are to please be at the ready in their ships. We will now begin the phased move to the starting line. All drivers are to please be at the...'

The grey-haired woman walked through the field, speaking through a megaphone. The small boy trotted behind her, his wheeled basket now empty.

'Well, here goes!' Baylor jumped up and landed in the driver's seat, still gazing at the Merenial's luminous burgundy carriage.

Fei took a breath. 'Here's hoping that James has already drunk his own body weight in champagne this morning.'

They watched as James's manager attempted to steer him towards the Millennial's cockpit.

'Good luck,' chorused Cora and Nessa. 'We'll be waiting for you in the winners' ring.' They hugged Fei tight.

'Puedes hacerlo. Nothing stays unbeaten forever.' Fei squeezed Nessa's arms and smiled.

Baylor reached over Catica's body and Fei took his hand, as he heaved her into the seat behind.

Cora gave her two thumbs-up.

Fei grinned and pulled her goggles down. Cora and Nessa stood back, and Baylor and Fei sat waiting in Catica.

The Merenial's driver suddenly appeared, marching towards the ship and jumping in expertly, a number twelve pinned to their dark brown jacket.

Baylor and Fei stared over at the surprisingly small person sitting with both hands firmly on the yoke. A tight brown curl poked out from under their aviator's hat, and a black scarf covered their nose and mouth. They looked round, stern intent in their eyes as they glared back at the them, their large blue eyes magnified behind their goggles.

'Anyone you know?' Fei asked.

'Nope.'

Baylor was fidgeting so much, his hands looked as if they were about to burst through his gloves. Fei put a calming hand on his shoulder. 'You've got this.'

Baylor nodded, his heart thundering as he fastened the strap of his aviator's cap under his chin.

A signaller stood in front of them, flapping them away with his paddles. Baylor pushed forward on the lever to his right and pulled up on the handles. Catica hummed and rose, following the other ships, behind the Merenial.

Nessa and Cora stood below, waving as hard as they could. Fei peered over and waved back as they joined the spiral of ships at the starting line.

# CHAPTER TWENTY-FOUR

A sea of ships bobbed in front of a long red ribbon. They could see more red ribbon and balloons positioned round the mountains in the distance, marking out the track. The roar of the crowd below was deafening. Hats were being thrown into the air, popping through the net, then dropping back down into the cheering crowd. Further up the side of one of the mountains, away from the crowd, sat a colossal golden balcony with a huge table covered in food in the middle. Divinely dressed men and women sat around it laughing and drinking.

Fei and Baylor watched as two men pulled an almost comically large loudspeaker to the front of the glistening balcony, which towered over the stadium.

The extravagant balloons quietened, waving and flapping lace handkerchiefs - some of which fell and floated into the roaring mass below. They laughed as people grabbed at the tiny pieces of cloth.

James D. Menillo, who had of course been directed to the front position in the Millennial, blew a deafening whistle, then stood and began waving at the gold balloons. Shrieks followed by several handkerchiefs flew out, missing James and dropping through the net.

'What's going on?' Fei shouted, staring at the balcony.

'Kiva,' Baylor muttered.

A tall, sinewy, grey-haired woman, dressed in purple velvet, emerged from the ornate double doors set into the mountainside, and glided across the balcony.

The crowd screamed as she waved, her sallow face splitting into a toothy grin. A white lace crest towered behind her small head and pearls and jewels hung from her dress. A thick layer of make-up had been plastered on her skeletal face. The people who had previously been eating and drinking on the balcony stood to clear her path to the box where the loudspeaker had been placed, two brawny bodyguards standing on either side of her.

She placed a bony, gloved hand on her chest and smiled. Lapping up the applause. The crowd fell silent as she raised her palm. Fei stared at the woman through some binoculars.

'Who is that?' she asked.

'Our glorious leader,' Baylor said bitterly.

'Good people of Leos, it is my absolute pleasure to open the twenty-seventh annual Leos Sky Chase,' Kiva rasped through the loudspeaker.

The crowd erupted. More hats and champagne corks flew up through the net. Kiva laughed and clapped, along with her drunk posse. She raised her palm again.

Silence.

'Eternal glory will be bestowed on the winner of this profound event, so use your powers wisely,' she giggled. 'No foul play now, I want a nice clean game; James, I'm looking at you, you naughty boy!' she cackled, bringing her hand to her emaciated chest as the stadium erupted with laughter.

James stood, beaming, flapping his hand down in mock modesty, before blowing Kiva a kiss. As he returned to his seat, he turned to look at Fei, tipped his cap and raised an eyebrow. She narrowed her eyes at him.

'Please don't tell me you've picked a fight with the three-time Sky Chase champion,' said Baylor.

'Sometimes all you need is a little competition.'

'I dunno, I'd be cool with less.'

'Also, it was either that or go out with him.'

'Fair enough.'

They pulled their goggles down over their eyes.

'On the sound of the third horn, the race will commence. Good luck!' bellowed Kiva.

'Here goes,' said Baylor. He gulped and gripped the yoke, staring ahead into the empty sky.

The crowd roared, and Fei and Baylor watched as Kiva's posse helped her down off the box, thrusting a champagne flute into her bony hand.

They stared at the number twelve driver sitting behind the wheel of the Merenial.

'Here goes,' echoed Fei, her heart beginning to lurch in her chest. Baylor's hands were fused to the handles.

They could see the flagger sitting in red balloon number one, a large horn in his hands. The roaring crowd seemed to quieten as they watched the flagger bring the horn to his mouth.

'Here goes,' said Cora, her eyes fixed on Catica.

Nessa squeezed Cora's arm as they stared at the flagger.

Fei took one last look at the burgundy ship hovering ahead of them.

Number twelve, staring ahead; James, fixed forward.

One.

Two.

Baylor pushed on the handles and Catica lurched forward, her exhaust popping with power. The crowd screamed with excitement as the ships whizzed off in a cloud of smoke. A couple of the more extravagant ships failed to move off and subsequently deflated, floating down into the net.

Catica steamed through the sky, sailing past the clouds. Fei watched as the numbers on the balloons gradually increased, a line of white flags behind them. She felt another, more intense, wave of adrenaline as three similar-looking ships pelted towards them.

The drivers were all dressed in black.

'Silgir!' she shouted.

'Every year.' Baylor bellowed over the engines.

A large burgundy blur bumped past them on the inside as they began to twist round a mountain peak and Fei jolted in her seat. James was already ahead of them, and number twelve was taking the lead.

'Dammit!' shouted Baylor. He twisted a small brass control, and Catica lurched into a higher gear, powering forward round the mountain. Flaggers with loudspeakers watched from the red balloons as ships bumped into the mountain and deflated down the side.

The Silgir were taking no prisoners.

And it was going unnoticed.

Fei growled. The Silgir were deliberately bumping into smaller ships; while the larger, more expensive ships were cumbersome; but doing better than they should.

However much the pair despised James, they had to admit he had impeccable technique as a driver: smooth transitions between gears, seamless pull-backs before corners, and he dodged deflaters with ease.

*Dammit.*

Baylor and Fei surged on, flying round the mountain peaks, passing the roaring crowds for the second and third time. As they dipped round again, the noise of the crowd was muffled by the mountain, and they felt a sudden bump on the back of Catica which jolted them forward in their seats.

'What was that?' Baylor shouted, his heart pounding as he attempted to steady the ship.

'Silgir,' Fei hissed, staring into the cold eyes of a driver on their tail.

Baylor turned to see the expressionless Silgir surging forward to ram into Catica once again, this time sending them wobbling back a little and allowing several ships to fly forward ahead of them.

James glanced over his shoulder, as Catica billowed away. He smiled and tipped his cap at Fei.

Number twelve thundered ahead.

Fei's blood began to boil as Baylor attempted to swerve, getting closer to the stadium. She looked around her seat, desperately searching for something to throw them off.

Baylor half-turned as she was rooting around.

'Spanner, side pocket!' he yelled.

She grabbed it.

A red balloon with a commentator was very close. Meanwhile, the Silgir continued to bump them.

'What are you waiting for? They're gonna knock us down!!' shouted Baylor in a panic.

'The flaggers can't see it happening!'

Fei glowered at the smirking eyes of the Silgir.

The second the red balloon had whizzed past and the white flag had gone up, Fei launched the spanner at the Silgir's cockpit.

It smashed straight through the glass screen.

The Silgir shielded themselves as splintered glass flew into their faces; their ship swerved outside the lines of the race and went spinning down the mountainside. Fei grinned and Baylor pushed Catica on. She sped off past several ships, the Millennial ahead of them in first place.

James had seen the Silgir ship tumbling down through the clouds. With a swift jerk down, the Millennial shot forward and he disappeared behind the mountain, the Merenial following shortly after.

***

'How are they doing?' asked Nessa.

Cora was following Catica's progress through binoculars. 'Not well enough,' she gulped.

'Maldita sea. Come on, Catica!'

\*\*\*

'WHAT A FANTASTIC RACE, FOLKS! WE ARE NOW HALFWAY THROUGH, SIX LAPS TO GO AND ONLY FIFTEEN OUT OF FORTY-EIGHT SHIPS REMAIN.' The voice of the main commentator boomed out of the loudspeaker as they flew through the stadium.

Baylor pushed Catica into a higher gear, her fins shaking in the wind.

'Dunstan? Binoculars, please,' Kiva clicked her fingers at a suited man and he helped her to the edge of the balcony. She held out her empty champagne flute, watching the ships pass through the main arena. Dunstan replaced the champagne glass with the binoculars. She brought them to her ashen eyes and watched as numbers eight and twelve took the lead, Catica not too far behind, and a group of Silgir and some of the grander ships following.

'Dunstan, who are the drivers in front?' she asked, looking sour.

'That would be number twelve, number eight, number eleven and number thirty-six ma'am.'

'I can see that, you damn idiot. What are their names and where are they from?' she hissed in disgust, flecks of spittle landing on Dunstan's face.

He apologised as Kiva continued to track their progress through her binoculars.

'That would be a Mr James D. Menillo in number eight, of course.'

'Obviously.'

'Ms Rabina Swiper in number twelve; a Mr Baylor Doone in number eleven, and Sir Peter Von Westhill in number thirty-six, Ma'am.'

Kiva grunted.

'"Swiper" and "Doone", who are they? This Swiper has the Merenial. Must be from money,' she wheezed, still watching them.

'Nobodies, Ma'am. Simple Leos folk."

Kiva's expression darkened. 'Well, see to it that these "simple Leos folk" remain "simple Leos folk".' She scowled at him, dropping the binoculars in his hands. 'Have our men waiting, round the other side of the mountain,' she commanded. 'I don't wish to congratulate sewer rats.'

'Right away, Ma'am.' Dunstan shuffled over to one of the guards and whispered urgently in his ear. The man nodded and beckoned to the other guard, and they disappeared through the double doors.

\*\*\*

'Four more laps, Bay. You can do this!' Fei shouted.

Baylor pushed Catica harder than ever as they roared towards the two ships ahead. The Silgir were hot on their tail, followed by a menagerie of large embellished ships.

Small flashes of light appeared on the side of the mountain as they flew, lighting up and then disappearing. Fei squinted into the distance: another flash. Then a whistling noise.

She gasped as an arrow pelted past her face, then another, piercing Catica's balloon.

They jerked sideways and Baylor watched, panic-stricken, as the pressure dial on the dashboard began to fall.

'What happened? We've lost momentum!!' he cried.

'Snipers on the mountains!'

Fei could see the smirking Silgir behind them, and more flashes ahead.

'Bastards!' Baylor desperately wrestled the controls in an attempt to steady Catica.

Air was rapidly escaping from their balloon.

'We need to plug the hole, I'll climb up!' Fei bellowed.

'Don't you dare! If you fall, you die!' Baylor yelled back. 'I can't keep her steady enough.'

'We're falling behind fast! Bay, if we lose this, we all die.'

Fei grabbed some tape from a cubbyhole next to her seat, leapt up and swung onto a rope ladder that hung down the side of the ship.

'FEI, NO!' Baylor saw her foot disappear up and round the balloon.

The Silgir hurtled closer, steadying beside them, then bumping them hard, pushing Catica into the red rope barrier; the red balloons swung out as they passed.

# CHAPTER TWENTY-FIVE

'Oh God!' shouted Cora.

'Qué, what is it? What is happening?'

'Something's happened to the balloon.'

Nessa grabbed the binoculars to see Fei climbing up the side of the ship. 'Dios mío!'

'We have to do something!'

'And what exactly do you suggest?'

***

As Fei dangled from the rope ladder, her foot shot through one of the rungs.

'FEI!' Baylor yelled, his palms soaked with sweat.

Fei gasped and stared wide-eyed at the abyss below. She forced herself up as an arrow shot past her leg, knocking her off balance.

*C'mon! Just a bit further, just a bit. You can do this.*

She clambered further and Baylor thrust the ship up and above the Silgir. She twisted the rope round her leg as her face drew level with the hole.

'LAST LAP, FOLKS. BOY, WHAT A CLOSE ONE!' the commentator boomed as they flew for the last time through the main arena.

The Silgir backed away as they powered through the stadium, the crowd watching their every move.

Fei clung desperately to the ropes.

'Fei, you hold on. You hear me? If you fall, I'll kill you!' Baylor yelled, as James in the Millennial and number twelve in the Merenial ripped through the sky.

Fei had the tape wedged between her teeth. She was shaking with the strain.

*Shit, c'mon Fei. C'MON!*

The closer they got to disappearing behind the mountain, the closer the Silgir soared up behind them, surrounding them on both sides. Fei ripped off a piece of tape and stretched out towards the hole, just as the Silgir closed in and knocked the ship on both sides, sending the tape flying from her hands and tumbling into the clouds below.

*No.*

Another whistling sound pierced the clouds, this time a lot further ahead; she saw an arrow strike the Merenial's balloon.

'The Merenial! FEI!' Baylor bellowed.

Clinging to her perch, Fei could see the Merenial falling back towards them. Number twelve was spinning furiously in the cockpit.

James punched a celebratory fist in the air.

Fei made a lunge and smacked her hand as firmly as she could over the hole in the balloon. She closed her eyes as the Silgir closed in on them again, knocking them hard.

Her hand slipped and she grabbed onto the rope ladder to steady herself.

*Oh God, oh God, oh God! C'mon, Fei, concentrate!*

She gasped, adrenaline surging through her. Her body ached with tension, her hand was trembling, and her breath was short as she attempted to steady herself. She peered through the clouds, faces rushed past, screaming with excitement and expectation. Exhaustion overwhelmed her.

A shot sounded ahead of them.

Fei felt the lump creeping back into her throat, her tired body beginning to give way.

*I can't ...*

'Fei, talk to me!' Baylor shouted desperately. 'Are you okay?'

As the Millennial neared Catica, James sneered gleefully. His expression was dripping with condescension as the Merenial closed in on them.

*They cannot win...*

Fei glared at James. She thrust her foot round the rope ladder, twisting it securely in place, then turned and slammed her arm back over the hole. The wind pounded into her beaten face.

Sparks flew out of a pistol in the carriage of the Merenial towards the mountainside.

Another shot.

Fei gawped as the flashes on the mountain stopped and the Merenial grew closer. She looked behind to see the large gold ship gaining on them. Clouds were thundering past and James was way out ahead.

*We can't lose now. We just can't.*

With her arm muscles straining to cover the hole, and her body pounded by the force of the wind, Fei closed her eyes.

\*\*\*

'No,' said Cora, her face paling.

Nessa grabbed the binoculars and pressed them to her panicked eyes. 'Do not be stupid, Feina!'

\*\*\*

But Fei had no choice. She faced the ship and allowed her eyes to glaze over. Baylor turned to see her eyes turning milky-white.

'NO, FEI!'

The Silgir narrowed their eyes; the Merenial was now sitting level with them. Number twelve was growling with rage, as the wind accelerated, mixed with the swirling gales.

Like a bullet out of a gun, a bird rocketed past.

Then another.

And another.

They flew directly into the Silgirs' heads, clawing at them. They roared in pain and flailed their arms as the birds tore at their faces.

As the birds flew into the Silgir, their ships began to slowly back off. Number twelve stared at Fei, who was gripping to the side of the ship, her eyes white, then at the mass of accumulating birds.

Number twelve gasped as a bird made a beeline for them. Then another, followed by several more. The Merenial was retreating behind Catica as number twelve pulled on the brakes.

James gulped as he watched birds soar into the Silgir's ships, he let out a small yelp as several birds twisted in the air, and began soaring towards him.

'IT'S SO CLOSE FOLKS! WHO DO WE THINK IT WILL BE? LAST LEG. WHAT A RACE IT HAS BEEN!' boomed the commentator.

\*\*\*

'Ma'am you may want to see this.'

Dunstan tapped Kiva's shoulder.

'What?' she flapped a hand at him.

His cheeks wobbled as he bent down and whispered in her ear. Kiva's eyes widened, and she shot up.

'Give me those.'

Snatching the binoculars from Dunstan, she tottered as fast as she could to the balcony, and focused the binoculars on the ships careering towards the finishing line.

\*\*\*

'FEI, STOP!' Baylor shouted, straining to keep up Catica's momentum.

James flailed as a flock of birds slammed into his cockpit, flapping their wings in his seething red face, stepping on buttons and squawking.

As the Millennial slowed, Baylor's eyes bulged. He gripped the accelerator, and pushed Catica towards the Millennial's looming rear.

The finishing line grew closer and the Silgir had fallen far behind. Fei clung on for dear life as Catica surged forward. One last bird shot at number twelve's head. The driver dodged it, squinted back at Fei, then pulled a small yellow stone out of a pocket. The stone was practically jumping out of the driver's hand.

Baylor thrust Catica into a lower gear, sending her storming ahead and swinging Fei round. Her back slammed into the side of the balloon, and for a second her milky-white eyes were thrust open.

As the birds continued to swarm in James's cockpit around his almost-purple face, the Millennial closed in beside Catica.

'We're gaining on him, Fei!' shouted Baylor excitedly.

*** 

Kiva gave a sinister grin as she saw Fei swing back round to face the balloon. Dunstan stepped beside her as she moved the binoculars away from her eyes.

'Call him,' she hissed, watching the ships career towards the finishing line.

'Yes, Ma'am,' said Dunstan, with a nod. He shuffled through the balcony doors and disappeared.

*** 

'Did she see it?' asked Cora.

'I cannot tell,' replied Nessa. 'There is not much happening. She is just standing there smiling.'

\*\*\*

Still temporarily blind, Fei gasped, bereft of energy.

James flustered to realign himself as he batted the birds out of his cockpit, roaring with frustration as he flicked switches and slammed buttons.

Catica and the Millennial were now neck and neck.

There it was: the finishing line, about a hundred metres ahead. Nessa and Cora stood transfixed as the ships jostled each other for the win.

Baylor peered over at James's red face. The last four years had led to this moment – he could not lose now.

'C'MON, BAY!' Fei roared.

Moving to the final gear, Baylor held his breath and powered down on the accelerator. The engine gave a loud bang and flames erupted from the exhaust pipe, making them hurtle forward and sending them flying over the line.

First.

\*\*\*

Nessa screamed, along with the crowd. Then she hugged Cora and they both hurried towards the winners' area.

\*\*\*

James exploded, slamming his fists on the dashboard, screaming, 'No, no, no, no, no!!'

Baylor felt the breath leave his body.

'AND THERE WE HAVE OUR WINNER, FOLKS!! NUMBER ELEVEN, BAYLOOOOR DOOOOONE!!'

Fei closed her eyes, allowing air to fill her lungs again.

'YES. WOOOOOO!' Baylor thrust his fist in the air.

Fei climbed down the ropes and landed in the carriage. They hugged, laughing and jumping as they descended down into the winner's area; waving arms, hats, streamers and confetti swirling to the ground around them.

Three large-bellied men in tuxedos swaggered into the area: one holding a large gold trophy in the shape of an airship; another holding a stupidly oversized bouquet; and the last holding an equally gigantic magnum of champagne. They bellowed with laughter as Catica bumped onto the green, followed shortly by James, who sat in his cockpit with his arms firmly crossed. His manager flew up beside him to cover his furious purple face and stroke his back as James proceeded to throw a tantrum.

Number twelve landed on the green beside them, ignoring the outstretched hands of the onlookers.

Fei and Baylor leapt out of their carriage, beaming, as hordes of people rushed towards them, wanting to shake their hands and pat them on the back. A brass band warmed up in the ring as more people gathered round.

Cora and Nessa powered their way through the crowd, heading towards the winning ships.

Cora felt a sharp yank on her sleeve. 'Stop...look.' Nessa nodded to her right, where the crowd had begun to split and quieten.

Kiva and two guards sauntered through the cleared path, waving. Two men rolled out a long purple carpet in front of her.

Nessa stared at Cora and shook her head.

Number twelve sloped off into the crowd as a small bronze trophy was being carried towards her, along with a bunch of flowers. She crept away, keeping out of sight as the usher carrying the silver trophy looked round in confusion.

James straightened his jacket and climbed out of his cockpit. His pink-faced manager was shooing away photographers as James shuffled forward. His jaw was twitching, and his fists were clenched, as he bowed.

Baylor dipped his head and pushed down on Fei's back.

The three large-bellied men and the crowd were bowing as well.

Kiva giggled. They looked up to see her beckoning them towards her. 'Ahh, congratulations, my young drivers.'

The crowd roared as she ambled over to the man holding the trophy; he bowed and placed it in her bony hands. She grinned at Fei, then beckoned Baylor towards her. He stepped out and Kiva placed the trophy in his shaky hands. 'What is your name my dear?'

'Uhh, Baylor, Ma'am. Baylor Doone.'

'Well, uh, Baylor, Ma'am, Baylor Doone, CONGRATULATIONS!'

The crowd erupted with laughter as Baylor grimaced and stepped back.

'Ma'am, I demand a rematch,' said a deep, furious voice. As James leapt towards Kiva, her bodyguards immediately intercepted him. Kiva laughed.

'Come now. It's only our James.' She flapped away the guards and hugged James's stiff body; her lips pursed feigning comfort.

'I would have won, had it not been for that damn flock of rogue birds!' he growled.

She stroked his cheek and patted his lapels. 'Come now, my dear, none of that now. Besides...' Her gaze rested on Fei. 'We cannot control nature, can we?' She gave a wry smile.

Fei glanced down, and Cora, Nessa and Baylor felt their pulses quicken.

James flashed Fei a look of rage and screamed.

'DANIEL!'

James's manager waffled through the crowd, spread out his arms, and herded James back through the ring. They watched as a bronze trophy flew into the air, followed by a tantrum.

Kiva laughed, the ring members following suit.

'So spirited,' she giggled.

Fei swiftly glanced down, followed shortly by the arrival of a perfectly manicured set of shrivelled purple toes appear in front of her.

'You might remove your goggles, dear. The race is over,' said Kiva in her silken voice.

Cora and Nessa scowled, and the crowd laughed once again as Fei pulled off her goggles. Kiva leaned forward and placed the large bouquet in her arms, smiling. 'Congratulations, my dear.'

'Thank you, Ma'am,' Fei nodded.

Kiva did not take her eyes off Fei, as the third large-bellied man ambled up beside them.

'Ma'am.' He bowed, holding out the magnum of champagne. Kiva raised her shoulders excitably and clicked her fingers at one of her guards. 'Bring it up to the balcony for us, darling.' Then she turned to Fei and Baylor. 'Join me on the balcony for some food and drinks,' she beamed.

Cora and Nessa shook their heads as subtly as they could.

'Uh, that's very kind of you, but – '

'I don't want to hear any buts. I *insist*, darlings,' she interrupted Baylor, pointing to the stairs leading up to her balcony.

Fei and Baylor nodded awkwardly. 'Um, okay,' Fei stuttered.

'Fabulous.'

Kiva sauntered towards the staircase while her guards closed in behind Fei and Baylor, ushering them forward.

Just as they were about to go up the stairs, Cora appeared. She grabbed Fei and Baylor's hands, shaking them erratically. 'Congratulations! I can't believe I'm meeting you!' She laughed nervously while the guard stood watching them.

Fei smiled and hugged Cora.

'We will be watching,' Cora whispered in her ear.

'No, go get supplies, then go back to Byrdy's. We will meet you there once we have Alfie.'

'I'm not leaving you here alone.'

'Ah, thank you so much!' said Fei loudly, pulling away and smiling at the guard. 'Do as I say,' she mouthed as he turned away.

Nessa nodded at them from the cheering crowd, and Fei and Baylor walked on after Kiva.

Number twelve watched, as Cora pulled away and joined Nessa, before retreating through the crowd.

Cora and Baylor followed Kiva up the stairs. The noise of the crowd faded as everyone returned to their merriment in the sunshine.

'One drink, then we leave, right?' muttered Fei.

Baylor nodded.

# CHAPTER TWENTY-SIX

Fei and Baylor arrived at the top and stepped out on to the vast golden balcony, draped in red and purple velvet. Kiva's posse were now a lot drunker and didn't notice their arrival.

Kiva clapped, laughing at her foolish followers. They wobbled in their seats and thrust their glasses in the air, sending champagne flying in all directions. One pale man with dark hair and moustache, dressed in a rich green tuxedo, leaned too heavily on a tray, making a mound of almond biscuits fall to the ground, at which they all roared with laughter.

Kiva cleared her throat. 'Allow me to introduce to you all, OUR CHAMPIONS!'

Fei and Baylor smiled awkwardly as she clapped and stared at them, her posse erupting into further merriment.

'Come now, have some food. You must be starving.' She pointed towards the vast golden table. At least they assumed it was gold. They could only really see the table legs, as the surface was completely covered in dishes of luscious-looking food: large, crisp loaves of bread, the juiciest pears and melons they'd ever seen, trays holding every variety of cheese, surrounding a huge roasted boar.

All barely touched.

'Jesus,' said Fei, her mouth open.

'I've never seen so much food. I don't even know what some of it is,' Baylor muttered, peering at some slimy looking little sea creatures in a squid ink sauce.

Kiva's friends and courtiers lounged around the table, throwing food at each other, and screaming with laughter. She pushed Fei and Baylor forward, and they slid onto two chairs.

'Eat, eat, please.'

A grape went flying past Baylor's head and Kiva flung up her arms, cackling. 'I do apologise. Please help yourselves.'

Fei and Baylor exchanged nervous looks as they stared at the mountain of food.

'Go on,' Kiva urged.

Fei gulped and reached for a piece of cheese. The texture – she remembered it well – was soft and crumbly between her fingers. She closed her eyes as the intoxicating smell wafted up her nose.

Baylor lifted his champagne flute and poured the delicious contents into his dry mouth. Fei followed suit. She felt herself floating away, as the delicious flavours consumed her.

*Death by cheese. Could be worse.*

Suddenly ravenous, she found herself reaching forward again, only just stopping herself from grabbing a whole block.

'Ma'am, we really cannot stay for long,' she managed to say. 'We must get back to our family, they're expecting us.'

'Oh, come now, don't be so glum. I'm sure they can do without you for a while longer.'

A single slice of bread sat in the middle of Baylor's plate and Kiva pursed her lips. 'Is there nothing else I can get you?' she said, looking a little offended.

'Oh no, thank you, Ma'am. I have a sensitive stomach. I'm not used to such rich food.' He gave an apologetic smile.

'Oh dear, what a shame,' she mocked, pouting. 'Not even a tiny bit of ham?' she speared a pink slice on a fork and wiggled it in the air in front of him, as the rest of the diners jeered.

'Fraid not.'

'Oh well. More for us, I suppose!' She howled with laughter, her posse following suit.

'Ma'am, there is something we wish to speak to you about,' said Fei, the delicious cheese still swirling around in her mouth.

'Oh, and what might that be?' Kiva replied, taking a large gulp of champagne.

'The matter of how we wish to spend our winnings.'

'Oh, I do apologise. Dunstan? Dunstan!' Kiva clicked her fingers and he shuffled over.

'Have someone bring them their winnings immediately,'

'Thank you. But, before they bring it out, you should know we intend to use it ... to pay bail for one of your prisoners,' Fei said, trying to sound firmer than she felt.

Kiva and Dunstan's faces froze.

'One of my prisoners? My dear, why on earth would you want to waste your winnings on one of them?'

'Um, Alfred Albonas.' Fei trembled slightly, as she felt beads of sweat begin to form on her brow.

'He's my cousin, and my family miss him terribly,' Baylor blurted out, sending a few breadcrumbs soaring past Kiva's head.

'Is that so?' she hissed. 'How unusual. I must say, this is a first. And how different you are from your cousin, my dear...' Kiva and Dunstan scanned Baylor's frail body. 'In all respects.'

Kiva and her followers laughed again as Baylor shifted uncomfortably.

'Shall I have him brought out, Ma'am?' Dunstan leaned down beside her.

'Indeed. What a reunion it shall be. He eats us out of house and home anyway.' Kiva clapped. 'And bring some wine, these bubbles have gone flat.'

The posse shrieked as Kiva and Dunstan walked out of earshot.

'How far away is he?' she muttered under her breath, smiling at the others.

'About three hours, Ma'am.'

At the banqueting table, Fei grabbed another piece of cheese and whispered to Baylor, 'I don't like the look of that.'

'Agreed.'

'Once we get Alfie, we go. No hanging around.'

Near the double doors, Kiva continued her conversation with Dunstan. 'Bring the lug from the cell, he is no use to me anyway. But once they have left the balcony, have them watched. He will arrive before they are able to leave the city. Besides, their ship is useless,' she snarled.

'Their ship is still in working order, Ma'am.'

'Did you not hear me? I said, "Their ship is useless".' Kiva shot Dunstan a piercing glare. He nodded in understanding and shuffled off.

Kiva smiled and sauntered back over to Fei and Baylor.

'My men will bring him up for you. Along with your remaining twenty-five thousand Pela.'

Fei sighed with relief and Baylor smiled.

'Thank you, Ma'am. Really, thank you,' said Fei.

'No thank you, my dear. Your money shall buy me a new car.' She cackled.

Kiva picked up her freshly poured glass of wine and tapped the side with a silver spoon. Her audience quietened, and one by one, picked up their glasses.

Kiva stared at Fei and Baylor. 'To our champions! May they continue to give us big chunks of their money!' Her followers screamed with laughter.

Fei grimaced and her eyes met Baylor's. Raising their glasses awkwardly, they took a small swig.

\*\*\*

Number twelve was standing behind a large post, one of many holding up a vast tent. Under its canopy a group of ladies in lacy white dresses stood with glasses of champagne, shielding themselves from the blazing sun. Scowling, number twelve watched the balcony through a small telescope.

'I say, Miss, what do you think you're doing?' A plump man tapped her on the leg with his cane, glaring at her. His bushy white moustache half-covered his wrinkly, pursed lips. A pompous woman, who was clutching his arm, stared down her nose.

Number twelve blinked and moved the telescope away from her eye to peer down at her leg, then slowly up at the man. Through the thick lenses of her goggles the look of utter disgust on her small, round face was clear.

'GRRR RUF RUF RUF!' she barked and snarled at the couple, jumping a little in their direction.

The man flinched and the woman shrieked, as they hurried off like two alarmed geese.

Number twelve gave a low, hoarse growl. 'Bluddy pompous halfwets,' she muttered.

Peering back through the telescope, she saw two guards approach Catica. She moved forward to hide behind another post. The guards circled the ship, as if they were checking it over; they patched up the hole in the balloon and fixed the dents in the back.

Then they looked around.

Everyone was too busy drinking and chatting to notice what they were up to. Number twelve watched as one of the guards opened the small hatch to the engine, the other quickly moving to hide him from view.

'Whit in the blazes?' Number twelve dropped to the ground, squinting through the telescope between the guard's legs. She could see the other guard stabbing a hole in the tank, sending a spurt of oil shooting out.

'Those sly devils!'

She moved her telescope back up to the balcony and shuffled forward to get a better look.

The ornate double doors in the mountainside swung open, slamming into the wall, as three figures appeared. The guards, who had seemed large earlier, now looked miniscule, as they appeared on either side of a huge man. His head flopped as they heaved his limp body through the doors, shoving him to the ground.

*** 

'I say, no need to be so rough,' Kiva giggled uncomfortably.

Fei and Baylor shot up and ran over to him. Fei kneeled beside his head and gave him a gentle shake.

'How sweet!' Kiva mocked.

'Alfie? Alfie?' Fei shook.

Easily six-foot-five, and as wide as he was tall. He dragged his muscular arms forward in an attempt to push himself up. He had jet black hair, shaved short at the sides but much longer down the middle, which wilted over his face.

He heaved himself up to sit, his brawny chest tight in his white shirt and his hands covered in dirt. He brought a huge arm to his face, shielding his weak eyes from the sun as he staggered to find his balance. Moving his arm, he met Fei's eyes, rendering the whole balcony speechless. He was, to put it mildly, ridiculously handsome.

The sun beamed down onto his tanned skin, sending goose bumps round his lightly bearded, chiselled face and low brow. Exhausted though he was, his bright hazel eyes shone as he scooped back his dark hair and gave Fei a confused look.

She couldn't help but laugh. Even Baylor was lost for words. Fei turned and wrapped her arms as far as she could reach round Alfie's bear-like body.

'Oh my goodness, it's so good to see you again. We've missed you so much!' she shouted.

He tilted his ear away from her mouth and gave her a bewildered hug in return.

'Ahh, such a sweet reunion!' Kiva interrupted, jolting all the onlookers out of their daze. The women fanned their flushed faces.

'My name is Feina Fourlise, Moth sent us. Just go with it,' Fei whispered in Alfie's ear.

His eyes widened. Dazzled by the sun, he smiled as Fei moved away.

'Cousin!' Baylor wrapped his arms around Alfie.

'The family will be so happy!' he shouted.

Alfie forced a smile. 'Oh, ooh, yes. I've missed you both so much as well.'

'Baylor Doone, nice to meet ya. I'm with her,' Baylor whispered.

'Well, you most certainly need a bath, dear Alfie. We must get you home and clean you up,' said Fei loudly.

'Oh, come now. Won't you let him eat first?' said Kiva, beckoning them over.

Alfie stared longingly at the vast array of food while Baylor strained to help him to his feet.

'We have already taken up too much of your time, Ma'am, and Baylor's family will be dying to see them both after today's win,' said Fei, edging towards the stairs.

Baylor put Alfie's tree-trunk arm around his shoulder and started walking him in the same direction. Kiva sauntered towards them.

'Oh, don't be silly. You are my champions! You must delight in your spoils.' Her tone grew more menacing.

'You are too kind, Ma'am, but we really must go; you have our eternal gratitude.' Fei continued her retreat to the stairs.

'My dear, aren't you forgetting something?' Kiva hissed, as Fei felt her heart drop.

Baylor and Alfie were rooted to the spot, hardly daring to breathe.

Finally, Kiva broke the silence. 'You almost forgot the last of your prize money,' she said softly, still smiling. Keeping her gaze fixed on Fei, she signalled to the guard to hand her a large wad of cash.

Fei took the money, her skin prickling.

'Silly me. Thank you, Ma'am.' Fei withdrew a strained breath, and joined Baylor and Alfie.

'Don't be sneaking into any more places you're not allowed in now, my silly little peach!' Kiva grinned and waved her finger at Alfie, as her posse once again shrieked with laughter.

Alfie's mouth twitched, and he forced a smile, as they began their descent.

Kiva watched Fei and Baylor strain to manoeuvre Alfie's huge body as he hobbled down the first step. Her sinewy arms were tightly folded.

Dunstan came up behind her. 'They will be watched till he arrives,' he said.

Kiva gave a large, menacing grin. 'She will be most pleased with me,' she said, fiddling with the string of pearls clinging on for dear life round her veiny neck.

'Indeed, Ma'am.'

# CHAPTER
# TWENTY-SEVEN

Fei, Baylor and Alfie hurried down the gleaming staircase, smiling as they passed people sitting outside the luxurious bars and restaurants on the hillside.

'Is she still watching?' muttered Fei.

Baylor gave a subtle glance over Alfie's huge arm. 'Yup.'

Their quickened their pace and Alfie groaned in pain.

\*\*\*

Number twelve watched through the telescope, as they stumbled down the staircase. She zoomed in on Alfie's face, gasped and almost dropped the telescope as another brown curl pinged from under her cap.

\*\*\*

'She knows something is up,' wheezed Alfie, wincing as his companions tugged his aching body.

Baylor was beginning to sweat under his weight.

'You think…?' said Fei, nodding at people who were lifting their glasses to toast them as they passed. Several pointing at Alfie's glistening face.

'We need to get back to Byrdy fast. And – I'm sorry, Bay – we can't take Catica, she's too easy to spot now.'

Baylor nodded. 'Yeah, I'll come back for 'er later. She'll be fine 'ere for a bit.'

'Byrdy?' asked Alfie, his sparkle returning a little. 'You know Byrdy?'

'Shh, yes, he's the one who told us where you were. That's why we entered the race; he gave us the entry fee.'

Alfie's plump lip began to wobble. 'Is he okay?'

'He misses you,' Fei smiled.

'You're one as well, aren't you?'

Fei nodded at Alfie and gave a small smile.

Baylor laughed.

Alfie smiled back. 'I knew it!'

'Shh,' Fei whispered, nodding at more bystanders.

'You don't also happen to know – '

Alfie was cut off by a large gentleman who placed himself in front of Fei as they arrived at the bottom of the staircase. He pushed past her to shake Baylor's hand.

'Congratulations, dear boy. What a spectacular run that was. I know a good ship when I see one, I had a rather large bet on you!' His breath smelt of wine as he chortled in Baylor's face. 'Now I'm spending it all on lunch, ha-ha-ha!' He slapped Baylor hard on the back, making him almost buckle under Alfie's weight.

The gentleman's companions laughed and cheered at the table behind them.

'Thank you, sir.' Baylor steered round the large man as Fei scanned the stadium, looking for the best way out.

'Say. What's happened to this chap? One too many perhaps? Good thing he wasn't driving, eh!' The man waved his glass in the air as the trio scurried off.

\*\*\*

'Don't go te th' bluddy ship, ye idiots,' muttered number twelve, peering through the telescope. She watched them stop for a second, look over at Catica, then turn the other way.

'Aye, good lads,' she grinned and placed the telescope back in the pocket of her brick-coloured woollen waistcoat. She took a step forward, then stopped as she noticed a dark figure following the group at a discreet distance.

Number twelve scowled as the three disappeared through some ornate golden gates, the dark figure shortly after. Number twelve's expression hardened, and she headed towards the field after them, keeping out of sight.

\*\*\*

'So, Baylor and Feina, ha. That kinda rhymes! Baylor and Feina, sweet.' Alfie grinned, as the sun warmed his handsome face.

Fei and Baylor smiled.

'Did you know there was a breed of warthog called a Baylor? Of course, they're extinct now, but they *loved* marshmallows. Best way to get a clear picture of one: scatter some marshmallows about. It never failed.' He limped along, looking questioningly at Baylor. 'Do you like marshmallows?'

'Never had one.'

'Shame.'

'You were gonna ask us something?' said Fei.

Alfie gave her an uneasy smile. 'To be honest I'm not entirely sure I want to know the answer, but how did you know I was in Leos? Why have you come to find me?'

Fei scanned the empty streets, which were covered in flyers for the race.

The figure following them darted behind a tall bush, trimmed into a balloon shape.

Fei moved to Alfie's other side and placed her shoulder under his other arm.

Baylor gave a sigh of relief.

'Moth told us.'

'And why exactly did she tell you to come and find me?'

***

Number twelve peered round the side of the gates, watching the figure creep out from behind the balloon-shaped bush and cross the road a little further up. She stopped, pondered for a moment, then made her way back to the Merenial. She marched through the messy crowd and powered towards her ship. Her dark brown jacket flew up, revealing two pistols strapped to her belt, while her black pantaloons flapped in the wind.

Several people were standing by the red rope surrounding the Merenial, reaching over to touch the ship and taking photos in front of it. Number twelve charged in front of a group having their picture taken, clambered over the rope barrier, and jumped into the carriage.

She jerked on the engine and the propellers began to spin. Women shrieked, men clung to their hats, and number twelve smirked as the Merenial hummed off the green towards the gate. Staying just out of sight, above the clouds, she followed the group's progress below.

\*\*\*

Alfie rubbed his forehead as they stumbled back into the city centre.

'For years I've known this day would come – we've heard the warnings, seen the changes – but you never actually expect it to arrive. Even with some previously thriving species dwindling, I didn't think it would be upon us so soon,' he muttered, now hobbling on his own.

'No one did. Least of all, me,' replied Fei.

'She 'ad to convince me too,' said Baylor. 'But at least there is one silver lining in this cloud.' He looked up at the glowing peach shop front and smiled as the setting sun illuminated the delicate gold lettering.

Alfie hobbled forward, looking eager. 'Six weeks is too long.'

They crossed the road and stepped into the alleyway beside Peaches, went round to the back entrance – and froze. The back door was slightly ajar, the windowpane smashed, and glass shards were spread across the porch.

'Byrdy?' said Fei, choked.

They stood, paralysed.

Alfie's pain was replaced by a surge of energy. His face darkened and his jaw clenched as he kicked the door open and stormed through the room and up the dark staircase.

More shards were scattered across the floor.

'Alfie, wait!' Fei raced up behind him.

Baylor stepped into the shop and peered round. A sewing machine sat on the counter, a half-sewn mauve jacket lying on it; Byrdy's little counter stool had been tipped over and there were scuff marks leading to the back door.

Baylor clenched his eyes shut.

Alfie flung open doors and hurled things everywhere, but there was nothing to be found. No one.

'Alfie, I'm so sorry.' Fei's voice shook and Alfie sniffed, his face hard as he dashed past her, back down the stairs.

***

The figure climbed up the side of Peaches and leapt onto the second-floor window ledge opposite the top of the inside stairs. He peered round, darting back again as Alfie stormed down the stairs.

The faint sound of whirring could be heard; the figure watched the Merenial emerge from the sky on the other side of the road and park in the courtyard of another house.

As its engines were switched off, the hidden figure stared back through the window at the group, who were standing over the sewing machine.

A tear fell down Alfie's perfect cheek.

Fei reached over to pull Nessa's half-sewn jacket from beneath the needle. 'I'm so sorry, Alfie,' she sobbed. 'They must have been watching him – us. They must know, somehow.'

'It's not your fault, believe me. We've never been welcome in this city. They were just waiting for an excuse to take him,' Alfie gulped.

Baylor rubbed his forehaed. 'I'll find a way to get 'im out. You've already done so much for me.' He mumbled, squeezing Alfie's shoulder. 'I promise, I'll find a way.'

'I thought you were coming with *us*?' Fei said, wiping her eyes.

'Lemme do this for you both. I'll find Byrdy, you find Yana.'

'I can't let you put yourself at risk like that,' said Alfie, sniffing.

'Believe me, there's nothing I hate more than feeling useless, and I'll probably get in the way if I come with you. I have my sources here – I can figure it out.' He gave a weak smile, then coughed as Alfie gave him a bear-hug. 'Besides, they can't be far behind, it's not safe for you here anymore.'

'You're right, we can't stay here. The others will be back soon, and we need to be ready to leave.' Fei squeezed Alfie's arm as he released Baylor's winded body.

Alfie wiped his eyes. 'Yes, I'll… uhh… just grab some things.'

Fei and Baylor followed him upstairs.

\*\*\*

Number twelve darted through the darkness, stopping just before the back door of Peaches. She looked round carefully and spotted the figure on the windowsill.

'Bluddy cockroaches,' she mumbled.

She clambered up the fence of the house next door, and tiptoed silently across the roof, until she saw two pairs of feet running towards the shop and round the back. She dropped down and glanced over the side in time to see a tallish, slim girl, with two red hair buns, and a short, curvy woman, with two long, dark braids, skid round the corner, their arms full of provisions.

She tiptoed to the back of the house as silently as she could and watched as the figure clung to the side of the building, frozen. The girl and the woman stared at the back door, then ran inside.

\*\*\*

'Fei!' Cora shouted, looking fretfully round the empty shop.

Fei rushed to the top of the stairs to see Cora's bright green eyes staring back up at her.

'What happened here? Where is Byrdy?' asked Nessa.

'They've taken him, we can't stay here,' Fei sniffed, beckoning them upstairs.

'You go, I will put these things in a bag and come up in a minute,' said Nessa. She took the food and hurried through to the shop.

When she saw her mauve coat laid over the counter, purple thread strewn across it, she blinked back tears. She tied up the thread and snipped off the end, then crouched under the counter and found some paper bags, with a little gold peach stamped on each one. She placed the food on the counter next to her jacket, pulled out the bags and began filling them, sniffing as she packed.

Cora blazed upstairs and hugged Fei.

'Come and meet Alfie,' Fei said.

They walked through to the bedroom, where Alfie was rooting through clothes in a drawer and pulling out various items.

'Alfie, this is my sister Cora.'

Alfie peered round. The moon beamed through the window onto his shining cheeks; and Cora raised an eyebrow, taken aback.

'Nice to meet you,' Alfie smiled, before returning to his packing.

Nessa joined them. 'We need to leave – now,' she said. Alfie turned, a pile of clothes in his arms. 'Where are we going?'

Nessa examined Alfie's face, and her lips curled into a small smile.

Alfie sniffed again.

'Irinvale. Remember?' said Fei. Alfie nodded slowly. 'This is Nessa, by the way...'

***

The figure took out a creased notepad and a pen from his jacket pocket. Flipping open the front page, he scrawled the word 'Irinvale'.

A crack echoed across the roof, and he slid the pad back into his pocket. He stared above him.

Nothing. Only the sound of the group talking inside. He lowered his head back to the window.

*\*\*\**

'Vanessa Marini, nice to finally meet you.' Nessa offered her hand.

Alfie smiled and squeezed it. 'Your accent? Are you from the Andal islands? I learnt the language years back, though I'm a little rusty now.'

'I am, yes. Has estado tú?'

'No, sadly never visited, but I wrote a research paper on the native Agate cat. Beautiful creatures, so misunderstood. Lovely name – Vanessa. I hadn't even met one other Nathair before today, let alone two. I'm usually more fun, I promise.'

'It's okay, I am usually less tense.'

Fei raised an eyebrow at her.

'Call me Nessa.'

They smiled at each other.

'Did you know our Cora plans to be a Sardan?' said Fei, giving Cora's arm a squeeze.

'A Sardan ...' Alfie's face dropped.

*\*\*\**

Number twelve crouched on the window's arch, grinning and peering down at the figure. 'Good day t' ye, laddy.'

The figure gasped and reached for his pistol.

*\*\*\**

'Hey you don't happen to know…' began Alfie.

***

Number twelve grabbed hold of the arch, swung down and kicked the figure through the window.

CRASH!

# CHAPTER
# TWENTY-EIGHT

Baylor jumped back and fell to the ground; and they all shot round to see a figure tumble down the hall and flop in front of Baylor's feet, in a pile of broken glass.

Fei shot out her daggers, Nessa clicked out her knives and Cora swung her crossbow; they aimed at the doorway, the sound of footsteps growing closer.

Baylor stared wide-eyed at the motionless figure, breathing heavily, as Alfie dropped the clothes and reached for two huge axes behind the dresser. They all stood with their eyes fixed on the doorway.

Number twelve strolled along the hall and stood over her victim. Her large, blue, eyes were magnified even more by another set of lenses over her goggles. Baylor squinted at her in sudden recognition, as did Fei.

Alfie's eyes widened.

'BINA!' he beamed and dropped his axes, flinging his arms wide with delight.

Rabina marched through the group. Though small in stature, her stride was purposeful. She stopped in front of Alfie's open arms, stood on tiptoe and smacked him round the head.

'What th' hell were ye thinkin, prancin round in Roc territory 'n' gettin yerself locked up? EEJIT!' she yelled, as he sheepishly rubbed his head.

The group stared at her in confusion as she glared at them furiously, her hands on her hips.

'An' ye lot! P'raps ye should be checkin around before ye start given away all yer plans, huh? That cockroach wis sittin on yer windowsill, list'nin t' everythin.' They looked at the limp body in the hallway, then awkwardly back at Rabina's scolding stance.

'Yer welcome,' she said, folding her arms crossly.

Alfie looked sheepish.

Baylor clambered to his feet and shuffled over to stand beside the others.

'Everyone, meet Rabina Swiper, my Sardan extraordinaire!' said Alfie, blushing.

Rabina bowed.

Fei, Nessa and Baylor nodded, embarrassed.

Cora beamed.

Alfie gestured to Baylor. 'This is Baylor Doone.'

'Ah, aye, I tip mah bunnet te yer win, my friend.' Bina crushed his hand in hers.

'Thanks. I very much enjoyed beating you,' Baylor grinned and Rabina chuckled. 'Aye, ye cheeky bastard.'

'This is Cora Fourlise.'

Cora stepped forward, shook Bina's hand firmly.

Alfie smiled. 'She hopes to be a Sardan one day.'

'Aye, is that right? Well, wi' a handshake that tough, ye'r halfwey thare, lassie.'

Cora smiled wider than ever.

'This is – '

'Feina Fourlise. Ah know who ye are, 'n' ye as well, Vanessa. I've heard about ye both, 'n' a'm chuffed tae finally meet ye.'

Her comforting grasp filled them with joy.

'Right, enough with th' niceties. We have tae go, now!'

'Right, yes.' Alfie swung round, stuffed his clothes into a bag and strapped his axes to his back.

'I will grab the food,' Nessa said, flying downstairs.

'I'll shove him in a cupboard. We don't want it to look as if we're on the run,' said Cora, placing her spindly arms under the prone Silgir's armpits.

'Wait. How are we supposed to outrun them, on all those steps down the mountain?' said Fei.

'Ah, that's where ah kin help.' Bina raised a hand.

'The Merenial?' asked Baylor, his eyes widening.

'Aye,' Bina nodded.

Fei and Baylor exchanged excited looks as Nessa returned with their clothes and the food she'd packed.

'We need to go out the back, we don't know who might be watching the house,' said Fei.

Cora nodded and ushered them all out.

Nessa, Cora and Rabina hurried down the stairs to the hallway, while Fei and Baylor took one last look at Alfie's bedroom. Alfie was standing in the corner, staring at the dresser, on which sat a small photo in a frame, of Byrdy and his mother. He reached forward and opened the frame. Behind the picture was another small, square photo. Alfie turned it over and looked at the blurry picture of him and Byrdy, clasped in each other's arms, smiling. A tear trickled down his cheek.

Fei placed her hand over his and closed it round the picture. 'Make sure to bring this with you. Baylor will find him.'

'I will, I promise.'

Alfie nodded, swallowing back tears. 'I can't lose him.'

'You won't,' said Fei, clutching his huge fist.

'Shift yer behinds, kiddos. We've got a ship tae catch!' Bina barked in the doorway.

'Let's do this,' said Fei, giving Alfie and Baylor an encouraging nod. They picked up their bags and hurried down the stairs. Cora, Nessa and Bina were already waiting outside.

'This wey.' It was dark and Bina beckoned them towards an alleyway at the end of the courtyard. They sneaked round the back of the houses, then held their breath as they saw four figures dressed in black creep across the road to Peaches.

They waited until the Silgir had disappeared down the alleyway before darting across the road.

*\*\**

A mangled eye peered round the side of the building, where the four Silgir had appeared. Harryn stared, his pale face stoic, as the group dashed across the road and down an alleyway. He crept out, six more Silgir behind him.

'Be ready.' His eyes were fixed on the road ahead, and he gripped the hilt of his sword. The four Silgir cocked their shotguns and silently followed their leader through the shadows, towards the alleyway.

\*\*\*

There it was: the carriage in all its burgundy beauty; the vast cream balloon glowing in the moonlight. Baylor gawped and ran his hand along the carriage.

'Right, e'yone in!' Bina flung her bag inside.

Nessa stared at her, bewildered.

Alfie smirked. 'Everyone in,' he smiled.

Nessa nodded, understanding.

'That's whit ah said.'

Alfie gave Nessa an encouraging nudge. Baylor watched them pile in; and Fei strode over, to give him a hug.

'Thank you, Bay, for everything,' she said, her chest tight as she placed a chunk of their winnings in his hands. 'This should at least get you out of here – '

'No way. You need this more than I do.'

'You won! And don't worry, we kept some.' Fei grinned and pushed his hands away.

'Thanks Fei.' He gave an awkward smile. 'I'll get Byrdy back, I promise.'

'And we'll get Yana back... *I* promise.'

'Now, get in, and go and save the world,' he said.

Fei climbed into the Merenial and shut the small door behind her, while Bina switched on the engine. The propellers began to whirl, and Baylor held onto his cap.

They all waved as the Merenial began to hum off the ground.

BANG!

A bullet soared out of the darkness behind Baylor and ripped through his calf. He cried out and dropped to the ground, clutching his leg, as three Silgir appeared behind him, aiming at the ship.

'No!' Fei screamed, flinging her arm over the side of the ship.

BANG, BANG!

Two more bullets slammed into the carriage. Fei leapt to open the door of the Merenial.

'Fei, no!' shouted Cora.

'Hold 'er in!' yelled Bina. We cannae risk her getting shot now.'

Bina eased the Merenial up between the buildings and Alfie wrapped his arms around Fei, holding her in as she grabbed at the carriage door. 'I'm so sorry, Fei.'

Fei writhed in agony as she saw Baylor's blood-soaked hands pull out the spanner he had hidden in his sock. Swinging with all his might, he smacked one of the Silgir hard in the side of the head, toppling him to the ground.

'We have to help him!' Fei screamed.

Baylor swung his arm up to the ship and yelled. 'GO, FEI!'

The group ducked as more bullets flew towards them.

'A'm sorry, lassie, but *yer* lyfe is far tae precious!' called Bina as she steered.

Cora pointed her crossbow at the black uniforms; her arrow whistled down and blasted through the skull of another Silgir, sending him flying backwards.

Baylor grimaced and squeezed his calf, struggling to stay upright as blood streamed down his leg.

The Merenial continued to ascend. Fei desperately looked around for any nearby trees, but there was nothing but darkness and emptiness. The remaining Silgir continued to send streams of bullets into the air.

Baylor swung again, narrowly missing another, who then shoved the butt of his gun into Baylor's stomach, making him double over. Two more Silgir rushed to restrain him and pulled his head up to face the ship, while his cap tumbled to the ground.

Fei watched in horror as Harryn strolled out of the darkness and glared up at her. He strode round to face Baylor, then looked back up at her, smirking.

'NO!' she screamed, in despair.

Harryn swung the butt of his pistol into Baylor's jaw, sending him slumping into the Silgir's arms.

He hung there motionless, blood seeping from his leg and forehead.

Fei closed her eyes as tears streamed down her cheeks. She watched as Harrin gave a wry smile, tipped his cap to them, then disappear beneath the clouds.

\*\*\*

Harryn stared up at the airship disappearing into the darkness, as cleaned the blood off his gun.

A Silgir shuffled up behind him. 'Where should we take him, sir?'

'Strap him in with the other one. Then take them both to her,' he instructed.

'And shall we follow the ship, sir?'

Harryn glared at the Silgir. 'Are you quite well?'

'Uh, yes, sir.'

'Do you know what ship that was?'

The guard stared at him blankly. 'Yes, sir.'

'Then you should know that is quite impossible. Take him away,' Harryn growled, then looked back up to where the Merenial had vanished. 'Besides, I believe I know where they are going...'

'Very good, sir.'

The Silgir shuffled off. Two of them dragged Baylor's limp body back through the alley, leaving a long trail of blood them.

\*\*\*

'We did not find anything, sir.' Four Silgir strode out of the house and stood behind him.

Harryn scowled and marched into Peaches, the troopers scattering out of his way. Glass crunched beneath his boots. He scanned the hallway and grimaced at the persistent aroma of Byrdy's scented candles.

Lip curled, he strode upstairs, crunching down once again on the glass scattered over the landing.

'What is this?' he glowered at the Silgir who had followed him.

'We're not sure, sir. We were informed the back door was the only damage made during his capture.'

Harryn examined the landing.

'Something else has happened. Has our man contacted us yet?'

'No, sir.'

Harryn peered into Alfie's room. 'He's still here.'

He stepped over the broken glass and narrowed his eyes at the bathroom doorway. Gliding forward, he studied the reflected light glinting off a scattering of shards. Then he pushed open the door and squinted at the faint bleached outline of a rectangle on the floor in front of the bath. Spotting a bathmat lying on the floor in the corner beneath a cupboard, the edge slightly folded over, he strode towards it.

'We checked the cupboard, sir.'

Harryn's jaw tightened as he grabbed hold of the bathmat and pulled it back, revealing a trapdoor.

The commander crouched, then turned to glare at the Silgir. He pulled on the trapdoor handle, and it flew open, knocking into the cupboard behind it, where two boots could be seen. He pulled open the other door, exposing the figure crumpled up inside.

'Apologies, sir. We did not think to look underneath.'

Rochford, the Silgir in front, was considerably more confident than his companion. He was tall and slim, with a slicked-back bun. He met Harryn's glare without flinching.

'Clearly. Perhaps you should spend more time planning and calculating, rather than tormenting the prisoner, if you are to progress any further. What a disappointment you are, Lieutenant!'

'That Peach prick called me a pillock, sir,' said Rochford, his face twitching.

Harryn edged closer. 'I fear for you, Lieutenant, if you allow yourself to be moved by mere words. Clearly, I have misjudged your capabilities,' he hissed.

'Apologies, sir, it won't happen again.' Rochford found himself sweating, under Harryn's piercing stare.

'Search him,' said Harryn.

Rochford nodded, scurried over to the figure in the hole and began rooting through his jacket. He put his hand inside a discreet pocket from which he withdrew a little worn notebook.

'Sir.'

Rochford flipped over a couple of pages, stopping at the one with 'Irinvale' scrawled across it, the end of the 'e' trailing off.

He handed the notebook to Harryn, the scrawled page facing up. 'What does it mean, sir?'

Harryn's scowl was replaced by a sinister smile, as he turned to look out of the window.

'Sir?'

Harryn's gaze met Rochford's dumb face. 'They're going after the dagger,' he said, and strode out of the room.

Rochford scurried after him.

# CHAPTER TWENTY-NINE

The impact of the hard dry ground began to hammer through Moth's dragging feet, sending painful jolts up her throbbing legs. Her mouth was bitterly dry, and she couldn't remember the last time she'd eaten. She stopped for a second and leaned against a tree. The pink imprints from her gas mask were now so deep that her cheeks and forehead were permanently bruised. She pulled it off and sank to the ground, letting her head flop back with exhaustion. She wasn't sure how long she had been walking – perhaps a week or two?

Staring up at the sky, she watched as a patch of grey tumbled aside in the distance, revealing the top of a dark turret. Her eyes widened, as she twisted round.

'Brunas,' she wheezed.

She wobbled to her feet, hauled up her weary body, and began trudging towards the turret, sweating into her jacket as the sun beat down.

The gravel desert stretched as far she could see, through pockets of twisted coal trees.

Another grey cloud rolled across the path ahead. Moth strained for her gas mask, wincing as she dragged it down over her aching face.

Tok, tok, tok.

She froze.

A long, spindly leg emerged from the grey, and her heart began to race. She limped as quickly and silently as she could behind a tree and fumbled for her pistol. Having managed to push the last six bullets inside the barrel, her hands were numb as she peered round the tree.

The Tok strode into the daylight and Moth's eyes widened in shock as it made its way down the path, its huge rippling back twitching in the dappled sun rays. It gave a low growl as it clawed the ground, scanning the area. Two more Toks appeared behind it. One was irritably scratching at its arm, which seemed to be smoking.

Moth peered round the trunk of the tree; the Tok with the smoking arm had taken a few steps; it growled and hissed at the first and largest Tok, which swiped at it in return and screeched. Moth darted back and rested against the tree, gasping for air, her heart pounding.

She clutched the pistol against her chest, cupping it with her hand, closed her eyes and breathed in. The smell of rotten food and damp stung her nose.

TOK.

Her eyes shot open to meet the skeletal chest of one of the beasts. It opened its bloodied jaws, staring at her with black, soulless eyes.

Gasping, she aimed her pistol and the Tok swiped out, it's thundering claws narrowly missing her face. Moth threw herself to the side, rolling away, then swung round and pulled the trigger.

*One.*

Missed!

She fired again as the Tok lunged towards her.

*Two.*

The bullet pounded into the Tok's chest, knocking it to the ground.

The sound ricocheted through the air, and Moth twisted her throbbing body to see the other three Toks careering towards her, screeching.

She scrambled up and began pelting towards the castle as fast as she could. Her ankles buckled and her muscles screamed with exhaustion as she ran through the twisted trees, stumbling over dried twigs and thick detritus. She could hear the Toks getting nearer, smashing their way through dead tree trunks. She stopped, pulled off her gas mask, and aimed at the closest Tok.

Her arm shook.

*Three.*

The bullet thrashed through the Tok's arm. It screeched and slowed but continued charging towards her. Her heart was thumping out of her chest as she reloaded her pistol, cocked it and moved her hand to steady her arm. Taking aim, she fired.

*Four.*

The bullet flew into its skull and the Tok tumbled to the ground, dead. The last Tok leapt over its body, undaunted.

Moth darted back, knocking her heel into a rock, as she fired again.

*Five.*

The bullet hit its leg. She fell back winded, and she watched in horror as the pistol tumbled away out of reach.

The Tok screeched as it grew closer, the ground vibrating with its pounding feet. Moth lay in terror, scanning desperately around her, and spotted a long, thick stick.

The Tok charged, spitting and snapping as Moth gathered all her remaining strength and thrust the stick into its mouth as it leapt forward.

A tear squeezed from her eye as she felt her arms failing, and the Tok's hammering jaw closing in. The Tok slashed her shoulder with its claw. She screamed and felt her arm give way as the Tok's head came crashing towards her. She felt herself losing consciousness, and her vision begin to tunnel.

BANG.

The Tok's body flopped onto hers, its weight crushing her rasping chest as she strained to take a breath. Her head flopped to one side, as she saw, through foggy eyes, two figures running towards her through the grey.

She exhaled and let her eyes close.

*** 

Cold. She felt so cold. She opened her eyes. It was dark and damp and she winced in pain as she attempted to move her shoulder.

'Oop, careful Mothy! Don't get that wet now, you've already used up your bandage ration,' a sarcastic voice shrilled, followed by a wheezing laugh.

Moth grimaced, as she turned her head – to see dark, damp cell walls.

She placed her hand on the floor, straining to push herself up. The pain in her shoulder was excruciating, and she groaned in agony. Looking with trepidation to her right, she saw the hazy outline of a man. He was holding a lantern, which lit up his grinning face, his pointy ginger beard wiggling with excitement. He stared at her.

Moth glared back.

'Wakey wakey, eggs and bakey,' he said mockingly, tapping on the cell bars with a long black cane. He clutched the top of the cane with his small hands covered in rings, which only made his hands look smaller.

He was sitting on a small stool beside the cell, wearing blue and brown checked trousers, shiny red shoes, a brown waistcoat over a white shirt, and a rather obnoxiously long black cape that was lined with the strangest black fur Moth had ever seen.

'Well haven't you made this easy for me, Mothy. I thought I'd have to come and find you and your merry band of bastards. But no, you've dropped yourself right on my doorstep!' He giggled like a naughty six-year-old, and rubbed his hands together, his ratty face quivering with delight.

Moth faced him, trying not to react to the pain that stabbed her shoulder every time she moved.

'Where is Jemiah, Konstantin?' she murmured.

Konstantin put a finger to his chin, with an expression of fake confusion. 'Hmm…I know, he's washing his hair. Wait. No, he's cooking tea. No, he's out shopping!' Konstantin gave another long, loud, wheezy laugh and slapped his thigh. 'Ah, things have changed around here, Mothy. For the better, this time.'

'What have you done to him?' Her jaw clenched.

Konstantin looked down. 'His failings were his own. He did it to himself,' he spat, examining one of his long, dirty nails.

'WHERE IS HE?' she barked, lunging forward, forgetting the pain in her shoulder.

Konstantin giggled as she clung to the bars, glaring at him. 'Ah, you haven't changed. Just like old daddio, eh?' He looked her up and down. 'Well, sort of.'

He wheezed again and stood, before bending back to meet her gaze. 'And you'll end up just like him.' His face darkened as he stared at Moth through the bars. 'At least you will, if I have anything to do with it.'

'You're a despicable cockroach and a traitor,' Moth hissed.

'Oooh, fighting words, Mothy. Call it what you like, I call it business. The second your buddies arrive, they're gonna find themselves in here with you.' Standing up, he waved his arm at the cell. 'One pretty package, and one pretty payment for me.' He rubbed his hands together.

Moth slumped back against the cell wall. 'And you were always so good at business weren't you, Konstantin,' she snarled.

Konstantin scowled. 'I have the city – what do you have? A new name and a wet arse.'

'At least I didn't have to kill daddy in his sleep to take power; I'm assuming that's how you did it, since you're in no shape to engage in any kind of combat.'

'I'd be quite happy to show you very soon, Mothy girl, the kind of combat I enjoy.' He squeezed the hilt of his cane.

'No, I'm tired, you're boring me now. Leave.' She waved dismissively.

Konstantin ground his teeth and smacked the railings with his cane. 'You have no idea what awaits you.'

'Bored.' Moth faced away from him.

Crunch.

Moth's nostrils picked up the piercingly sweet smell of a ripe apple; she closed her eyes in an attempt to block out the sound of Konstantin slurping.

'Yum, yum, yummy. They don't make 'em like this anymore.' He took another large bite.

Moth turned to see him slicing off small bits of cheese and jamming them onto a fork, along with another piece of apple. Her mouth began to water as Konstantin looked at her, shrugged his shoulders and wiggled his brow grinning. He then reached for a cup beside him and slurped down what looked like creamy milk, spilling most of it down his front.

Moth's stomach growled in agony.

'Oh dear, messy me. Never mind, got plenty more upstairs,' he smirked. He flung the half-eaten apple across the floor. 'I think this was all yours, I'm so sorry. I guess you'll just have to wait till... we can find you some more, and who knows how long that will take? Upstairs is sooo far away.' He stuck out his bottom lip.

A large brown dog trotted down the stairs towards him, licking its lips and staring at the block of cheese in his hands.

'Aww, baby want some cheese? Here you go, baby. Aww precious boo boo!'

Moth watched, tormented, as Konstantin fed the block of cheese to the dog, while tickling its large, drooling chin.

'You see, Mothy, in this castle we like to have a hierarchy, so everyone knows where they stand. Notice how my Reggie is on this side of the bars...' He gave her a menacing grin as he stroked the dog, which was now lapping up the remainder of the milk. 'You sit below the bottom. Or below *his* bottom, if you like.' He giggled and Moth dragged herself across the cell, pulling herself up to face him.

'You have thrust yourself into the firing line, fool. And you can be sure we will not miss that stupid shiny head of yours,' she hissed.

Konstantin stood face-to-face with her, his expression unmoving.

Then he suddenly burst out laughing, wheezing and spitting. Moth glared at him as he slapped his hands on his knees. Reggie was bounding around him, barking excitably.

'Oh Mothy, no wonder you've found yourself in this pickle, if it's my barnet, or lack thereof, that you're focusing on!' He sighed, patted Reggie on the head, picked up his cane and shook his head, grinning at her. 'You have no idea, do you? Ahh, this is just fantastic.'

Moth's eye twitched with confusion, and Konstantin's grin shifted to a scowl. 'Did you really think Ela was just gonna sit back and let you all band together, without retaliating in any way?' He walked back towards her. 'And do you really think the Aon is the most formidable force in the world?' He rolled his eyes at the word 'Aon' and planted his face close to hers. His breath stank of wine and tobacco and Moth scrunched her face in disgust. 'You have sorely underestimated the status quo here, Mothy. She's closer than ever,' he whispered.

'Well, I hope for Ela's sake, Abel has been taking better care of his oral hygiene than you have,' she smirked.

Konstantin scowled and thrust his arm through the bars, grabbing her shoulder, squeezing it hard, and pulling her towards him. Her face slammed into the metal, and she winced as Konstantin whispered in her ear.

'You think this is pain? You don't know what pain is.' He threw her back, sending her flying onto the cold, wet cell floor. 'My brother would never have ended up like this,' he growled.

Moth's face twitched. 'You've never had a brother.'

'That's for damn sure!' he snarled.

A small cloud of blood began to work its way through her shirt. She clutched it and turned to face the window again.

Konstantin looked down at Reggie, who wagged his tail. He straightened his jacket, puckered his lips and reached down to scratch the dog on the head.

'Aww, precious boo boo, who's my good boy? Who's my good boy? Go on, get it!'

Taking a dog biscuit from his inside pocket, Konstantin threw it towards the stairs. Reggie bounded over and began crunching out of sight. Konstantin gave a loud and dramatic sigh, arching his eyebrows as he clapped his hands together.

'Right, well, enjoy your stay. Lovely to have you! Can't wait to meet your friends, heard so much about them. Nighty night!'

He picked up the lantern, and backed out of the cell, slamming the door behind him.

A moment later the door opened again, and Konstantin popped his head round. 'Oh, and try not to die overnight, or do... Whatever!'

The door closed again, and Moth could hear his wheezing laughter echoing down the corridor. She hung her head as tears trickled down her cheeks.

She'd never felt so alone.

But then she remembered, the others would not be far behind. She could not let them walk into this trap.

Mustering her last reserves of energy, she lifted her head, gazed out of the window, then dragged her body into a kneeling position. She pressed her trembling thumb hard onto the red haze on her shirt where it covered her shoulder. Her face contorted and her eyes welled as she pressed the blood on her thumb into a small dot over her heart.

She pressed her palms to the ground and closed her eyes, picturing Bisou's face, as she whispered, 'Do not come here, do not try to find me, stay away from this place.'

A tear fell and soaked into the wet floor, sending gentle shockwaves through the ground.

\*\*\*

Bisou, who had been munching on a rare yellowing patch of grass with Clyde, jolted and raised his head, whining. This shocked Clyde, but not enough to stop him returning to his meal. Bisou paced, whining and sniffing the ground as a gust of wind from the West flowed through his fur and nostrils. He lifted his head and sniffed again. Pricking his ears, he barked, staring in the direction of the breeze.

\*\*\*

Moth gasped and fell back onto the floor. Tears of frustration rolled down her cheeks as she lay back, and closed her eyes.

# CHAPTER THIRTY

The Merenial spiralled through the clouds, down the side of Solas Mountain. The light was dwindling, and the air became thicker and greyer, making them cough.

Fei sat at the back, staring over the side. Her arms were wrapped round her legs, with wet circles on each knee. Her stomach twisted with nausea, while they all sat in silence.

The Merenial bumped onto the dry, cracked earth beside the mill and Fei jumped over the side, making for the forest.

'Fei, wait!' Cora jumped out and caught her up. 'What are you doing?'

'We need to find Clyde and Bisou – and the dagger.' She sniffed.

Bina, Nessa and Alfie watched from afar as they clambered out of the carriage and started heaving their bags onto their backs.

'He will be fine.'

'We don't know that.'

'You're right, we don't, but worrying about it isn't going to help.

'I know. But we have a promise to keep. We *have* to get that dagger,' said Fei, burying her face in her hands.

Cora nodded, her eyes moving past her sister, and beaming as a gentle bark sounded behind her. Fei spun round to see Bisou wagging his tail.

'B!' they chorused as the Paodin lurched forward, licking their faces and running round them in a frenzy of excitement.

Alfie lifted his bag over the side of the carriage and turned to see where the shouting was coming from.

His jaw dropped, as he let his bag fall to the floor. 'Stop!' he muttered under his breath, edging towards Bisou, watching as he bounded round Fei and Cora. The edges of his smile almost in his ears.

'B!' Nessa beamed and hurried past Alfie to scratch Bisou's chin and receive a long lick on the face.

'Oh boy,' said Bina, shaking her head as she watched Alfie edge closer, awestruck.

'And no one thought to tell me we had a Paodin joining us!' he said in wonder.

Fei, Cora and Nessa laughed as they brushed the dried mud off themselves.

'I think I'm gonna cry.' Alfie's lip wobbled as he stopped in front of Bisou, who sat staring at him, tipping his head to the side. Alfie bowed his head, his eyes fixed on Bisou's. Bisou continued to stare at him.

Bina chuckled to herself while she tinkered with the Merenial's engine.

'Bow, yes bow. Oh god, what was next?' he mumbled. He raised his head up to find Bisou right up in his face, panting. Alfie gulped and Bisou whined, furiously wagging his tail.

'Oh my,' he gawped. 'Hello,' he said, his voice trembling with joy.

That was all the invitation Bisou needed. Bisou lunged, knocking Alfie back, and began licking his face, wagging his tail at top speed.

'Bluddy eejit,' muttered Bina, giggling to herself.

The unmistakable sound of Clyde's hooves ricocheted through the ground and Fei turned to see him plod out of the forest.

'Clyde!' She wrapped her arms round his thick neck as far as she could reach and squeezed him tight. He snorted and nudged her with his nose, nodding at the ground.

'So one-track minded,' she smiled and kneeled down to place her hand on the yellowish grass.

It sprouted immediately and Clyde buried his head in it. Fei chuckled and returned to the others.

Bisou sat panting on the ground, his mouth steaming; Alfie had crouched beside him, and was now examining him carefully.

'Did you know a Paodin has the digestive system of a carnivore *and* a herbivore? Like a cow, they have a caecum, which allows them to survive primarily on grass, if they need to. But they don't however, have four stomachs like a cow.' Alfie ran his hands along Bisou's antlers.

The others nodded with interest.

No, they didn't know that.

'And did you know they steam after long periods of exertion? Along with panting, that's how they regain their energy, you know, quicker.'

Again, they nodded.

'Have you seen him breathe fire yet? The fire is said to have magical properties, but we have no data on exactly what it can do,' he said, running his hands through Bisou's mossy green fur.

Alfie looked up at Fei and Cora, who stood nodding.

'Yeah, he exorcised a dryad with it,' said Cora.

'Amazing. That probably means he'll be around thirteen or fourteen years old. The lush colour of his fur suggests he's still very young. Paodin can only breathe fire after they have reached sexual maturity, which is usually around twelve to fourteen years old. They live a long time. The oldest recorded Paodin was one hundred and twenty-one years old.'

Alfie stroked Bisou's head, while Bisou gave Alfie's face a gentle lick.

'Fourteen years?' Fei's brow furrowed.

'Give or take a couple of years.'

'That's when Gee died. Mum's Paodin.' Fei looked thoughtful and Cora nodded.

'I'm sorry, another Paodin? Do you know how rare they are? And you're telling me there are two?'

'There's only ever one Paodin in the world at a time,' Fei said.

'Who told you that?'

'Moth. She said they can't go extinct, but there's only ever one in the world.'

'Well, that would explain why they're so hard to find. They tend to have bonded relationships with particular humans. Almost imprinted, you might say. This one is Moth's?'

The girls nodded.

'Pfft, she kept that one quiet!'

'Imagine if she had tried to take him up there,' said Nessa.

'True. Well, honestly, I'm surprised he came with you and didn't stay with Moth.'

Bisou licked Alfie's face again, then trotted over to Cora, who began scratching behind his ear, making him tap his back leg on the ground.

'Fascinating. Byrdy would have loved to meet him.' Alfie stood and gave a weak smile. 'Honestly, if I see him breathe fire, I may die of amazement. Just forewarning you.'

'We better get a shift on sharpish, kiddos, if we wanna dodge the cockroaches.' Rabina stood with her hands on her hips.

A few minutes later, Alfie shuffled back to the ship and peered over the side of the carriage to see Rabina with her rump in the air, fiddling with something under the dashboard of the merenial.

'Bluddy wiring, so bloody dark down here. Godamm it!' she growled, her voice muffled. Sparks flew out and around her grumbling face.

'Anything I can help you with?' Alfie offered, reaching down for his bag.

'We need tae mak' sure they cannae use her against us. A'm twistin th' wiring. Ahh, hell's bells!' A particularly vibrant spark flew out and landed on her arm.

'We should probably deflate her and drag her into the forest then,' he said, looking up at the cream balloon.

'Aye, we'll strap her to a pair o' carthorses. Clyde 'n' ye will be perfect!' she chuckled.

'Hilarious.'

'Ahh, thare we go! Huv a go a' drivin her noo, ye Silgir scum!' She popped out from under the dashboard and Alfie reached his arm down to help her out of the rather small space she had squeezed herself into.

'A'm fine, a'm fine. Got maself in 'ere, ah can get maself out.' She clambered up.

'How we gonna do this?' Alfie examined the balloon hovering above them.

Rabina tapped her foot thoughtfully, then whipped out her pistol and shot several holes in it, making the air gush out with a whoosh. The group shot round to see the balloon deflating into the carriage.

'That'll do it. But it will have also alerted every Tok within a five-kilometre radius, so we'd best get going.' Alfie made his way to Clyde.

'Aye, c'mon pony.' Bina jumped out of the carriage and skipped behind Alfie, clicking her fingers at him.

'Okay,' Alfie smiled ruefully and pushed Rabina to the side as she chuckled.

He looked over to see Bisou bounding around with the girls, barking. Blinking back tears, he quietly fiddled with the straps of his bag.

'He *wull* meet him one day.'

'What?'

'Byrdy 'n' Bisou. They'll meet, 'n' ye'll see him again, too, ah promise.' Rabina gave Alfie a warm smile.

Alfie nodded and sniffed, cupped his hand over hers and gave it a squeeze.

'Besides, he's git mah jacket tae finish.'

Alfie laughed. 'He's had a lot on!'

'That's nae excuse.'

She grinned and Alfie squeezed her tight.

*** 

It was dark now and the group had pulled the Merenial deep into the forest, having decided to rest for a while before travelling on to Irinvale. They sat round a fire, compliments of Bisou. Alfie had almost fainted in awe, watching him light a pile of branches.

For a time, they relaxed and thought about nothing much. It was quiet and peaceful. This was something none of them had experienced for a while, and wholly welcome. They ate some of the bread and cheese Cora and Nessa had bought.

Although they had all been in desperate need of a break, Fei couldn't help thinking about Moth, Baylor and Byrdy. And, judging by Alfie's sad expression, Byrdy was on his mind too.

'Byrdy loves cheese,' he said. 'We had a cheese platter the first evening we ever spent together.'

'How long have you been together?' asked Cora.

'Three years.'

'Long time,' Nessa smiled.

'Yeah. See, if we lived in another world, I would've asked him to marry me ages ago.' Alfie hung his head. 'I hope I will get the chance one day.'

'You will. Byrdy will be okay,' Fei reassured him.

'Aye, Byrdy's a pure tough laddie. Ain't nae Silgir gonnae get to him.' Rabina agreed, ripping through her cheese.

Bisou, having already gotten some small cheese blocks from Cora, lifted his head and looked up at the spinning piece in Alfie's hands.

He licked his lips.

'I wish I had your faith; and you're right, he is strong, but there's only so much torment anyone can take. I just hope I find him before he reaches his limit.'

Fei was fiddling with her bread. 'Faith is all we have. If we don't believe we can actually do this, there's no point and she's already won. Blind delusion, whatever. We have to keep imagining the day we succeed – especially now.' She laughed to herself. 'God I've changed!'

Nessa spoke up. 'I never imagined I would be thrust from my comfortable life like this. In fact, as you well know, I resisted it at first. But I would not have it any other way now. If it were not for this, I would have continued with my head in the sand, thinking I was happy. But now it is obvious, I understand my purpose in life.' She stared into the fire after exchanging a smile with Fei.

'So, how did you two meet?' Cora asked Bina and Alfie.

Rabina, with a large hunk of cheese in her mouth, smirked and nodded her head at Alfie. 'Well, five years ago, this one was jailed for flipping over the tables of traders selling illegal bush meat. Her cousin Jero – '

'Prat,' muttered Bina.

\*\*\*

Jero's eyes flashed open.

\*\*\*

' – was refusing to bail her out. During my time at university, I studied the Roc bird. Hence why I entered the restricted zone in Leos: Roc meat was what the poachers were after. It's said to have magical properties, or some rubbish like that. I had planned to track the poachers and take them out … subtly.' He raised an eyebrow at Bina, who frowned.

'You know, so they couldn't keep selling it,' Alfie continued.

'Ye did a week after. Dinnae be scowlin at me,' she said, through a mouthful of bread and cheese.

The group chuckled.

'But of course, that didn't go to plan, and they scarpered.'

'Ah wis in th' area because ah wis tracking this one.' Bina pointed at Alfie. 'We traced his energy, found out he had ne Sardan lookin out for him. So ah went after him, 'n' ah got a bit side tracked.' She gave a toothy grin and shoved another large piece of bread in her mouth.

'I was there in the marketplace when it happened, saw everything. The drama: it was fantastic.' Alfie grinned and Bina shook her head. 'Safe to say I knew she was someone I could get on with. But I found out she would be going away for – '

'Five bloody years, th' bastards! Fur disrupting th' peace!' She shook her head, spitting out some breadcrumbs.

'Yeah, and I couldn't have that. So, a couple of nights later I broke into the cell and got her out. And we've been inseparable ever since. Right, buddy?'

Alfie gave Rabina a bearhug. She attempted a smile, as her cheeks – puffed out with food – squashed against his chest, to which she gave his arm an agreeable tap.

'What made you want to become a Sardan?' asked Cora edging towards Bina.

'Mah brother Roger, God rest him, was hunted 'n' executed by Silgir whin he wis eighteen. Ah wis ten whin he died. Ah've had some Mage in mah family line ower th' years, 'n' whin thay cam tae investigate our house, he wis branded undesirable 'n' dealt weth. Ah swore that day ah wid dedicate mah lyfe t'ensurin ne one is hunted 'n' murdurred fur bein' something thay cannae help.'

Fei, Nessa and Alfie hung their heads.

'So, do all Nathair have a Sardan?' asked Fei.

'All th' ones we know aboot, lassie. Th' Prime Minister wis adamant she watched ower ye, an' has done all yer lyfe.' Bina gave her a warm smile. 'She never wanted tae reveal herself 'til ye wur ready. She worried, after yer mother passed, that th' weight o' responsibility wid nae allow ye a normal childhood. She hoped never to bring ye in at all.'

Fei swallowed. 'I wish I had known, then perhaps something could've been done sooner.'

'Thengs wur always gonna happen th' wey thay have, whether ye'd known or not. Th' important thing is wur together now, 'n' our eyes ur more open than ever!'

Fei smiled as Bina reached forward and squeezed her hand tight.

Very tight.

Fei winced, but it was the loveliest pain she had felt for a while.

Cora leaned forward. 'We have to think of it this way: if literally no one cared, this would have happened a long time ago.'

The group nodded.

'Aye, thare's a lot more folk out thare wanting change. Thay just dinnae know how thay kin help, 'n' tis scary. Thare are those who simply can't.'

'Sí, It is not just about stopping one thing; it is about making a long-lasting change. There will be more Elas in our lifetimes, we just have to make it very hard for them to gain any momentum.'

Fei shuffled closer to the fire, spreading out her palms to its warmth. 'I feel I've known you all my whole life. Everything you're saying, it's always been there, waiting for me. I just needed that push.'

Cora smiled at her sister.

'No estás solo. We all did.'

Alfie and Rabina nodded.

Fei took both Alfie and Nessa's hands in hers. Bisou barked and wagged his tail as the grass beneath the group bloomed bright under the fire. Small shoots opened and they looked up to see the leaves on the dry trees fluttering in the breeze. Even the fire seemed to pick up a little.

Fei's eyes bulged. 'We almost forgot. There's a fourth.'

'A fourth what?' asked Alfie, bewildered.

'A fourth Nathair,' said Cora.

Alfie and Bina drew back, Bina's mouth so wide open they could see exactly what she had been eating all night.

'That cannae be,' she whispered, through a mass of half-chewed food.

'How do you know this?' asked Alfie.

'When Ela possessed that dryad, she must have thought we knew as much as she did. She said, 'With thousands of us, and four of you...' We assumed she meant Nathair.'

'But we've only traced th' energy of three. Ah dinnae understand.' Bina swallowed.

Nessa looked thoughtful. 'Whoever they are, they must have buried that part of them so deeply, their Nathair is almost dead.'

'Can that happen?' wondered Cora.

Alfie choked back tears. 'If you're threatened and condemned enough times for being something you can't help, you sometimes want nothing more than for that side of you to die; for it never to have existed. Desire it enough and it can happen. There are parts of me I used to wish were dead. They must be terrified.'

'We gotta find that bloody dagger!' Fei said and gulped the wine Nessa had poured her.

'Aye, lassie, we bluddy doo.' Bina thrust her fist in the air, and also took a swig of wine.

Nessa and Alfie raised their cups over the fire, and Fei and Bina followed suit, while Cora shrugged and raised her cup of water.

# CHAPTER THIRTY-ONE

The group took it in turns to keep watch as they rested for
the night. It was decided that Fei should not be allowed to
take watch on her own, and was subsequently grounded.
The effects of the grey were gradually worsening: even
with the five of them there, the trees were taking longer to
turn green, and small shoots strained to break through the
hard, dry ground. They did not see any stars that night and
the grey seemed to hover over them, like a suffocating
oven. They found themselves in no need of their blankets,
and Bisou was steaming noticeably more.

*So warm, urgh.*

Fei opened one eye and looked round. Nessa was
using her dagger to carve an animal that looked like
Bisou out of a piece of wood. The fire sent glowing
orange blooms over her face as she concentrated. Cora
was lying down, hugging Bisou and her crossbow. Bisou
was on his back, hooves in the air, and tongue flopping
over his twitching mouth.

*A Paodin dream perhaps? Cute.*

Rabina was sitting against a tree, sleeping, arms crossed, with a pistol in each hand. Her head lolled to one side, and she was snoring loudly. Alfie seemed to be the only one who felt cold, his muscular body creating a hill of blankets next to the fire. Even asleep he was beautiful.

The next morning, they moved off again, and the next, and the next... After a while they lost count of how many days they had been walking; their feet ached and their shoes rubbed. Clyde grew more and more disgruntled, even though Alfie was there to share the load. They trudged on, wandering through the overgrown ruins of an old village.

A sad, hollow sensation passed through them as they imagined the lives of the people who had once lived there – stories, families, a community.

Expelled.

It really wasn't that long ago. A time they could remember, and a time that sometimes felt like a dream. They had grown so used to their strange new world, they hardly ever talked about the time before. In polite society an individual who started such a conversation would be swiftly ostracised.

The group arrived in another of the many abandoned villages. A red and white sun canopy poked through a large brown bush and Fei spotted a sign saying 'reamery'. She assumed the 'C' was hidden by the mass of dried-up ivy stems which, although practically leafless, lay thick all around the village. Walking on a little further, they past what looked like a clinic. The windows had been smashed and vines were protruding in and out. Fei squinted at a dirty piece of paper nailed to the front door.

It said:

### FEELING SICK?

*Due to a lack of resources, this establishment is now closed. Please report to Ms Fre...*

The writing trailed off.

*Sick? Hmm...*

A memory struck her. She had been so distracted by her sadness when they were descending in the Merenial, she had shrugged off a feeling of sickness. The vibrations of the ship had somewhat clouded the sensation, but she did remember feeling nauseous, although not a kind of nausea she had ever felt before. It was like the feeling you get after eating something that hasn't agreed with you – a warning not to eat it again.

Having dropped behind a little, she caught up with the others as they trundled through another village, towards a rather precarious-looking bridge over a deep canyon.

'Did any of you feel weird when we were coming down in the Merenial? I felt sick, and I don't normally get motion sickness,' she said.

Cora faced her. 'Yeah, I did. You felt it too?'

'Yeah, it was so odd. I thought I was the only one. I just assumed it was cos I was really sad or something.'

'Me too, I didn't wanna say anything, as it didn't feel that bad.'

The sisters exchanged confused looks.

'Anyone else?' asked Fei.

Rabina and Alfie shook their heads.

'Sí, a little,' said Nessa, 'But I get motion sickness.'

'Hmm.' Bina frowned and walked towards Fei. 'Did ye feel dizzy?'

'Um, a little, yeah. But I just assumed it was because we were spiralling down,' said Fei, drawing back as Rabina came closer, examining her.

'Whin we landed 'n' ye got oot 'n' walked in th' opposite direction tae where ye'd bin facing, did ye feel better?'

Alfie's eyes widened and he walked up behind Bina.

'I did actually, yeah.'

An' you?' Rabina stared at Cora, who nodded.

'You don't think...?' asked Alfie.

'What is going on?' Nessa shuffled beside them.

'You don't think ... what?' Fei said.

'Ah think someone tried tae contact ye. An' ye must've all picked it up. It cannae be an old Sardan.' Bina rubbed her chin and marched over to a large rock beside the entrance to the bridge. 'D'ye remember what direction ye were facing in th' ship, lassie?'

'No idea, the sickness came and went in waves as we twirled round the mountain. I'm sorry? A Sardan tried to contact us? And why can't it have been an old one?'

Cora raised a finger. 'Because if it had been an older, stronger Sardan, Alfie would've felt it. Like a drug. Alfie requires a higher dosage to feel an effect.'

Rabina beamed at her and nodded.

'Why did you not feel it?' Nessa said to Rabina.

'Tummy of an ox, me lassie. Dinnae feel a thing. Always been a nuisance.' Rabina shook her head.

'Who could it have been?' asked Alfie.

'We only know two Sardan,' said Nessa.

Fei's eyes widened. 'Moth? But surely she would have known she wouldn't be able to contact Alfie?'

'And she would also have known that none of us would recognise the call,' said Nessa.

Bisou whined and wagged his tail. They looked at him, realisation dawning.

'Th' pup.'

'We haven't been walking in the direction of Brunas Peak, have we?' said Fei.

'Nae, lassie. Brunas Peak is west, we're headin north.'

'Alfie, try facing him west,' said Fei.

Alfie took a few steps back. 'Bisou, come here,' he trilled, crouching.

Bisou turned. Took one step. Then stopped and put his ears back.

He whined and snorted before lying down on the ground, resting his head on his leg.

'That's not like him,' said Cora, moving to stand next to Alfie. 'C'mon, B.'

He sat up, wagged his tail and gave a shrill, frustrated bark.

Alfie and Cora walked behind him.

'Come, B,' they called in unison.

Bisou spun and bounded over.

Fei's face dropped as the emptiness crept back. 'Moth's in trouble.' She faced west, and it sent her stomach churning.

Cora clutched at her stomach as she stood next to Fei. 'We've been walking north for so long we didn't notice.'

'I knew we shouldn't have separated.' Fei hung her head.

'Once we've got th' dagger, she'll be at th' top o' th' list.' Rabina looked stern.

'I'm so sorry, Moth.' Fei's stomach flipped again.

*I can't lose her.*

'How far from Irinvale are we?' asked Cora.

'Ah'd say another day's walk. Nae too far now.'

Fei sniffed. 'When we get there, I'll offer myself as bait. We have to sneak in somehow. The sooner we get in and out, the sooner we can get Moth, Baylor and Byrdy back.'

'No seas estúpida, Fei. Harryn may be there. He will recognise you and this will all have been for nothing.'

'I don't care, I'll be fine.'

Nessa huffed.

'No one knows me,' said Cora, quietly raising her hand.

Bisou whined.

'No way,' said Fei, pointing at her sharply.

'But none of them will know me. I'll just be thrown in a cell. And believe me, I've picked enough locks in my time,' she grinned.

'You're not going in there alone.' Fei stepped towards her, while the others watched awkwardly.

'I came in through the back when we were in the club. It was dark, and Harryn never saw my face properly. The crossbow covered my face in the ship. The only time he may have seen me was outside the forest, from behind, when he was aiming at Nessa. If we cut my hair and I wear a different coat, he won't have any idea who I am.

Besides...' Cora finished, 'I'm just a standard human anyway, so they won't bat an eyelid at me.'

'You're not *standard*, and you're not going.'

The group looked at Fei.

Alfie pulled a face. 'It's actually not a bad idea.'

'Not happening.' Fei slumped against a large rock.

Cora moved towards her sister. 'It's the only way one of us can get into the castle without alerting them. Don't worry, I'll be able to escape.'

'I would never forgive myself if something happened to you.'

'Nothing will happen to me. I'll just be locked away.'

The others all nodded in agreement. Fei hung her head and sighed. 'Fine. But you do *exactly* what we say. Not a step different!'

Cora grinned and Fei gripped her spindly arms. 'Don't go thinking this is gonna be some solo mission, cos it's not. I'll be watching you like a hawk.'

'Or a Roc,' muttered Alfie.

# CHAPTER THIRTY-TWO

The landscape grew darker as they trudged further north; they felt a long way from the glamour of Leos and the comforts of Valkyrios as they dragged their feet through the woods surrounding Irinvale. The twisted trees loomed over them like predators and the ground cracked under their feet as they walked. And they were finding it increasingly difficult to breathe.

They hadn't seen any sign of life for days – apart from Toks, which now appeared fairly regularly. The group swiftly dispatched each one, though this was beginning to take its toll.

They had decided to leave Clyde and Bisou waiting further behind, as the closer they got, the drier and harder the land became.

Cora was finding her mask particularly annoying; Nessa had chopped her hair into a bob that sat level with her chin. Although her hair was straight, the ends always curled up, so strands of hair kept getting trapped inside the mask and tickling her eyelids.

Irinvale was just ahead of them, lodged between two dark, jagged cliffs. If it hadn't been for the lights in the tall, thin windows, it would have been hard to tell where the castle ended, and the cliffs began. Thin spires loomed above, almost appearing to sway with the swirls of grey. Colossal rocks from the cliff stuck out around the castle, camouflaging the monstrous fortress.

The rocky path to the castle zigzagged above a lake. Oily waves crashed against the dark weathered rocks; while the sun struggled through the clouds, creating an ominous grey glow behind the castle.

They watched as Toks patrolled outside the ramparts. There was a fetid smell of wet rock; and the lights flickered between the castle turrets, which rose up, long and spindly as a Tok's fingers.

They looked down at the murky lake they would have to wade through to get to the main door.

'Whit a dump!' Rabina's lip curled.

'How many Toks are there?' Nessa squinted at the beasts trundling around the castle, screeching and swiping at one another.

Fei sighed. 'It looks as if there are three, maybe four? Big ones.'

They watched as a bird fell from the sky and slammed down on the rocks. The Toks roared and charged towards it, slashing and biting, blood flying everywhere as the bird was ripped to shreds. Each Tok took a portion, then moved away from the others to eat.

The group gulped.

Alfie turned to the rest of the group. 'We need to distract them so Cora can get close enough for the guards to notice her.'

Fei looked over to the lake shore, a little way round the side of the castle. She could see a lump of rock protruding from the ground, like a large, thick stalagmite.

'I know what we can do,' she said.

An hour later, Rabina's jacket sat tight across Cora's shoulders as she stepped into the murky lake. The water seemed to consume her foot – it was like stepping into cold custard that stank of rotting fish.

The others had sneaked on ahead, and were hiding behind the large stalagmite-like rock, watching the Toks shuffle round, screeching. Two guards stood behind them at the double front doors.

They had not enjoyed wading through the lake one bit. Alfie particularly hated the cold, and the thick oily film on the surface of the water still clung to his boots. They stood in the shallows, with the ripples sloshing against their legs, watching Cora get closer to the Toks.

Alfie whistled through his hands, mimicking a bird call, as he peered round the rock. Fei, Rabina and Nessa stood, weapons at the ready, behind him. He whistled again, a little louder this time.

The Toks froze and turned in the direction of the group, as Alfie whistled again. Digging their claws into the ground, they careered towards the group. The guards spun round, looking confused as the Toks charged off. Unable to see the cause of their flight, they assumed it was another fallen bird, and continued chatting.

As Cora moved out from behind a rock to wade through the bleak lake, the Toks came tearing round the side of the stalagmite rock. Rabina silently fired a dagger into the forehead of the first. The guards blinked at the whimpering screech that followed, belatedly aiming their guns. The second Tok tumbled over the body of the first, and the third leapt over. Nessa sliced at its legs as it jumped, sending it crumpling to the ground with a scream.

The guards edged towards the noises, as Alfie slammed down on the third Tok's head with his axe, crushing its skull, and sending blood splattering across his face.

Meanwhile, the second Tok jumped to its feet and screeched, opening its bloodied jaws. The guards stopped dead, eyes wide, guns shaking against their cheeks.

Fei lunged and ducked as the Tok swung at her head. She skidded beneath it and shoved her dagger into its gut.

The guards edged closer, and Fei, Alfie and Nessa pushed the Toks' bodies into the water, watching as they disappeared into the murky abyss.

The group crept further round the rocks. Finding a foothold, they climbed up, and slid into a shadowy crevasse; Alfie craned his neck as he squeezed his body into the nook. The guards peered round the corner, pointing their guns at every splash from the lake.

The group held their breath as they watched from above, hearts pounding.

'Stupid buggers must've drowned, fighting over a bloody bird,' said one of the guards, shaking his head as one of the dead Toks bobbed just beneath the surface.

'They've only been here a week. But there's plenty more where they came from.'

'I really hate them.'

They made their way back to the castle.

*\*\*\**

Cora tiptoed towards the doors, which grew larger and darker, the closer she got. The grey seemed thicker and more alive as it swirled around her. She stood for a moment, transfixed, as the lights in the vast windows flickered.

'Hey!'

'Don't move!'

The sound of two guns being cocked rang through her ears as she raised her hands.

'Turn around!' another voice boomed.

She spun round to find two barrels pointing straight at her.

*\*\*\**

Fei didn't blink. She just ground her teeth as she watched Cora turn; patches of moss began to sprout from cracks in the rock beneath her. Rabina, noticing the bed of green, reached over to her hand and squeezed it tight. Fei felt the familiar comforting pain of her grasp, and met her eyes. Rabina nodded as she gripped, and Fei looked back at her sister.

*\*\*\**

'Please don't shoot, I'm lost,' said Cora.

'Lost? You stupid girl. How did you end up here?' said one of the guards, lowering his gun a little. 'Who are you? What's your name?' he barked.

'My name is Samantha Lynch. I'm a baker's daughter from Prior's Wall, not far from here – '

'We know where it is,' interrupted the second guard. 'What we don't understand is how you found yourself here.'

'I'll just be going then, sorry.' Cora took a step, and both guards immediately aimed their guns at her again.

'Oh, I don't think so,' snarled the first guard. 'Turn around and put your arms behind your back.'

Cora turned and brought her fists together behind her. The guards grabbed her wrists and she winced, as they placed some cold, heavy irons around them. One of the guards knocked on the big wooden doors.

\*\*\*

The group watched from their hiding place as the doors opened to reveal a long torch-lit hallway. Orange light shone in Cora's eyes as the guards pushed her in.

'Bastards!' Fei's jaw twitched and Bina squeezed her arm again as the moss began to sprout little pink flowers.

The heavy doors shut behind Cora, the crash reverberating round the lake, sending ripples towards the group.

'And now, we wait,' said Nessa, slumping against the rock.

Fei buried her face in her hands and Alfie placed a large, warm hand on her back.

The lake settled.

# CHAPTER THIRTY-THREE

The inside of the castle was quite different from what Cora had been expecting. She stood on a long, dark-green carpet, which stretched so far she could barely see the end of the hallway. The walls were covered in paintings depicting angels and demons, and golden gargoyles glared down from the ceiling.

On either side of the carpet, torches were mounted on gold pillars, the flames crackling at the top. High above, there was a glass ceiling, and Cora could see the swirls of grey bouncing off and drifting across the top.

As they walked, Cora noticed the sad faces of stuffed animals' heads below the gargoyles. She felt her stomach turn when she stared into their dark, bleak eyes.

They continued along the carpet towards a large domed glass ceiling, from which hung a vast chandelier. It appeared to be made of antlers, some of which looked uncomfortably similar to Bisou's. A shiver of disgust travelled down her spine; the further they walked, the sicker she felt.

Finally, they approached a wide marble staircase; at the top was a vast doorway. Arriving at the bottom step, Cora looked up at the ceiling. It seemed to go on forever, into darkness, and the wall with the door, disappeared up with it, into nothingness.

'C'mon,' grunted one of the guards, as they pushed her up the stairs and through the doorway. It grew colder and Cora shivered as they arrived in a huge, round room, painted red.

'Not a word, you hear,' the guard growled under his breath, as he tightened his grip on her arm.

The carpet continued to a circular dais at the top, where an iron ring stuck out of the floor; just behind it was the most disgusting-looking creature she'd ever seen, sitting in a large gold throne, glaring at them.

Chichenache

*So he was real!*

Cora's pulse quickened.

He was so tall, but gangly and uncomfortably thin, and his unnaturally long fingers resembled those of a Tok. A bony hand was clawed round the gold lion's head on one arm of the throne, while he tapped a long, twisted fingernail against the other.

His face was a horrifying sight, as the blood vessels were visible, purple and throbbing, beneath his transparent skin. A long gold cane was balanced against the side of his throne, and he wore a tweed suit and shiny black shoes. His trousers were too short for his legs, the bottom of which revealed his ankles, which looked like something you might pick up from the butchers to feed your dog.

Cora moved her gaze up to his long oval head. He had tufts of wispy hair and a large, wide mouth, out of which poked small, sharp, white teeth. His beady black eyes watched as Cora and the guards approached, and Cora felt one of the guards begin to tremble. They stopped just in front of the iron ring that was poking out of the floor. The guards both kneeled and bowed their heads.

Chichenache stared at Cora, who stared back.

'And who might you be?' his booming voice bounced off the walls of the large room.

'We found her outside the castle, sire, claiming she was lost.'

'Lost? Well you can't be from round here, otherwise you would exhibit better manners in my presence.'

He glared and leaned down towards Cora. She lowered her head and descended onto one knee.

'She claims to be from Prior's Wall, sire.

'Is that so? Then you should know who I am. How did you arrive here?'

Cora looked into his empty black eyes, while the guards kept their heads down.

'I was out looking for wheat when the grey came, and I lost my way. My father is a baker,' she said, her eyes flicking between him and the floor.

Chichenache grinned, revealing rows of shark-like teeth. He reached for his cane and pushed himself up. Skulking towards Cora, he bent and placed the end of his cane under her chin, loomed closer, and sniffed her face. He sniffed her face, narrowed his eyes, then loomed closer to her face. Cora blinked as his coat slid back and she saw her mother's silver dagger glinting beneath.

'Who *are* you?' he hissed, examining her.

Cora felt beads of sweat form on her forehead.

'As I said before, sir, I'm a baker's daughter.'

'You smell ... different,' he growled.

'Just – just a baker.'

Chichenache drew back, scanning Cora's whole body. 'I'm rather in need of a baker... Perhaps you shall stay with me, let's see if you are any good.' He moved away, flapping a skeletal hand at the guards. 'Take her to the cells! She'll need a night alone to think of some good recipes,' he grinned, and licked his pale, thin lips.

'No, please, my father – he'll be wondering where I am!' Cora called, as the guards grabbed her arms.

'Quiet!' The guards pushed her forward.

A knock came from the door behind them. Chichenache motioned for the guards to open it, and Cora saw a tall, muscular, bald man, with a dark moustache, dressed all in black, stride confidently into the room. A large pink scar spread diagonally across his cheek.

Cora looked down, her breathing short.

'Ah, Yaeffe, you have come to join us for dinner. Always on time.'

Chichenache opened his arms in greeting. Harryn stopped and bowed. Rochford, and another Silgir behind him, followed suit.

Harryn nodded, then looked at Cora. Her heart began to pound as she swiftly turned away.

'Who's this?' he said, scowling as he looked her up and down, focusing on the faint yellow bruise on the side of her face.

'Oh, just some brat we found wandering outside the castle. Claims to be the daughter of a baker. I've asked for her to be sent to the cells...' He shot the guards a chilling look.

The guards trembled and shoved her forward again.

'Wandering around outside?' asked Harryn, as the guards walked her to the doors.

'Indeed. Curious, I must say. Claims to be from Prior's Wall.' Chichenache scratched his razor-sharp chin.

'A girl of her age from Prior's Wall should know these parts, should she not, sire?' said Harryn, his jaw clenched.

Cora and the guards were almost out of the room, her heart hammering and her pace quickening.

Chichenache frowned. 'Indeed.'

'Only extended periods of time unprotected in the grey can cause delusion, sire. The markings on her face suggest she was not unaware of the dangers.' Harryn glared at the back of Cora's head. 'Perhaps she *meant* to find herself here.'

'STOP!' Chichenache boomed.

Cora shut her eyes, her foot hovering over the threshold as the guards halted.

'Bring her back!'

The guards pushed Cora round, back to Harryn and Chichenache; while she kept looking down.

Harryn stepped towards her. He stared at the guards, who caught his eye as he beckoned them away. They retreated, leaving Cora standing in front of the iron ring on the floor.

'Who is she, Yaeffe?' hissed Chichenache.

Harryn began to walk in a circle, keeping his eyes fixed on Cora's face. He stopped behind her.

'Sixteen days ago I watched an airship fly away with some particularly valuable cargo. Then I discovered the destination of said ship in the pocket of one of my men, whose dead body was hidden in a shop in Leos.'

Cora tried to look calm as Chichenache studied her face.

Harryn stepped closer. 'Now, as it happens, you have arrived the day after myself, and found wandering around outside. Do you think this a coincidence, sire?'' Harryn continued staring at the back of Cora's head.

'Coincidence indeed!' Chichenache snarled.

'I am the daughter of a baker in Prior's Wall, I swear. I got lost,' said Cora, as evenly as she could.

Harryn moved his gaze to the nape of Cora's neck, where he saw tiny, cut hairs behind her ear. Then down her back, where a few more small hairs lay scattered over four pin marks in the shape of a square in the centre of her back. He smiled and walked back round to face her.

'Who is she, Yaeffe? Tell me. I thought I smelled something odd on her when she was brought in.'

'That, sire, would be the smell of her sister. Her Nathair sister, Feina Fourlise.'

Chichenache's eyes widened.

'My name is Samantha Lynch, of the Lynch bakery at Prior's Wall. I have no sister; only a brother, I swear it.'

The veins in Chichenache's face throbbed. 'Fourlise,' he whispered. 'You cannot mean...?'

'As in the daughter of Dhalia Fourlise,' said Harryn.

Chichenache stared at the floor, his face twitching.

'I do not know this "Dhalia", sire,'' insisted Cora. 'I swear my name is Samantha Lynch!'

Harryn bent to face her. 'I preferred the two buns, baker girl.'

He grinned and Cora's face dropped. She stared back into his piercing eyes and glowered back.

'I knew it. I thought I recognised that smell, that disgusting stench!' growled Chichenache, his face flushed red and purple. He roared and struck one of his guards, who shrieked and went flying. Then he shoved Harryn to one side.

Harryn jolted as he watched Chichenache wrap his spindly fingers round Cora's neck and lift her off the ground. 'No, sire!' he shouted, as Cora gasped for air, her hands still tied and her legs dangling.

'I rejoiced the day your filthy mother died. My only regret is that I was not there to watch the light leave her eyes myself,' Chichenache spat in her face. 'Now I shall enjoy watching you die.'

His grip tightened and Cora fiddled under her coat for the dagger Rabina had hidden in the back of her trousers. Gasping for air, she felt herself growing weak.

'We need her alive, sire,' said Harryn, calmly. 'They sent her in here for a reason, and I know why. We must use her against them.'

Chichenache glared at him as Cora fumbled more frantically for the knife, her lips turning blue.

'Why should I deny myself this pleasure?' Chichenache snarled. 'I can already see her glow fading.'

'They've come for the dagger, sire,' said Harryn.

Chichenache finally loosened his grip, allowing Cora to retrieve the knife from her trousers and catch her breath.

'My dagger?' he asked.

Cora's limbs felt numb; with her last shred of strength, she threaded the knife down into one of her sleeves.

'This girl is no use to us, but the others are most valuable. We must use this one to our advantage. No doubt they are close by – they would not have sent her here alone,' said Harryn.

Chichenache let Cora's body drop to the floor, his eye twitching.

She fell in a heap; her legs buckled under her. As pain seared through her head and neck, she strained to focus her blurred vision, gasping as Chichenache moved his long fingers to the bottom of his jacket, and pulled it back to reveal a long, thin, silver dagger. He gripped the ornate hilt, engraved with tiny ivy stems, meeting at a small emerald at the top that glinted in the light.

'This dagger has never left my side,' he whispered.

'And it never will, sire, so long as we are careful. Keep her chained up here. Place her on 24-hour watch, add more men to the wall, and let them come to us,' said Harryn.

'Mark my words, Fourlise, once you are of no further use, I will snuff out your light myself,' Chichenache snarled in Cora's face, before marching to the double doors.

'Chain her up in the main hall! I WANT EYES ON HER AT ALL TIMES!'

He slammed the door behind him, making the room shudder, as the guards hurried towards the iron ring.

Harryn smiled at Cora. He stepped over her and reached down for the small knife she had half hidden in her sleeve. He pulled it out, cutting her hand as he did.

Cora growled as blood dripped down her palm. Harryn stood above her, laughing.

'Whoops,' he hissed.

The guards grabbed her lapels and dragged her to the iron ring on the floor. Harryn watched as they ripped off her jacket, searched her pockets and removed her shoes, flinging them to the side, out of reach. One of them produced an iron chain and threaded it through the ring, before attaching each end to Cora's cuffs. When she moved one arm up, the other was pulled down.

The guards positioned themselves evenly round the carpet, with Cora in the middle.

'I imagine you would have carried out your plan later tonight?' asked Harryn, stepping closer.

Cora scowled at him through bloodshot eyes.

'You would have picked the locks, and let 'em in?'

She remained silent.

'I'm very much looking forward to presenting your Leos friends to her. She does love a good hanging.'

Cora shot one arm towards Harryn's face, but he caught her wrist, and grabbed her neck with his other hand, kicking her legs from beneath her and slamming her into the ground.

'Don't make the mistake of believing that you have any chance of winning this one, child. You have indeed placed yourself in the eye of the storm. She sees your every move. And you will all die!' he spat.

Cora held her breath, as he released his hold on her neck and plucked out a pin buried in her hair.

'How predictable you all are! I must say, I find you rather entertaining. It's like watching my dogs run for kills on a hunt,' he sneered, twirling the pin, then sliding it into his pocket. 'No doubt we shall see the rest of your pack soon.'

Cora pushed herself up, with difficulty. 'Don't worry ... you will.' She shot him a wry smile.

Harryn sobered and turned to the guards. 'Don't take your eyes off her for a second, do you understand?'

'Yes, sir,' the guard nodded.

The commander turned and left.

Cora exhaled and hung her head as the lights in the vast, cold empty room began to dim.

# CHAPTER THIRTY-FOUR

'What the hell is going on? She was supposed to signal us from the wall over three hours ago,' said Fei, pacing anxiously.

'There's more guards on th' wall now. Ah counted ten whin we got here, there's at least double now.'

'Something's happened, I just know it.' Fei stared in terror at the castle, her heart pounding as moss continued to cover the rock like a glistening green blanket.

'That can't be a coincidence,' said Alfie, exchanging a concerned look with Rabina.

'No, it's not a bloody coincidence... Something's happened!' Fei stared up at the castle, tapping her foot.

'Fei, tranquila. Perhaps the timing was not right, we have to trust her. We cannot lose our heads now.'

They studied the guards walking back and forth along the castle wall. Fei focused on her breathing as the water they were standing in grew clearer and less sticky.

'Aye, lassie, we cannae flap now.'

*Stay calm, stay calm ... stay ... calm, dammit.*

Fei closed her eyes and rubbed her forehead. 'You're right.' She slumped helplessly against the cold, wet rock. 'We wait.'

\*\*\*

Chichenache grabbed a turkey leg and shoved it into his mouth, bits of skin and meat falling into his lap. 'It's been over twenty-four hours, Yaeffe. Where are the scum?' he growled, flinging the bone across the table.

Harryn remained silent and the guards at the door kept their eyes on the floor. Chichenache slammed his hand down on the table angrily. Apples and oranges, which the guards didn't dare touch, bounced and tumbled by their feet.

'Sire, we must consider they are waiting, exactly as we are. I do not believe, however useless this one is, that they will leave her to die,' said Harryn, as an apple made contact with his boot. He gave it a kick, sending it flying under the table.

'Then let's do it, I'm tired of waiting! Send the guards out to find them.' Chichenache flung back his chair and swept across the room to look out of the window. His back was hunched and rigid as he examined the cliffs outside, growling under his breath.

'In order to overthrow them efficiently, sire, we need them to enter the castle. We know it far better than they do. We must fight on favourable ground.' Harryn's lip twitched.

'Their stench sickens me. I will enjoy watching them all strung up. Your plan had better work, Yaeffe; otherwise

I will hold you personally responsible.' Chichenache glared at Harryn, then strolled back to the table and bit the head off a baked fish.

'For twenty years I have been tormented by her existence; for twenty years her daughter has walked this earth and I have been sitting here, like a FOOL. Oblivious!'

Small, wet globules of food dropped from Chichenache's mouth as he stared at the dark window.

'You will have vengeance, sire.'

'Indeed! I will spill every last drop of Fourlise blood on the blade of my sword. I will have all their heads mounted in my home,' he hissed. 'The day she took my heart was the day she signed her death warrant.'

Harryn bowed stiffly, his face flushed, and his hands clenched. Chichenache waved him away with a greasy hand and he marched from the room, his Silgir troopers close behind.

\*\*\*

Fei's face was blank. The cliffs were covered in terrifying cracks and sharp pieces of rock that jutted out like claws. Any of those rocks could break off and fall at any moment, and the mass of scattered rocks at the base suggested this was a regular occurrence.

'The number of times she's said, "trust me", and it's been fine, I can't even count. And yet, when it really counts, I'm terrified.'

Fei sat with her back to the rock. They had been taking it in turns to watch for a signal from Cora from the castle.

Nessa picked at her jacket sleeve. 'I never had a sister. I always wanted one, but after my parents had me and I turned out to be what I am, they could not risk it happening again, especially living through the Crusades. It became almost impossible to hide my father and me. I would be scared too, but as you said, we have to trust that she is okay.'

Fei continued to stare blankly ahead. 'I do. I just don't trust myself. I'm like my father in that respect. I'm learning, though. It's funny – only Cora could make me feel so calm yet so panicked, at the same time.' She forced a half-smile.

Alfie turned to the others. 'We should wait till morning, call their bluff.'

Fei and Rabina nodded.

'Question is, how valuable are we to them?' asked Fei, meeting Rabina's thoughtful gaze. 'She's alive. I can feel it.'

'Aye, lassie, she's alive.'

The sky grew darker and still the group waited. And watched.

The waves had calmed and turned into ripples that were gently washing in and out. The group paced back and forth from the safety of a cave, which was now almost covered in moss.

\*\*\*

Harryn sat in a tall, red leather chair by a window in one of the long hallways in the castle, watching as waves hugged the cliffs, and rocks plummeted into the depths of the lake.

He gripped the arms of the chair, his mottled fingers white with tension as small cracks began to form along the leather. His eyes were fixed on the water below and his jaw twitched as more seaweed appeared, winding through the waves, the glint of its long green tentacles tormenting him. He felt his body getting hotter and moved his hand to unbutton the top of his uniform.

Suddenly Chichenache burst through a door at the end of the hall, bellowing. His face was purple with rage. Harryn shot up as Chichenache thundered towards him.

'Where are they, Silgir? I've had enough of your games!' he bellowed. Spitting as he marched.

'Sire, I have a plan,' said Harryn calmly.

The ground rumbled with Chichenache's footsteps.

'It is clear to me your plans are futile, Yaeffe. Still, we harbour the useless one whilst those scum could be outside right now, plotting! I say we chop off her hand and send it out to them. That ought to get things moving!' Chichenache spat in Harryn's face.

Harryn ground his teeth. 'We shall give them twelve hours, sire. If they do not present themselves within that time, we shall do as you suggest,' he said smoothly.

'Six,' Chichenache hissed, drawing closer. 'Six hours, Silgir!' He turned and swung round his large black fur cape, sending it smacking into Harryn's face. 'I WILL NOT SEE ANOTHER NIGHT PASS WITH NO BLOOD SHED!'

He stormed out, slamming the door.

Harryn felt his anger rising. The paintings in the hallway jumped on their hooks as Chichenache blasted down the stairs. Rochford and the other Silgir shuffled up behind him.

'What will you have us do, sir?' asked Rochford.

'You can stay out of my way and do your job! That's what you can do,' he growled. Rochford nodded as Harryn stormed off.

\*\*\*

Cora sat in the hall, looking round the large, empty room.

*What a waste of space.*

She now knew the exact number of panes within each window, the probable amount of pressure needed to break each pane cleanly, and which ones to break, causing minimal disturbance. She had counted the exact number of antlers attached to the chandelier, and the number of different guards who had come in to watch her, also noting their height, muscle mass, potential fighting ability and experience.

She had had not been impressed by any of them. They looked terrified when they heard any noise above. Which made her chuckle.

As she began to count the antlers for the fiftieth time, she noticed the chandelier shaking a little more aggressively, making the bulbs flicker.

Heavy footsteps vibrated through the room, growing closer, making the lamps on the walls rattle.

The guards shifted their gaze between her and the doors. She had lost count of how many times she had heard Chichenache storm through the halls, but these strides were different: shorter, more direct.

Cora's pulse quickened and she stood, staring at the doors.

Harryn came crashing through, his glare fixed on Cora. The guards shuffled as he marched towards her.

While doing her best to remain stoic in face, Cora's heart began to pound as his pace quickened; he was only a few steps away.

She kicked out at his stomach but he caught her foot in his open palm, and twisted it away. Cora stumbled back, grimacing as she swung out a fist. Clasping her wrist, Harryn punched her cheek with full force.

Pain shot through her eye as her head went flying to the side. Another, sharper, wave of pain shot through her stomach as Harryn buried his fist in her ribs.

She doubled over, blood pouring from her nose as he swiped at the other side of her face. Her ears piercing, she fell to the ground, gasping for air.

The guards gulped as they saw Cora splutter through the blood cascading down her face.

Harryn began to circle her, his breathing short. Wiping his bloodied knuckles on his jacket, he watched her attempt to push herself back up. Rage filled him and he kicked her in the stomach again.

The pain was excruciating, and Cora slumped to the ground once more. She coughed, as blood spattered from her mouth and disappeared into the red carpet.

Harryn kneeled beside her and grabbed the side of her head, his thumb digging into her cheek as he whispered in her ear. 'I'm going to make you watch me kill your sister. And you can be sure I'll make it slow and painful.'

He pushed down on the side of her head as he stood, his lip twitching. Closing his eyes, he took a deep, snarling breath, the sound of muttering surrounding him. He opened his eyes to see the guards staring at the floor. His fists shook as he turned and made for the door.

'OUT OF MY WAY!' he shouted as he careered through the guards. The guards frantically parted.

Cora lay on the carpet. She felt a lump forming in her throat as her eyes began to swell and blood trickled down her face. Forcing back tears, she rolled onto her back, her vision blurring as the chandelier swung above her, the many antlers blending into one.

She tried to push herself up. Pain stabbed through her stomach and she winced, clutching her side as she thumped back down onto the carpet, now soaked with her blood. She watched it seep down her little blue tie, then closed her eyes.

Harryn slammed the door behind him, leaving Cora's limp body on the floor, illuminated by the swaying chandelier.

*Sister...*

***

Harryn stared at the mirror above the sink; and his dishevelled reflection glared back. Hanging up his jacket, he examined his cracked red knuckles as he turned on the tap. He moved his hand beneath the flow of the water, which was searingly hot.

He groaned in agony and punched the mirror. It shattered in the middle, tiny shards lodging in his knuckles.

Rochford and the other Silgir stood outside the door, listening to the commander's groans and the sounds of breaking glass.

Harryn carefully picked the shards from his fingers, wincing as blood and water stained his shirt. He ripped a towel from a hook on the wall and dabbed his hand. It stung and he hissed, and pulled on his jacket. He ground his teeth and blinked as the image of Cora's small beaten body flashed through his mind.

Leaning on the cold sink, he stared at his reflection, distorted by the jagged edges of the shattered mirror. He closed his eyes as someone else knocked at the door. It was Rochford, offering him a bandage.

'For your hands, sir,' he said, not meeting Harryn's eyes.

The commander took the roll of bandage and began wrapping it round his knuckles. 'Find me a loudspeaker. I'll be at the main wall, don't keep me waiting,' he muttered.

'Yes, sir. Right away, sir.' Rochford nodded and left with the other Silgir.

Tying a knot in his bandage, Harryn watched from a window in the corridor, as the ripples in the lake made their way back towards the castle.

# CHAPTER THIRTY-FIVE

The group sat watching from their cave as the ripples in the lake moved away, towards the castle. They were all chilled to the bone. Drained of energy and shivering, they jumped as a shrill alarm sounded behind them. They shot round to squint through the crack they had been monitoring.

Harryn was standing on the castle wall, above the doors.

'That bastard!' said Rabina, practically foaming at the mouth.

'Qué está haciendo?'

Alfie paled. 'It looks as if he's going to announce something.'

Rochford appeared with a huge loudspeaker, which he positioned next to Harryn. Fei crouched, open-mouthed, adrenaline cascading through her.

'Feina Fourlise?' Harryn bellowed. 'I have your lovely little sister here.'

Fei felt her jaw tighten and dread flood through her.

'I must say, though, she won't be looking lovely for much longer. In fact, to be honest, she is already a little less "lovely".' Harryn gave a menacing smile.

Fei's body jolted, her eyes narrowed as she leapt up, her gaze fixated in an emotionless dazed rage as Alfie grabbed her arm.

'I'm giving you six hours. If you do not give yourself up, your sister will be killed.'

Fei closed her eyes as she felt the oxygen leave her lungs. The group exchanged despairing looks and Alfie clutched Fei's trembling body close.

'Believe me when I tell you, an execution is about the only entertainment this castle gets, so it won't be quick,' Harryn continued. 'Death by fifty blades is a particular favourite here. You have six hours, Mage.'

The commander stepped away from the loudspeaker and turned to Rochford.

'Have the prisoner brought out to the courtyard, and chain her to the iron in the middle. Twenty-five guards are to watch her at all times. If *they* do not reveal themselves in six hours, bring down another twenty guards.'

Rochford swallowed and nodded as he made his way back to the hall where Cora was chained.

Fei pulsated with fury. The waves crashed against her legs as she buried her face in her hands. Rabina shook her head and signalled for Alfie to loosen his grip.

Nessa sighed. 'We need to tread carefully now. We – '

Fei shook her head, sniffing. 'We need to wait.'

They stared at her.

'How many guards did you say were up on the wall, Bina?' she muttered.

'Aboot thirty, give or take.'

'When we got here there were about fifteen, you reckon?' said Fei.

The group looked perplexed.

'Aye, aboot.'

'So, when they commence this, "death by fifty blades",' Fei ground her teeth and peered back up. 'They'll have to take them, and likely more, back inside. All eyes will be on that courtyard, expecting us to burst in at any moment. So we wait.'

'Till th' guards on th' wall are called below, then we sneak in! Brilliant! Although it dinnae leave us much time.'

'What other choice do we have?' asked Fei, trembling.

'She's right,' said Alfie.

Nessa nodded.

'Aye.' Rabina gave Fei a loving smack on her back. It hurt, but in a good way.

'So we wait,' smiled Alfie, nodding at Fei.

'We wait.' Fei muttered, dropping her face back in her hands.

\*\*\*

Three hours had passed. Harryn was sitting in the large red leather chair by the window, picking at the seams with his bandaged hand, when Rochford shuffled up beside him.

'Perhaps they are not outside, sir?' he said, his voice shaking slightly.

'*Perhaps* you should keep your theories to yourself. Call the guards off the wall, leaving the best six. Position them round the prisoner. I've waited long enough.'

Twenty-five of the guards made their way down to the courtyard, leaving six behind to patrol the wall. Two guards heaved out a wooden throne and dropped it in the courtyard facing Cora, whose arms had been chained through an iron ring, as before.

She gazed round at the eyes watching her, through her own slightly swollen pair. After a moment, Chichenache strode out and flicked up his cloak, before sitting. He rested his silver cane against the side of the wooden throne and reclined, looking at Cora with an expression of cruel satisfaction, his hand gripping the dagger tightly.

She was surrounded by fifty guards, each holding a large knife. From the castle turrets around the courtyard, eyes peered down through the tall, thin windows, hoping to catch a glimpse of the action.

*Bastards. My goddam cheek kills.*

At each end of the courtyard were double doors, held shut with a plank of wood. Burning torches lined the dank walls, shedding a flickering light on the pit of despair in the centre.

It stank of death; every cobble encrusted with blood.

No way out.

*Stay calm.*

Her skin prickled.

\*\*\*

Alfie watched the guards disappear from the wall before giving the others the go-ahead.

'Right, they've gone. We need to leave now.'

'A'right, see ye in a few,' Rabina grinned, smacked them all on the back, then made her way towards the lake.

Nessa hugged Fei. 'Be careful. I have not had friends until now, and I have decided I like it, te veré pronto,' she smiled.

Nessa gripped Alfie's hand and followed Rabina. They waded round the rocks protruding through the surface and made their way towards the castle.

\*\*\*

Cora opened her eyes to see Chichenache rubbing his hands together excitedly. Harryn was standing next to him. She glared at him and Chichenache chuckled. He waved his bony hand, hitting Harryn in the stomach.

'That dirty brat won't be able to look at you like that for much longer, Yaeffe.' He shuffled impatiently in his throne. 'I have waited too long to watch Fourlise blood spilt. And in my own home no less, what a treat!' He was almost drooling with anticipation. 'Yaeffe, even if the scum present themselves, this one will still be dispatched. I will have my spoils.'

Cora looked away.

'As you wish, sire,' Harryn muttered, looking up at one of the six remaining guards on the wall. He sighed as the guard shook his head. Harryn kept his gaze fixed on the six-man patrol and re-counted them every few minutes. Cora tried to stay calm, also keeping an eye on the wall, while the pale sun peeked through the huge grey cloud rolling towards them.

\*\*\*

Rabina and Nessa moved swiftly through the water, keeping their eyes fixed on the pacing guards. Soon they could see one of the side doors to the castle, two black-uniformed figures standing stiffly either side.

They floated closer. Gliding silently, they stopped behind a large rock that stood between them and the shore. Two more guards marched along, towards the grey cloud that was closing in on the wall. They reached down for their gas masks and pulled them over their faces.

'Soon as they are through, we go,' whispered Nessa, her eyes fixed on the uniforms.

'A'right lassie, I'm right behind ye.' Rabina squeezed Nessa's shoulder and placed a smooth, palm-sized rock in her hand.

The two guards disappeared into the cloud and the girls listened as their footsteps quietened, eventually disappearing altogether.

Nessa nodded and threw the rock, sending it smashing into the castle wall.

The two guards at the door shot round as tiny fragments of brick crumbled to the ground. Nessa pelted out of the water, stopping just in front of them, clasping the hilts of her knives.

The bewildered guards turned to see Nessa, waving at them. They gasped and went for their guns as she released one of her knives, wrapping the cord round the neck of one. The other was stunned as the throttled guard's head careered into him. Knocking him out cold.

They dropped like bags of sand.

Nessa signalled to Rabina and was shocked to find her standing right behind her, beaming.

'Dios mío! You want to get stabbed?'

'Crackin' work lassie. Mah turn now.' She grinned and pulled what looked like a small screwdriver with a strange shaped jagged end out of her boot.

They hurried towards the heavily barred door.

Rabina dropped down to the lock, pulled a small magnifying lens over her already heavily magnified glasses, and shoved in the strange metal tool, twisting and jabbing it around.

Nessa scanned the area, and noticed the grey cloud crawling towards them, and the muttering sound emerging from its depths.

'Bina, hurry up. I think they are coming back,' she whispered, tapping Rabina on the shoulder. Rabina jiggled a bit faster.

'Ah'm trying, lassie, bit these bloody iron locks are rusty as hell.' She strained as she twisted. And the muttering grew louder, accompanied by the sound of footsteps.

'Vamos.'

Click.

'Ha.' Rabina beamed as the door squeaked open.

As three guards stepped out of the grey, the pair heaved the two slumped guards into the castle and pulled the door back, leaving a small gap.

They hid in the shadows inside the castle wall, waiting for the footsteps to fade away.

'They've gone,' Nessa whispered, before feeling a tap on her arm and turning to see the barrel of a gun pointing at her face.

'Don't move, hands up where I can see them,' said a guard, his hands shaking as the girls slowly moved their hands.

'Move and I'll shoot.'

'Calm yerself now, laddie.'

'Quiet. Faces to the wall.'

He indicated with the gun for them to turn, beads of sweat trickling down his forehead.

'Alright, laddie.'

Rabina and Nessa turned as the guard edged towards them. Rabina still with the lockpick in her hand; swung her arm and jammed it in the guard's neck. Catching him as he fell, they laid him on the floor. Rabina smothered his groans with her hands as he clutched his spurting neck. Finally, he lay limp.

Nessa peered through the doorway. The cloud had smothered the light, and more muttering could be heard from its depths. 'I can't see the others anymore, and I can hear more Silgir coming.'

'Blast.' Rabina replied, as the cloud began to creep up the sides of the castle.

They craned their necks to look at the top of the wall. The last few rays of sun illuminated the dark, dank bricks at the top.

'Th' wall. We'll have tae signal them from up thare.'

Nessa rolled her eyes, 'Of course!'

'No one said this wis gonna be easy.' Rabina squeezed her arm.

Nessa sighed and nodded. 'You go that way, I will go this way. First one to the top will signal the group.'

'Good luck, lassie.' Rabina turned to hurry down the dark corridor.

Nessa soon found a towering, twisting staircase in front of her, with a tiny beam of light showing under a door at the top. The staircase seemed to stretch for miles; the pinhole of light at the top unchanging as she removed her shoes and silently began climbing the stairs. Each step felt like a block of ice beneath her feet as she clawed the wall, trying not to fall.

She stopped by a narrow opening in the bricks; and squinted through the slit into the courtyard below.

'Cora,' she whispered, horrified. The sight of Cora's small body, surrounded by a sea of glinting knives, made her heart ache.

*Mantente fuerte mi hermana.*

She refocussed. Her short, sharp breaths leapt from her body as she forced herself forward, twisting upwards round the bleak tower.

Her body prickled, as a large shadow obscured the light from the door.

The guard at the top froze, his eyes wide. He stared down at Nessa, while the grey cloud continued creeping towards him, slowly snuffing out the light.

'He – '

Before he could make another sound, Nessa sent a knife spinning towards him, and twirled it tightly around his thick neck.

He grabbed it and twisted it round his muscular arm, pulling Nessa towards him. His neck muscles pulsated as he shoved a finger between the twisted cords.

Nessa's wet toes slipped on the icy stairs as the guard twisted the cord further around his arm and pulled harder. Slidding closer to his grasp, she was almost within arm's reach of the burly man, as he continued to twist and pull.

The grey cloud crept up; the light at the top was just a few steps away. Slowly fading.

Her fingers were bleeding, and her cuff ripped at her skin. She cried out and flung her second dagger.

The guard grabbed it with his other arm and twisted it once again round his meaty forearm. Yanking hard, he sent Nessa flying towards him. At the last moment, she twisted up her legs and kicked him in the stomach, making him double over. She swiped at him wildly, only to be met by his large hand, cupping her fist.

The light from the door dimmed even more as the grey wound its way further up the turret, obscuring any remaining pockets of light.

He threw the cords to one side and blasted his fist into Nessa's face, sending a shrill ringing through her ears. She gasped for air as blood shot from her cheek. With a final burst of adrenaline, she twisted her body and jumped to kick him in the side of the head.

He plummeted to the floor in a crumpled heap.

Nessa's eyes darted between the encroaching grey cloud and the guard as he groaned and attempted to refocus. Summoning up her last shred of energy, she yanked the cords around his neck hard, and rammed his head into the wall, knocking him out.

Nessa winced as she touched her cheek, pain shooting through her eye socket.

The grey crept towards the last window at the top, its light fading.

She ran, charging through the doorway as two large grey clouds closed in on either side of her, bringing with them the sound of footsteps.

Knife in hand and chest heaving, she thrust her arm into the last dying ray of sun.

The glow bounced off the knife as she twisted it; and she slumped to the ground, her heart pounding as the footsteps grew louder.

Far below, a small smile crept across Cora's face, as she saw the tip of Nessa's knife glint from the turrets at the top of the tower, then swiftly drop beneath the grey.

Harryn was too focussed on the patrolling guard to noctice.

\*\*\*

'There it is,' said Alfie.

'Let's go,' Fei nodded.

They waded into the lake, dropped below the surface and made their way to the castle.

# CHAPTER THIRTY-SIX

Nessa sat with her back against the cold brick of the walkway at the top of the castle wall. She coughed as a wisp of grey cloud wafted over her shoulder. She fanned it away with a frail arm; the footsteps were almost upon her.

A guard had stopped in the doorway of the tower, and he was standing there, staring at her. She wheezed with the strain of pushing herself up, the grey waterfalling over the castle wall walk. She drew a sharp breath as he aimed his shotgun at her.

Her eyes bulged as she saw the guard collapse on the ground – a knife protruding from his back.

Two black leather boots strode through the grey-covered doorway. Rabina stood over him, hands on her hips. She tipped her cap back and pointed down. Nessa nodded, leant against the wall to catch her breath and rub her raw wrists.

The grey tumbled past them and floated down into the courtyard.

Nessa crouched and hobbled towards the wall to peer down. Cora was still alone in the centre.

'Mantente fuerte mi hermana,' she whispered, her jaw searing with pain, before disappearing back down the stairs.

***

'How much longer Yaeffe? I'm bored,' drawled Chichenache. He glared at Cora as she watched the grey swirl towards them.

'Thirty minutes,' muttered Harryn shortly, scanning the battlements and doors.

Chichenache turned. 'Do not take that tone with me, Silgir. You forget your place. I only respect your judgement because *she* trusts you.'

He got out of his chair, glowering at Harryn, who still had his eyes fixed on the wall walkway.

'I could have snapped my fingers and had that little brat's head on a plate hours ago!' Chichenache loomed closer, his voice filled with frustrated rage.

Harryn turned to meet his gaze. 'That would have been a mistake,' he scowled.

Chichenache's lip twitched, and his bony arm shot out, gripping Harryn round the neck and lifting him off the ground.

'Perhaps I shall snap my fingers and have *your* head on a plate instead!' he boomed.

The grey tumbled down the wall behind him.

Harryn, grimacing, flicked his eyes up; two guards were missing.

"WHY DON'T YOU LOOK ME IN THE EYE, SILGIR?! YOU HAVE NO RESPECT!' Chichenache screamed, spitting with fury.

Harryn's eyes widened. 'They're in the castle,' he whispered, straining through Chichenache's grasp.

Chichenache swung his head round, his black eyes squinting at the empty walls; the grey cloud rolled towards them, and the guards began to cough.

He let Harryn's body drop to the ground, his mouth wide, revealing a mass of pointed teeth. 'Find them! FIND THEM NOW!' he roared, gripping the dagger on his belt.

The guards shuffled out of the way as Harryn disappeared through the large doors behind Chichenache and pelted up the twisting staircase. His face red with wrath as he climbed. The Silgir followed.

Chichenache looked at Cora, who stood tall and glared back at him. His lip twitched again and a vein in his forehead began to throb.

\*\*\*

'Did you hear that?' whispered Fei, as Chichenache's thunderous roar escaped the castle.

'Mmm hmm. We'd best get a move on,' said Alfie, scanning the cliffs.

They sped out of the water towards the side door, checking for guards as they pulled it open and hurried in.

Nessa jumped down beside them and Alfie gasped, flinging up his axes in shock.

'Ahh!' Fei jumped, lowering her daggers and catching her breath.

'Perdón, I know how annoying that is.'

'Cora?' asked Fei, her eyes wide.

'She is okay for now. They have chained her up in the courtyard. She is surrounded by fifty guards. We have, maybe, ten minutes at most.'

Fei's fingers were white with tension, as she clutched her daggers.

'How do we get there?' asked Alfie.

'That wey! Ah passed th' courtyard door on mah wey back,' Bina panted behind them.

'Ahh!' Alfie jumped, flinging up his axes again.

'Sorry.'

Nessa raised an eyebrow.

'There's two doors either side of th' courtyard. Ah reckon th' north one's yur best bet.'

'Okay. Alfie and I will make our way to the north door, you two go to the south for the dagger, and when the time comes ... we surround them,' said Fei, smiling weakly.

They all nodded, turned and ran for the doors.

\*\*\*

Harryn blasted up the stairs and through the turret doorway at the top, shooting his gaze round to each guard as he flew. The grey obscured his feet as he ran along the wall walk, before turning into the turret to find the two unconscious guards collapsed against the stairwell.

His heart raced as he stared at their useless bodies. Another guard stepped through the doorway, took in the slumped uniforms and caught Harryn's piercing stare.

The guard gulped.

'Sir, I'm sorry. I didn't see anything, I swear,' he said, shaking.

'That is precisely the problem,' Harryn hissed, and lunged forward to grab the guard's collar. He shoved him against the wall. 'Find them, or it'll be you in that courtyard next,' he growled, throwing the guard aside.

The guard stumbled away, blowing furiously on a small trumpet. 'THERE'S BEEN A BREACH!' he bellowed.

Chichenache spun round to see the guard pelting across the wall, then back at Cora, who let a small smile creep across her face.

He had never felt rage like this. He ground his sharp teeth together.

'Kill her now,' he muttered.

The guards shifted uneasily.

'KILL HER NOW!'

A shudder seemed to run round the courtyard, and the guards raised their long knives. Harryn froze as Chichenache's roar thundered up the castle walls. He sped out of the turret and skidded to a halt; as he stared down into the foggy courtyard, the guards stepped forward.

***

Fei and Alfie jolted as Chichenache's cry boomed through the hallway.

They looked at each other and pounded ahead. When they noticed the glare from a window reflecting onto the hallway floor, they ran towards it and squinted into the courtyard.

Fei felt as if her heart had left her body as she saw the guards make their way towards Cora, knives out, pointing at her.

'CORA!' Fei screamed.

'Oh, God,' muttered Alfie.

Fei ran, her body shaking with adrenaline as Alfie struggled to keep up. Cora's beaten face was branded in her head.

*Stay strong, sister.*

She thought of Cora's little blue tie, splattered with blood…

\*\*\*

Alone, chained in the centre of the courtyard, Cora watched in wonder as a tiny blue flower squeezed through the black bricks on the ground between her feet; her little blue tie flopped down in front of her face and hung over its delicate petals.

*Anything can be a weapon.*

She began to subtly pull off her tie, twisting the ends round her fists. Her breaths accelerating as the apprehensive guards edged towards her. The grey beginning to obscure them one by one.

\*\*\*

Rabina and Nessa careered round the castle, past the entrance to a hall in which a huge fireplace crackled. Rabina stopped and backed up, grinning at the flames.

'What are you doing?' cried Nessa.

'Ah will catch up with ye at th' end, lassie. There's someone else who needs sortin,' said Rabina.

'We do not have time for this! We have to get the dagger!'

'Just trust me, lassie. Go on, I'm right behind ye.'

'Maldita sea. Don't do something stupid, Bina!' Nessa shook her head and ran on.

'Ah wouldn't dream of it.' She grinned. Rabina crept into the hall and reached for a gas lamp perched on the wall beside the door. She lifted it out and turned to stare at what was hanging on the chimney breast: the largest shotgun she'd ever seen.

'Whit a beauty!' she breathed. She unhooked it and checked the barrel. Two shells. It landed heavily in her arms as she strained to lift it onto her shoulder.

As she jogged back to the doorway, she smashed the gas lamp across the carpet.

The fire soon caught.

She sent more waves of oil scattering across the room, smirked, spat on the floor, slammed the hall doors shut and hurried after Nessa, leaving smoke billowing under the doors behind her.

Fei and Alfie raced down the corridor, blasting their way through the guards who appeared intermittently as they ran.

They turned a corner to see the north gate at the end.

'There!' Alfie shouted.

Fei darted forward.

Rochford sprang out from behind a column and shot at Fei. The bullet grazed her arm and she flew back, crying out as blood sprayed in Alfie's face. Alfie gasped and his eyes bulged as he glared at their assailant, who was already reloading.

'Dirty Mage. You're filth!' Rochford spat, then looked up to see Alfie's axe thundering towards him. It blasted into his side, sending him crashing into the wall behind. Alfie dashed over to Fei as she tried to stand.

'Are you alright?'

'I'm okay, I'm okay. We need to get Cora NOW!'

Her skin was prickling with anxiety.

They stared at the door, as the grey tumbled in through the bars.

\*\*\*

'MAKE IT PAINFUL!,' Chichenache boomed, as the only few guards left not surrounded by grey stepped towards Cora.

The first lunged towards her. His long knife swung back as he leaped and Cora lashed out with her tie, snapping the end into his eyes. He bellowed in pain.

Another trembling guard made his way towards her. Quick as a flash, she blinded him as well.

Another.

Cora ducked and spun her tie round his arm, twisting it back and breaking his elbow.

'WHAT THE HELL ARE YOU DOING, YOU USELESS SCUM? KILL HER!' Chichenache roared as the obscured guards manoeuvred theirs masks over their faces.

Cora began to sweat as her eyes darted through the grey surrounding her for her potential next attack.

Harryn watched over the wall, his blood boiling as Chichenache leapt forward.

'SHOOT HER!' he roared.

Harrin felt his breath leave him, and he blinked. He watched, open mouthed as Nessa crept through the grey towards Chichenache from behind. His knuckled paled as his fingertips dug into the castle bricks. He ground his jaw as he turned and silently made his way back down the turret.

# CHAPTER THIRTY-SEVEN

Fei and Alfie skidded to a halt and Alfie shoved his shoulder into the huge stiff doors. Fei's face twisted in pain as she strapped a handkerchief tightly round her arm.

'Dammit, they've locked it.'

Fei panicked. She squinted through the bars into the grey mass, coughing, her arm limp at her side.

'Stand back,' Alfie gripped the handles of his axes and passed Cora's crossbow to Fei. She took it and stumbled back, wincing at its weight.

The grey had almost entirely obscured the door. Alfie leapt forward with his axes up and brought them crashing down on the lock. The iron crumbled and the door buckled.

The door burst open.

They pulled on their masks and dashed through the doorway into the courtyard.

Chichenache stood, seething, as the remaining guards attempted to aim their crossbows through those who stumbled, lost and coughing, in the cloud.

Nessa's fingers brushed the hilt of the dagger strapped to Chichenache's belt as he stood bellowing at the guards.

*Vamos. Tan cerca.*

She held her breath as she pushed forward, out of the blanket of grey, her hands trembling.

Harryn crept towards the south door as Nessa's hand closed round the hilt and gently pulled it from its sheath. She shot back and hid behind the chair, clapped her hand over her mouth and closed her eyes, holding back a cough as the grey made her lungs tighten. She clasped the hilt to her pounding chest and scurried towards the door. As she sped round the corner, a fist slammed into her face.


'YOU IMBECILES, GIVE THAT TO ME!' Chichenache lunged and his spindly legs wobbled as he grabbed a crossbow from a nearby guard.

He aimed at Cora. She spun and locked eyes with Chichenache as he released a short arrow. Two other arrows whistled towards her at the same moment, and she dropped to the ground, hiding behind the body of a guard as the arrows pounded into his chest.

She cried out as one of the arrows lodged in her calf; while Chichenache trembled with joy at the sound.

Then he sniffed the air and his face dropped. His beady eyes landed on two masked figures who had appeared at the other end of the courtyard.

The grey began to disperse, and all those left standing in the courtyard stared at Alfie and Fei. Cora smiled and Chichenache froze, the pulsating vein on his head close to bursting as he flung his skeletal arms in the air.

'GET THEM!' he screamed, pointing at the trio.

Fei and Alfie lunged forward, as the guards charged towards them.

Alfie blasted through, sending the guards flying into the grey, while Fei skidded and sliced at their legs and ankles. Chichenache growled, frantically shooting as they ducked in and out of the grey.

An arrow punched into Alfie's thigh. He bellowed and wrenched it out, snapping it in half, and pulled the crossbow from his back.

'CORA!' he bellowed.

Alfie flung the crossbow towards her. Cora followed her weapon as it plummeted, her hands steady, waiting.

Time seemed to slow as the crossbow flew – and landed in her grasp.

She cocked it and aimed.

As the guards charged, Cora fired arrows at their heads and chests. Fei ran, fumbling for the lockpick in her pocket. She skidded down beside Cora.

'Hey, sister,' Cora panted, firing arrows into the black uniforms.

'Hey,' Fei gasped back, manoeuvring the lockpick with one arm.

'Feeling like that "one day" yet?'

'A smidge!'

A guard charged at Fei, only to drop to the ground beside her, an axe sticking out of the back of his head.

One of Cora's cuffs fell to the ground.

Chichenache grabbed a nearby guard and snatched his shield.

Fei fumbled with the lock of Cora's second iron cuff as Chichenache grew closer.

It unlocked and dropped.

Cora pulled her trigger. The sound of emptiness knocked her as she peered through the gaping holes where there should have been arrows.

'C'MON!' Fei bellowed beneath her mask.

The few remaining guards had begun to retreat, as Alfie scooped Cora up into his arms and charged towards the north gate.

*The dagger.*

Fei stopped in her tracks when she saw Chichenache pounding towards her. He gripped the end of his cane and pulled out a long, thin, silver rapier.

She ground her feet into the cobbles and drew out a dagger.

'WHAT ARE YOU DOING?' Cora yelled.

'I have to check we got the dagger. Otherwise this was all for nothing!' Fei prepared as Chichenache swung back his arm.

*** 

Nessa rolled along the floor as the dagger spiralled out of her hand. Her cheek searing, she looked up to see Harryn's red face looming over her.

Smoke crept from under the castle doors as he swung his boot into her stomach. She grimaced, flung out her arm and sliced into his leg with her knife.

Harryn howled, grabbed Nessa by the neck and hurled her against the brick wall. She crumpled to the floor, and he kicked her in the jaw, blood flying from her mouth. Then he squeezed her neck and lifted her bloodied face off the ground.

'Did you really think you could run from me? Did you think I would not eventually find you?'

Nessa spat a stream of blood into his eye.

His mouth contorted, and he slammed his other hand into her neck, lifting her higher off the ground and crushing her back against the wall. Nessa gasped for breath as she clawed at Harryn's hands.

Flames began to appear, like flickering red tongues, under the doors.

'You are nothing,' he hissed.

Nessa weakly thrust her dagger at his neck but he grabbed her wrist and smashed it against the wall beside her head.

She felt her eyes closing.

'Look into my eyes. I want to watch the life leave you, just as I watched the life leave your foul Mage parents,' he whispered.

The smoke began to form large clouds which mixed with the grey, the heat of the roaring fire in the great hall sending sweat dripping from Harryn's brow onto Nessa's face, which was rapidly turning blue.

*\*\*\**

Chichenache swung his sword and Fei leapt back as the tip of his blade whistled past her chin, and again as he swung back, bellowing.

More guards raced towards them.

Chichenache brought his sword down on Fei, at which she pulled out her second dagger and crossed them above her head. They clashed, and her arm gave way as she crumpled to the ground.

'FEI!' cried Cora. She limped and swiped as the guards kept coming.

Fei rolled to the side, narrowly dodging Chichenache's sword. She twisted and sliced his arm; he roared and swung down, cutting into her leg. He shook with glee as Fei shrieked, blood pooling out, agony ripping through her.

Her arm crumpled as Chichenache's blade swung close to her neck. She cried out, kicked him in the face, then sliced at his belt.

It dropped to the ground. Empty.

Fei stared and pulled it towards her, as Chichenache spun round and saw the empty sheath in her hands.

'No,' he whispered.

Cora and Alfie limped up beside Fei.

Fury surged through Chichenache and he raised his arms, his sword primed to drop.

'SISTER!' Cora attempted to hobble back.

'Cora, stay back!' Fei smacked her palm into the cobbles, ready to dodge the sword, when a loud blast ricocheted round the courtyard.

Chichenache jolted. Blood waterfalled from a gaping hole in his chest, his arms dropped to his sides, and he fell to the ground.

Rabina's curly head poked out from behind a shotgun in the hot, glowing passage next to the courtyard, the barrel still smoking.

Alfie beamed as Rabina disappeared and made her way through the passage, after furiously signalling them in the direction of the gates.

'We need to leave NOW!' said Fei, as flames burst through the windows of the castle and the walls started crashing to the ground. The grey and the smoke swirled together into a tornado.

Getting to their feet, they hurried towards the north door. Not a moment too soon. Heat was consuming the courtyard, melting the mortar between the bricks.

Harryn buckled, bellowing hoarsely, as a bullet blasted across his back. Rabina stood further down the passage, her shotgun smoking. Nessa dropped to the floor, unconscious, beside Harryn.

Rabina darted over, wheezing as smoke continued to fill the castle, and flames burst through the doors to the great hall. She grabbed the dagger and latched it to her belt.

'C'mon, lassie! Wake up, wake up!' Rabina tapped Nessa's blue cheek.

'Nessa! Wake up, c'mon now!' Rabina's forehead was dripping with sweat as she put an ear to Nessa's mouth.

After a moment, Nessa gasped, and spluttered.

'There she is! C'mon, lassie. Ah've got ye, we have tae go!'

Rabina pushed her arms under Nessa's limp body and heaved her up. Nessa's head fell forward as Harryn grabbed Rabina's ankle.

Flames burst through the doors and began to spread towards him, as he sprawled on the floor.

'I will find you all, and I will watch you die,' he grimaced as the flames crept closer.

Rabina lifted her mask and glared at him. 'Not unless ye kin find yer wey out this pure burnin hell first, ya bastard!'

She kicked his hand away as the flames began to circle him. Pulling Nessa's mask over her pale face, she dragged her through the corridor towards the side door.

Rabina gulped as the sound of Harryn's cries soared through the passage, the flames clawing at his feet.

\*\*\*

The castle was crumbling, and Alfie, Fei and Cora hobbled towards the door.

Alfie grabbed the door first, jumping as Rabina shuffled round the corner towards them with Nessa hanging over her shoulder.

'Bina!' Alfie shouted.

'Get out th' door, ye great stoatin lug!' she bellowed, swinging her free arm, the dagger glinting on her belt.

Alfie nodded, scooped Nessa's frail body up into his arms and dashed out.

Cora and Fei ran ahead, clutching their wounds as the fire caught onto the oily water, leaving a sea of flames behind them.

They skidded to a halt at the bottom of the hill and turned to watch the castle collapse. Flames roared up and around the cliffs on either side; the sky was almost black with swirls of grey, and they ran for the forest.

Behind them, Rochford hobbled through the courtyard, clutching his shoulder with a bloodied hand, as great walls of flame loomed above.

'Sir? Sir!' he coughed, hobbling towards the south door. He skidded through to find Harryn lying on the ground, burning.

'Sir!'

He flung his jacket over Harryn's legs, smothering the flames and began shaking Harryn's limp body.

'Sir? SIR, WAKE UP!!'

Harryn stirred and winced. He peeled open his singed eyes, looked up at the black sky and roared in agony as Rochford turned him over and dragged him away.

\*\*\*

The group staggered through the forest for as long as they could, until Alfie's legs began to throb with the extra weight of Nessa's weak body in his arms.

'Wait, I have to stop.' Alfie stood panting as the others continued running.

'STOP!' Rabina shouted, her hands on her knees as she too halted to catch her breath.

Fei and Cora slowed and turned to see Rabina and Alfie laying Nessa down against a tree. They hobbled back.

In the distance they could see the bridge they had crossed to get to the castle, and the hills on either side of it.

*So close.*

Fei took a breath.

The group gasped as they heard a gentle whine behind them, and turned to see Bisou wagging his tail and Clyde thumping towards them.

Bisou could not contain himself and proceeded to gift each of them an enthusiastic lick across the face.

Fei's eyes filled as she hobbled over to scratch Clyde's thick neck and bury her face in his mane.

Cora rushed to Bisou, who barked excitedly and bounded around her. She grabbed him and he sniffed her bruised face, then eagerly licked her hands.

'We're so close,' said Fei, as Clyde munched the grass at her feet.

'Sí. About two hundred metres, I would say.' Nessa felt her bruised neck as she coughed.

The group beamed.

'Give ur tak,' grinned Bina, giving Nessa an affectionate pat on the back.

They smiled and looked at the sunlit hill ahead of them.

'Shall we?' asked Cora, taking in their weary faces.

'We shall,' said Alfie.

Bisou leapt into the air and wagged his tail, leading the way. Bina walked with Alfie and Cora, holding up Nessa; and Fei and Clyde strolled along together at the back.

Their thighs ached as they climbed the hill, which grew grassier the higher they went. Much to Clyde's joy, they stopped in the centre of a particularly lush, sunny patch at the top. They could see mountains, hills and cities in the distance. Lights flickered as patches of grey rolled across the sky.

Fei viewed the vast expanse in front of them, then winced as Bina came up behind her and clutched her shoulder.

She held out her hand, the dagger laid across her open palm.

Fei stared at it. It was so long since she had last seen it. A lifetime ago.

*Finally.*

She reached down and grabbed the hilt, pulling it towards her, she ran her trembling fingers across the gleaming edge.

The group watched as she turned her head towards the sun and lifted the dagger high into the air.

The sun beamed onto the blade, and the light reflected brightly round them. Fei's skin prickled with anticipation.

A sense of relief washed over them all, as they watched a beam of light shoot from the dagger into the distance – towards the heart of the forest.

# ACKNOWLEDGEMENTS

To my mum. Thank you for always instilling in me the value of gentleness, kindness and fighting for a cause. Without you I'd probably be a lot more scrappy, and this book would probably still not be out. Love you more than words.

To my little sister. Thank you for being part of the reason I wrote this book. You're stronger than you think. Also thank you for not running away from me a much as you did as a toddler. I sleep soundly at night knowing you're not going to disappear every two seconds.

To my partner Nathan. Thank you for telling me every day how much you love me and for humouring me when I force you to give me your opinions on sections of the book. I do listen I promise. Although I must admit it does go over my head every time you impress upon the importance of dishes going in the dishwasher and not the sink. Love you!

To my dad. Thank you for constantly telling me I can do anything I want in life. I did it. I took the bull by the horns and I'm certainly closer to the 'grizzly bear' mindset.

To Mike. !!!...Plethora. Plethora. Plethora. Sorry I couldn't help myself. Thank you for coming into my life at a point where I really wasn't sure which direction I was going in or even if my book was any good. You have no idea how much when you said 'The story itself is great - if it wasn't I'd have made my excuses months ago' meant to me, as I know how busy you are and totally believed you! You truly have been the bestest of bossmen friend. Thank you. @m.w.craven

To Jo. What else is there to say other than you are an utter angel. I'll never forget your offer of editing my first draft as honestly your kindness dumbfounded me somewhat. To arrive in my life and offer such a gift was so stunning, still to this day as I sit here writing this it makes me well up. (Yup still an emotional mess!) Thank you endlessly, you gave this wee writer a sprig of hope, and I've carried it with me ever since.

To my amazing editor Kelly. Thank you for being a truly inspiring woman of the arts. I grew up admiring women like you who harnessed the power of a creative life. Your poetry I see weaved into Sardan, so thank you for incorporating your beautiful words into the story.

I don't think you've realised what a mistake you made being so good at what you do, I'm never letting you go now! @kellyc.davis

To Letta. Thank you for being, literally the best painter in the world. I can feel you cringing as you read this, but I don't care, I'm gonna keep saying it till I'm blue in the face and you believe me. Cos it's true, you are the best, you gave the book soul and I see you every time I look at the cover. Literally exploding with and love and gratitude for your existence. @lettalopez_art

To Zach. The best graphic designer in the biz. Thank you for remaining so calm as I rambled over messenger about the silliest little details like 'the title colour needs to be dustier' honestly I hang my head in control freak shame. You've outdone yourself friend thank you so much! @zach.loera.design

To Clare. Thank you for capturing a photo of me that I can confidently say I really love, and I believe that's mostly because I was truly happy in that moment. Getting a photo taken of myself was something I never thought I would do, but I am sooo glad I did. Other than being another inspiringly influential woman in the arts, you were wonderful to chat to, and made me feel so comfortable, so thank you thank you thank you for that. I will be back for sure! @clareparkphoto

And finally to my tattoo clients. Thank you doesn't quite cut it and it never really will. You are the reason I was even able to write this book. You kept me in work to a point I was able to take enough time off to fully channel all my energy into the story, and the characters. In which I hope some of you will see yourselves. As in short, to me, you are the Sardan. And without you, there would be no story. You have my eternal gratitude. Love Indie x

To my wonderful readers. Thank you from the bottom of my wee soul for picking up a copy. To say this book has been a passion project would be a major understatement! It only took seven years to get to this point, but wowzers have you guys made it all worth it. I really do hope you've enjoyed it, I never set out to write the next tome we're all forced to study at GCSE. I just wanted to write a fun story, and that is the main thing I hope you've experienced in these pages. Fun. Because that's all I had writing it. Love you more than the words in this book...And the next two still to come...

Indie x

@clareparkphoto

Indie was born in Camden in East London and grew up in Hackney. After twenty years, she finally decided city life was not for her. She moved to Carlisle in the North of England for university where she studied Wildlife Media at Cumbria University, and subsequently also where she met her partner of ten years Nathan. In 2016 after deciding the likelihood of her becoming the next David Attenborough were slim, she decided to begin a tattoo apprenticeship. Having been surrounded by creatives for the better part of a year, during her walks to work, the characters within Sardan's world began to make themselves known. After writing the full layout for the trilogy in 2018, two years later the world was locked down, so she wrote Volume One.

If you can't find her at work drawing pictures on people's bodies. Then you'll most likely find her at home sipping on a peach iced tea with a cat on her lap, YouTubing her next creative project or watching Godzilla for the hundredth time.